PENGUIN BOOKS

OUR HOUSE IN THE LAST WORLD

Oscar Hijuelos was born in New York, where he now lives. *Our House in the Last World*, his first book, received stunning acclaim when it first appeared and won him the prestigious Rome Fellowship of the American Academy and Institute of Arts and Letters. His second novel, *The Mambo Kings Play Songs of Love*, also published by Penguin, was winner of the 1989 Pulitzer Prize for literature.

OSCAR HIJUELOS

OUR HOUSE IN THE
LAST WORLD

PENGUIN BOOKS

PENGUIN BOOKS

Published by the Penguin Group
Penguin Books Ltd, 27 Wrights Lane, London W8 5TZ, England
Penguin Books USA Inc., 375 Hudson Street, New York, New York 10014, USA
Penguin Books Australia Ltd, Ringwood, Victoria, Australia
Penguin Books Canada Ltd, 10 Alcorn Avenue, Toronto, Ontario, Canada M4V 3B2
Penguin Books (NZ) Ltd, 182–190 Wairau Road, Auckland 10, New Zealand

Penguin Books Ltd, Registered Offices: Harmondsworth, Middlesex, England

First published in the USA by Persea Books Inc., New York, 1983
First published in Great Britain by Serpent's Tail 1987
Published in Penguin Books 1992
1 3 5 7 9 10 8 6 4 2

Printed in England by Clays Ltd, St Ives plc

To my mother and to the memory of my father

CONTENTS

Cuba, 1929–1943

1

Hector's mother met Alejo Santinio, his Pop, in 1939 when she was twenty-seven years old and working as a ticket girl in the Neptuna movie theater in Holguín, Cuba. At that time she was still living with her mother, Doña Maria, in a small limestone house with a tin roof off Arachoa Street, where there was a bakery. Her name was Mercedes Sorrea, and she was the second of three daughters and not married because her last *prometido*, or "intended," who worked in a Cuban sour-milk factory, was a louse. At first, he would take her dancing on Saturday nights to the social club or Spanish Society, sweet-talk her, make her laugh, and then afterward bring her out on the iron balcony to discuss the marriage. But he never went through with the wedding; he disappeared for days at a time, and when he was around, he fought with her so that she had to come home and cry on her mother's lap. After a year Mercedes and this man broke up, and she resigned herself to spending a quiet old maid's life with Doña Maria and the ghost of her father, Teodoro, and with her dreams of the much grander house in which they had once lived.

Before her father died in 1929, the Sorrea family owned an immense house of white stone, in the best residential district of Holguín, across

11

the way from a park with towering royal palms and fountains and a bandstand where an epauleted orchestra played Sousa marches, fox trots, and rumbas on Sunday afternoons. Holguín was a city of about twenty-five thousand people, situated on a plain and surrounded by hills in the interior of Oriente province in eastern Cuba, a thickly forested region with its chief commerce in sugar, tobacco, wood, and cattle. Holguín was a center of this trade with a large marketplace and rail lines south to Santiago de Cuba and north to the port towns of Belen and Gibara. An old city, it had always been a center of Cuban insurgency against the Spanish and had seen much death. It was a city of white-, light blue-, and pink-walled houses with tin roofs, well-shaded squares, parks, slaughterhouses, churches, and ghosts.

Life was quiet in Holguín. The world was different then. People believed in God, and children died at early ages of the fever and tuberculosis. Saints and angels walked in gardens. The living called to the dead through spiritualists, horses were left dead in the streets, and honking automobiles frightened swarms of birds off the treetops. Priests were respected, and there were very few robberies, especially in Mercedes's town, and the poor were provided for by charities and fed with scraps of food given out after the last meal of the day. People were more polite, more elegant, and they liked to go promenading in the park on sunny afternoons. Because people died more easily, there was more praying and there were more funerals, which twisted through the streets with coachmen and pallbearers dressed in long black robes and wide three-cornered hats, and everyone but everyone knew one another's name and gave greetings as they passed.

In those days Mercedes was a little girl with a Cleopatra hairdo and a red ribbon in her hair. She spent her afternoons roller-skating in front of her house, watching people come and go through the park, waving to them and to the farmers and leather-pantalooned soldiers who traveled the road. She loved the family's house, all her life she would always remember it. It had twenty rooms and carved mahogany arabesque doors, fine iron grillwork of stars and flowers. It had a large central gallery, a shaded rear patio of pink and blue tiles, and a courtyard with large potted palms and an arched entranceway. Her father had filled that house with wagonloads of furniture: tables and chairs with animal feet, a piano, mirrors, Chinese vases, and crystal everywhere to capture light. There were wide, pleated curtains and high arched windows that let in a serene white light, strongest in the parlor. The house was surrounded by bushes with flame blossoms and by tamarind and orange trees. Everywhere there was sunlight. Blossoms streamed down the walls and between the slats of the white picket fence. Flowers were everywhere. And from everywhere it seemed her father, Teodoro, was looking at her and smiling.

Teodoro Sorrea was a bald, plump, distinguished-looking man with an aristocrat's nose and dark intense eyes. He dressed like a gentleman, with a stiff collar and lace bow in the Victorian fashion, and he wore a perfectly folded *pañuelo*, "handkerchief," in his vest pocket. Despite the tropical climate, he never abandoned his formal attire and maintained the image of the proper señor until the day he died. He was in the timber business and knew the names of all the dark and light woods of the forest. He always carried a cane and a ledger book and would sit on a pile of white stones by the Jigüe River, giving orders to his men who hacked down trees with machetes and loaded them into the truck that would carry the timber into Holguín. Twenty men worked for his business. At home Teodoro employed a cook, a laundress, a seamstress, and a maid. He paid decent wages and was known as a good *patrón*. At the day's end he would ride homeward on a squat, shaggy-maned palomino that he loved very much. He was fond of animals. He kept a parrot and six German hounds that he and his daughters took walking in the park at night.

Teodoro came to Cuba in 1897 with the Spanish army and was posted as a captain of the guard on the main road into Holguín. He liked Oriente enough to emigrate from Majorca with Doña Maria, who would never get over leaving her family back in Spain. Remembered over the years for his pro-Cuban sympathies, Teodoro came to be well respected in Holguín. He held local magisterial posts, was highly placed in the Masonic society, and knew all the politicians of the province. And he was regarded as a greatly cultured man. In Spain the Sorreas had owned a tannery and an orthopedic shoe business, and had always been patrons of the arts. Teodoro's father had had some fame as an opera singer in Madrid, and his talent had passed

13

down to Teodoro and to Hector's mother, Mercedes, both of whom had fine voices. Teodoro also wrote poetry. Carrying a pad of bleached newsprint and a pencil, he would sit in the garden composing verse. He published regularly in the Holguín *Sol*, and poets and professors from the province often visited him and would sit in the parlor to hear him recite poetry. He wrote about the world as a garden where people were like blossoms that fell from the most aromatic trees when they died.

When Teodoro sat at a small desk in his study, composing, the house seemed to fill with light. Curiously watching him work on rainy afternoons, Mercedes sometimes noticed a frightened butterfly lingering by the dry glass of the window, as if waiting to be carried into the refuge of one of Señor Sorrea's poems.

> We live in the garden
> butterflies resplendent
> in the sun
> joyful because one day
> our brilliant wings will
> carry us upward
> and we will not burn
> but prosper.

Imitating him, Mercedes wrote her own verse and gloried in the applause of their refined, educated visitors. She lived for her father's approval and followed him everywhere, proud to be a Sorrea. She wrote so well that she won prize after prize for composition and poetry, and dreamed of going to the university to become a poet or a teacher. When she was seventeen years old, she won first prize in a province-wide Catholic essay contest. Her winning essay was called "On the Lost Souls of the Titanic," in which she compared the world to a ship heading into an iceberg of sin. The award ceremony was held in the park and broadcast over the radio. Stands with seating for a thousand people were erected on the green, and the prize-winner in each category was given a blue ribbon bearing an image of our Blessed Mother and a bouquet of roses. Mercedes would always remember sitting beside the Bishop of Havana and shaking his hand, and that when she looked down at her classmates in their white and blue dresses, she saw her sisters and mother and father proudly smiling. Standing before the microphone, Mercedes gave a little speech in which she said she had never been so honored in her life, and this message boomed and echoed across the park and was met with great clapping from the crowd.

She was very happy in those days, but then things started to come down around her.

Teodoro Sorrea, good businessman and poet, was not a good judge of character. His troubles started in the 1920s when he involved himself in politics, giving out loans and making campaign contributions to liberal party candidates. Among mayors, senators, and ministers he had a reputation for reliability. During elections he often went out on a truck, making speeches through a megaphone to the people of small towns. One of the men he supported with an enormous loan eventually became the eighth president of the Republic of Cuba. This was President Machado, who once visited the house and bounced Mercedes on his knees. His first term, from 1925 to 1929, was considered most productive. He built the Central Highway that linked Cuba east to west, brought new electrical generators to Havana, and increased economic investment by Americans in Cuba. But during his second term he began to seek total power. Fighting widespread opposition, President Machado shut down schools, tried to disband labor unions, set up torture prisons, and almost brought the economy to ruin.

He was given a nickname by the poor people: "Second Nero."

Machado owed Teodoro a large sum of money that was supposed to be paid in a tax-skimming scheme. Teodoro waited and waited but never received a cent. He had overinvested in a number of projects and was on the verge of bankruptcy when he decided to approach Machado personally. One day in 1929 Teodoro arrived in Havana and roamed the halls of the presidential palace. It was a most opulent mansion with glittering chandeliers, Venetian mirrors, and Greek statues adorning the halls. With so much wealth in evidence, Teodoro thought Machado would surely be able to pay him back. But after three days of patient waiting, after making countless requests to one minister after the other, Teodoro did not meet with Machado. He returned to Holguín, sick from worry and depression. Unable to sleep at night, he paced the floors, smoking cigar after cigar, until morning. He did not spend the usual time before the mirror, looking himself over; his eyes were heavy with sadness.

One evening he heard Mercedes crying out from a bad dream. He went to her room. In the dark he was as wide and high as a mountain:

"Mercita, what's wrong?"

"Nothing, Papa. I was having a dream."

"Don't be worried."

"But it was terrible," she told him. "There were dead butterflies in my dream."

"Your dream was made of air," he told her. "Just remember when you see the butterflies, they are made of air."

But during the succeeding nights the air filled with more of the dead butterflies that weren't there, and one evening an immense butterfly fluttered down the hallway and fell to the floor, crying. The next day Teodoro came home, ate dinner, sat in the patio with his pad of bleached newsprint and pencil, grew drowsy, went to bed, and died in his sleep.

There was tremendous confusion that week, and many flowers were brought into the house. A line of mourners that stretched past twenty of the largest houses went from the street to the door and into the parlor where Teodoro rested in his coffin on a bedding of lilies and orchids. Farmers and poor people came dressed in clean *guayaberas*. The poets came and then military men and politicos, Teodoro's workers and his banker, the local priests and merchants, fellow members of the Masonic lodge, his doctors, young señoritas who carried parasols, the tough young *machos* of town with their mothers, nuns and the local prostitute, feeble old women and the youngest children, who did not know about death. Inside the room they looked into the coffin and prayed for his soul. Mercedes, who greeted the mourners without looking at their faces, sat beside her mother, trembling.

The funeral paralyzed the main road of Holguín for the several hours the procession of wagons and horses needed to make its way to El Campo Santo, the cemetery where Teodoro Sorrea was buried in a fine white tomb in the shade of a tree. Mercedes would not too quickly accept his death. She would not believe it even though she had run her fingers through his hair and touched the bucket of ice that was kept under the coffin as it stood in the parlor, not after she had touched his face and he still did not move, not when they took him out and the procession wound through the streets, past countless mourners who crowded the walkways, and not even when he was put in the ground and she watched a basket of flowers float down into the dark of his tomb.

The years that followed Teodoro's death were not good to the Sorrea family. Never paid by Machado and without an income, Doña Maria had to finally sell off the house, the furniture, and the grand decorations and move away to Arachoa Street, one of the roads the farmers took on their way to market. Mercedes's days were spent quietly on the porch with Doña Maria, reading romantic novels, the Bible, and movie magazines. She wanted to be with her father, but he was gone, and so she sometimes saw his ghost. Resting in bed, she would hear a noise and see on the wall a sprinkling of light, like the sun rippling on water, and her father would appear for a moment, shaking his head. Or she and Doña Maria would go to the cemetery, pray for his soul, and then come home to find him in the living room looking for something. For years she could not stop thinking about him and their old life together. That is the way with the dead, she thought, see him one day and not see him the next. It turned her into a nervous prankster. She played tricks on her sisters and loved to show them how she could still laugh. But at night she dreamed about Teodoro: about walking with him up the white steps of Palo Alto, a mountain in Holguín, to sit before a statue of Jesus; about being a little girl again with a Cleopatra hairdo, happy as a mouse by his side; about feeling his kisses on her face and hearing his voice when she went to bed.

Thinking of him influenced her life. One day, after a long bus ride, she arrived in Santiago to take a scholarship exam for a teacher's school. This was her great hope, and she was certain to pass the exam with ease. But in the middle of the exam she began to think about her dead father, and soon she couldn't answer the questions or decipher the numbers on the pages, and she broke down crying, excused herself, and ran from the examination room. She never attempted the scholarship exam again. So she remained with her mother, Maria, and watched her sisters Rina and Luisa find men, get married, and move into their own houses. When she became bored at home, she went to work as an accountant's assistant for a family friend with a tobacco concern in Holguín. She passed a few years in this job. But in the riots of 1933 the building she worked in burned down. Then she didn't do very much for three years. She spent time with a few different *novios*, but these romances amounted to nothing. Sometimes she dabbled in prophecy and entertained herself and friends with predictions about love. One afternoon Mercedes decided to go to the movies at the Neptuna movie theater, where *Snow White* was playing. Just as she was going inside, the manager of the theater came out and asked if she would like a job as a ticket girl. She accepted.

There is much more to be told... One day Hector and his older brother Horacio would hear all the different stories, and it would amaze them that for all her ability and talent their mother ended up tearing tickets off a spool and pushing them out under the window of a gold painted booth. She sold those tickets for a peseta each. Sometimes she looked up to find the god Neptune with trident staring back down at her from the marquee, and she would leave the theater and walk the street, sad because she did not have a good man, sighing as the other couples passed by her and strolled to the park where they held hands and kissed behind the trees.

Sometimes, as she waited in the booth, blossoms blew over from the park. One whiff of the enlarging fragrances and she began to think about her father, Teodoro Sorrea, standing in the parlor of the grand house, in all the sunlight, with the famous poets and other admiring visitors. And she would hear his fine voice speaking of nightingales and stars. She would daydream about these things until someone rapped at the window and interrupted her, saying, "Señorita? Señorita?" or someone caught her eye, like Alejo Santinio, whom she saw one day standing a few feet away from her.

18

2

In those days, on Sundays, Alejo Santinio used to take the bus into Holguín from his town of San Pedro, about ten miles away, and go walking down the avenue by the park. San Pedro was a nothing town, known long ago as a center for trading and selling slaves. It had a town square of pounded-down dirt that sent up clouds of dust any time a strong wind came along. Going into Holguín was thrilling to Alejo because that city, surrounded by hills, had everything from a movie theater to an enormous dance hall. On Sundays there were crowds and music in the park and young couples strolling and friends to be met, sweets and fruit to be eaten.

For a small town dandy, Alejo was a good dresser. He usually wore an embroidered guayabera but sometimes put on a flashy linen suit with light blue stripes and a pair of black and white spatted shoes. He was tall, nearly six feet in height, with broad shoulders, a large nose, dark eyes and hair, and a typically sad Galician expression. Several generations back his family had emigrated from Galicia, Spain, to the Canary Islands and then to Cuba. Then his grandfather had done something in the slave trade. He had sailed the seas between the Canaries and Santiago de Cuba with that terrible cargo, made some money, and settled in San Pedro where he bought up farmland. Alejo was not a handsome man. Nor did he look particularly Cuban or Spanish. His immense ears and longish face gave him the air of a gypsy. But he was very clean, well manicured, and well shaven, with skin fragrant with a lilac after-shave lotion that attracted the stingless bees of the park as he walked along.

One Sunday his girl had refused to go kissing with him behind one of the trees, so he left her alone—to hell with her, she was a prissy virgin—and crossed the wide avenue and walked down the side street until he found himself on the corner where the Neptuna movie theater stood. Looking around, he noticed the ticket girl staring at him, so he smiled and nodded and called out, "Señorita, Señorita," which made her blush and return to counting the receipts. But she kept taking peeks at him, and seeing this, Alejo decided to make her acquaintance.

An Edward G. Robinson double feature was playing, and the big posters that fluttered like ghosts off the theater pillars showed a gangland floozie hanging from the leg of her man. This must have put certain thoughts into Alejo's mind. He straightened his hat and walked over. Noticing blossoms on the sidewalk, he stepped down and gathered them into a bouquet, went to the booth, and shoved the flowers into the opening saying, "Señorita, if I may be forward, my name is Alejo Santinio and these flowers are for you. Flowers for the flower. Señorita, you are very pretty."

She blushed and, giggling, said, "And I think you're a little crazy, Señor."

From this beginning sprang their romance. She kept the flowers and he went into the movies free. This was a good deal for him, and he returned week after week. He liked the movies and he liked Mercedes. Soon he began to take her out. She would meet him in the back of the theater and sit beside him in a creaky chair, fanning herself as they watched the newsreels. In those days there were Nazis marching arrogantly down European squares and shots of a scowling Hitler and movie stars and shots of Eastern European refugees, so poor and lost. "Persecuted," as Mercedes would say, "even though they believe in God, too." They would see cartoons and then Laurel and Hardy (*El Flaco y el Gordo*), funny enough because when Alejo would grow older and world-weary, his face would grow round and heavy, and he would begin to resemble Mr. Hardy more and more each day. After the movies they would get lost in the park and wander in the orange grove, watching the moon in the wash of stars. They kissed behind prickly trees and under gaslights as bright as the moon. They walked under luminous clouds, sighing and speaking in whispers. In little cafeterias, they feasted on rum-drenched sweet cakes and guava paste, then went to the dance halls and the three-hundred-year-old Central Gallego with its Spanish pillars, endless mirrors, and archways. They inhaled each other's breath, kissed under the shadows of church walls, and wandered in the cemetery among the white tombs held aloft by apostolic hands and by exhausted saints, and they sat on the low white benches of the *placitas* throughout town ecstatic in their mutual love.

Who knows what caused the original love. Was it the taste of the tongue that had been sipping a creamy *café con leche*? The weight of his body pressing her fearful body, thin and soft, against a stone wall? Gentlemanliness on his part, ladylikeness on hers? Was it religion? The shadows on the street? Or the fact that when she mentioned her father's name, Alejo took hold of both her hands? Or was it the twisted, deformed elbow he had gotten from a childhood fall? His sad eyes? The air of chivalrous melancholy about him? Her fears? Was it because he took her to a friend's house, or to a shed in the slaughterhouse part of town, or up north to the beach whenever he pleased? Did she ever try to resist?

Who knows? But when Alejo brought Mercedes home to Arachoa Street, they would find Doña Maria sitting by the front window watching the street and shaking her head because so many of the young people of the 1930s were starting to go where they pleased without a chaperoning aunt or mother—a *dueña*—to keep an eye on them. In Maria's youth she could go nowhere with a male unless her mother accompanied her. But now things were different. Poor Doña Maria, even though she was infuriated by this change, she wanted Mercedes to find a man and have a life of her own. Even though she was very old herself and might be left alone if Mercedes married.

So when she saw them coming to the house, holding hands and playing around, she remained silent. As they sat on the porch, Maria's head would appear silhouetted behind the curtains and then disappear. She constantly spied on them and rarely smiled. When Alejo called out to her from the porch in a cheerful voice, "Good evening, Señora!" she remained silent, perhaps nodding. The only emotion she seemed to show was sadness, which had been her way since she first came to Cuba with Teodoro. That sadness had made her very strict with Mercedes and her sisters. Perhaps it had turned her hair white. Even though she loved Cuba, Maria refused to forget Spain, and this stubbornness made her suffer.

"Good evening, Señora," Alejo always said a second time, waving until her face left the window. Then he and Mercedes followed a tile path through bushes and hanging lianas to the yard behind' the house, where Teodoro Sorrea's ghost sometimes became visible.

"My father comes here when it's very late at night. And then he's quiet. A good man doesn't like to frighten people. It's just that spirits want to be near people so much they can't help themselves."

"When did he die?"

"When I was younger and prettier. He died from a bad heart."

"My father's dead, too. He passed on two years ago, but it's just as well because he said we were all trouble to him. It's just as well that he stays in the ground."

"Dios mío, don't say that. Or he'll cry. It'll make him suffer and then you won't know what to expect from him."

"Psssh," he said. "I don't really believe in all those superstitions. And besides, the world is hard enough. Why do you have to think about ghosts?"

"Because they are there," she said wistfully.

"You think too much."

In those days, being young and strong, Alejo did not think too much about death or cry in the evenings fearing the end of things. It's hard but pleasurable to imagine him that way. No tears. Instead he preferred to think about the opportunities in his life. He had some money. His father, Isidro Santinio, had left the family some fruit and livestock farms. All but one had been sold and the money divided up among his family. They were nine daughters and two sons, Alejo and his older brother after whom Hector would be named. Alejo's share came to about five thousand dollars. When he met Mercedes he was thinking about what he would do with the money. All he knew was that he wanted to leave San Pedro and head out into the world, to break away from the small town life he sometimes found so boring.

"Then why don't you go?"

"Why? Because I feel tied to this place. I want to go and I want to stay." He looked down into his hands. "And there's also my family."

"Is that all you're afraid of?" She laughed. "Ai, leave them when you want to!"

She was prone to say what he wanted to hear and to compliment him on the way he dressed and carried himself and on his soft voice.

This pleased him. Being the youngest he was used to having affection and praise lavished upon him. And he was accustomed to having his way and generally doing what he pleased. The accident that deformed his right arm as a younger man had exempted him from the hard work of the farms. His brother, Hector Santinio, managed the farms and was the patriarch of the family after Isidro. He was always after Alejo to do something more with himself. But Alejo liked the easy life, the big parties his mother enjoyed giving, cock fights, gambling, domino games, the movies, women, dancing, lazy naps, suckling pig with large platters of saffron rice and black beans... Go away? Yes, he would like to go, but in San Pedro he could work only when he felt the urge. He had an occasional job taking mail into the mountains by mule. For two days he would travel south through the countryside to reach the mountains. Then he would stop to eat and drink with the people who lived there and give them news about the outside world. To them, as to the people of San Pedro, he was a big man. If he remained he would never have to worry about friends, food, or money. The Santinios had been in Oriente for more than seventy-five years. They were respected and their life was good.

"Yes I think I would like to go somewhere," he told Mercedes. "These towns are too small; maybe one day I will go somewhere." And then he looked around at the windows and up into the trees where little bell frogs were chirping, and he pulled her close and kissed her.

3

They were going together for a long time. Generally speaking, she let him have his way with her. Who knew where they would go, groping and kissing one another? Maybe into the parlor after Doña Maria had fallen asleep, perhaps to the rear patio where they could hide behind jade plants and creepers. Mercedes did not mind Alejo's forwardness. She always waited anxiously for their evenings together at the Neptuna, in the dance halls, and for their romantic walks in the park and then home.

On Saturdays he would bring her out to San Pedro. He lived on a farm outside the town. The main house was in the old Spanish style, with iron balconies, winding stairways, a central gallery, and a little garden by the entrance that led into a courtyard. The Santinios always held big parties in the house for their friends from town. Tables and chairs and Chinese lanterns were carried out through the gallery into the central courtyard. So many delicious foods were cooked: suckling pig with garlic sauce, chicken fricassee with rice and black beans, yucca and plantain soups, platters of beef *picadillo*. Mercedes would remain until midnight, spending much of her time with Alejo's mother, Doña Isabel. They would sit in the shade, laughing and chatting, watching the maid and the cook prepare the courtyard for the festivities. Isabel would come out in a red dress with beads and a flamingo plume in her hair, in the style of the flappers of the 1920s. A wind-up phonograph played tangos, and dance contests were held, all for the amusement of Doña Isabel, who needed such festivity to forget the death of her husband. Nearly a hundred people would come from town to dance and eat. Doña Isabel and Mercedes would sit together talking about life.

Isabel's husband, Don Isidro, had died abruptly one day, and this fact drew Isabel close to Mercedes.

"Sometimes I wonder where he is," Isabel said sadly.

"In heaven," Mercedes answered, looking up at the sky with wide-open eyes. "Up there it's like a park, so very nice with benches and trees and streams. There's plenty of sunshine and tables set with food. The leaves have little pictures of Jesus Christ on them."

Isabel laughed. "And how do you know this is so?"

"Because I know, as sure as I am here." Then Mercedes took a rose and gave it to Isabel. "Take a deep breath, Isabel. That is what heaven is like."

"Ai, but you're a funny woman," Isabel said to Mercedes. "But you're a good one, just the same. Alejo is making a good choice."

As Mercedes always knew, Doña Isabel liked her. And she was well liked by almost everyone in Alejo's family. The exception was Alejo's eldest sister, Buita, who hated Mercedes from the start. They were opposites. Mercedes was thin and dainty with a mermaid's amazed face; she liked to laugh, easily felt the pain of others, and had a delicate soul. But Buita was harsh and liked to give orders; she was physically huge, good-looking but not pretty. A jealous woman, she criticized people easily. Although she was fervently religious and owned a chest of crucifixes, she had no real interest in the suffering of others; her soul was eight feet high and made of chain mail and armor.

Buita was married to a musician whom she had met in Havana on a shopping trip, but he was always going away. He was the leader of *Los Bufos Cubanos*—"The Jolly Cubans"—and his name was Alberto Piñon. He was popular in the States, where he sometimes toured, and occasionally he asked her along. But just as often Buita remained in San Pedro taking care of her mother and watching over the household. During his absences, Buita liked to pass her time with Alejo, with whom she was very close. But sometimes she would embarrass him by giving him too many orders, and so Alejo tried to avoid her, sneaking out to spend time in Holguín with friends or with Mercedes at the Neptuna. Sometimes Buita would go looking for him, cursing Mercedes and calling her a witch who had put Alejo under a spell.

Buita was thirty-five years old. Being the eldest, she had the power of a substitute mother over her brothers and sisters. When Mercedes came to visit, Buita said whatever she pleased, and Alejo never protested.

"Chica," Buita would often say, "how can my brother want someone like you?"

"Well, Buita, he does have eyes."

"But not much of a brain."

Things never improved. Whenever Mercedes came to visit, Buita interrogated her. "And can you sew? Do you know how to clean a house? Can you cook?"

"Oh yes, of course, I know how to do those things," Mercedes assured her.

But when Buita, treating her like a house servant, put her to work, Mercedes burned up a pig in the oven, stripped off the finish of an old German cabinet with metal polish, and dropped an old family mirror, shattering it into pieces on the floor.

"Dios mío," Buita said. "How can my poor brother want you?"

Because she grew up in a house with servants, Mercedes never learned how to cook or sew or clean properly. Whenever she mentioned her "other life," her life before her father's death, and offered it as an excuse, Buita would laugh and say, "You? You never had anything!"

"Oh, but we had a grand house with a cook from Cienfuegos and three others to do the work," she answered Buita. "We had two coaches and a car, three horses, and six German hounds."

"Psssssh, no tenia nada! You had nothing. Ni pío! Nothing!"

"We did!"

"Then why do you look at everything in this house with such big eyes?"

"I don't."

"You know what she's up to, don't you?" she asked Alejo, who pretended that nothing was being said. "She's like a little cat who wants to lick up all the milk in our family because her family had none. She's not interested in you but in your plata." Buita was rubbing her fingers together as a fly rubs its legs. "She's a lower kind of woman, and you would be better off without her."

Soon Buita took to spreading vicious gossip around San Pedro and Holguín, calling Mercedes "a stupid ticket girl," "a cheap harlot," "a lowlife," and a "seducer," as if she had taken Alejo's innocence from him. Buita hated Mercedes so much that she went up to Alejo one day and bluntly told him, "If you marry that girl, you will lose the family."

Torn between Mercedes and Buita, whose power over the others was strong, Alejo tried to avoid the subject of marriage. But the rivalry continued until finally one day Mercedes went to the Santinio house to have a talk with Doña Isabel about Alejo.

"Of course you know the things people are saying about us are not true," Mercedes told Isabel, "but there is one way of stopping this gossip, and that is a wedding. I wouldn't ask unless I thought it would be for the good—otherwise people will continue to talk, and all our names will be shamed...."

Mercedes probably shocked Isabel with stories of their love. She may have even said she was carrying Alejo's baby. Like in the romance

26

novels. In any case, after this, Doña Isabel more or less ordered Alejo
to marry Mercedes.

4

The ceremony was held in an old colonial church with cool stone
floors and walls with saintly figures recessed into stone, under a ceiling
of cracked crossbeams and fresco depictions of celestial battles. Everyone from both families attended the wedding, except Buita and two
of her sisters who were no longer living in Cuba—Lolita, who had
moved from San Pedro to Havana to California, and Margarita, who
was living in New York. Doñas Isabel and Maria sat together and
chatted like friendly widows, and both sides of the family were smiling
at each other. Alejo looked very handsome. He wore a one-hundred-
stitch-per-inch cotton suit and a pair of gleaming black shoes. Mercedes wore a plain blue cotton dress, dotted with little flowers, and
a pair of simple low-heeled shoes. Alejo held both her hands because
Mercedes was trembling and also giggling as the priest, Father Julio
Verdad, an old family friend, read the marriage vows. Mercedes was
thinking about so many things, feeling the warmth of blood in Alejo's
hands and watching the faces around her nod and blink, and soon her
mind really started to wander, so that she saw the statues of saints
and angels look around and blink their eyes, and then beyond the
windows, it began to rain even though it was not raining. Then the
ceremony was suddenly over. The priest gave the final blessing. Alejo
kissed her, and everyone kissed her, and they left the church and found
themselves outside, being serenaded by a troupe of singers from San
Pedro playing guitars and violins, and then they got into a noisy,
blossom-covered white automobile and drove off into town.

They went to the Spanish Society and danced all night to a *charanga*
band. Mercedes kissed her sisters, and her sisters, Luisa and Rina,
kissed Doña Isabel and Hector, who kissed Doña Maria, and she kissed
the other Santinios, Juanita, Sarita, Consuelo, Vivian, Linda, and
Concepción, and then friends and neighbors. Everyone danced and
ate and drank, toasting the new couple, and this went on until long

past midnight when they left the Spanish Society for their hotel room, which happened to be around the corner from the Neptuna in Holguín.

During the honeymoon night the unrestrained act of love inspired a kind of hysteria in Mercedes. She got up from bed, which was made of squeaky metal, to hang a cloth over the mirror, and later, as Alejo was being his most forceful with her, she seemed to drift away, floating off the bed, becoming more a spirit than a wife, weightless and without a body. She was thinking about so many things: the lariats of hair that curled up from his belly, over his chest, and behind his neck; the strength of his body; his good looks; his wishes for the future. She thought about the taste of his salty sweat while he whispered his love and looked at her with sad, angelic eyes. She imagined birds circling the garden of her childhood house and saw her father walking up the path to their house with gifts for her in his arms, and this made Mercedes shiver. And she found herself looking down over the hotel room at herself and Alejo in bed. She began to shake from loving and kisses, and when they were finished, Mercedes sighed and Alejo murmured, "Mi querida, mi querida." "My love, my love." Entangled in each other, they caressed and kissed until they fell asleep.

Mercedes dreamed that she was a flower in her father's hands, and Alejo, standing on the bow of a ship under a sky of gently spinning stars, felt an ocean breeze cooling his face.

Later that night their peace was broken by a violent pounding, as if a bull were trying to knock down the door. They sat up in bed, holding each other, and then Alejo called out, "Go away!" But neither he nor Mercedes dared to move from the bed. They remained there, holding each other, for another half hour, until finally the pounding ceased. Alejo smoked a cigarette and then they went back to sleep. Years later Mercedes would tell her sons, Hector and Horacio, "It was some poor lost soul who was jealous of our love.... Ask your Papa if you don't believe me, and he will tell you the same."

They were very happy. The uncertain future was open to them. Alejo was thin and tall, with hope in his eyes. Like a character from a romance novel, he promised Mercedes the world. And Mercedes, frail and vulnerable, with long curly mermaid's hair, wanted to believe in him. In those days she would do anything for him. She was a willing slave and never wanted to let him go.... They spent a week honeymooning up at Gibara beach, but after that they had no real plans. What were they going to do? It was 1941. There was a war in Europe, and a new crooked president in Havana. They rented a little house with running water outside San Pedro, within walking distance of the bus stop, bought a radio, and for a time spent their afternoons loving on their rickety bed. Sometimes Alejo went into the mountains with his mule, carrying mail, and Mercedes passed the evenings at the Neptuna, tearing tickets off a spool. It was around this time that Alejo started thinking seriously about coming to America.

5

Alejo's sister, Margarita, lived in New York, and she would send Alejo letters that spoke of her loneliness for the family and practically begged him to visit her. She was married to Eduardo Delgado, a tobacco exporter from Cienfuegos. They had been living in America since 1932, when Eduardo had opened a shop on Madison Avenue and started retailing cigars for the Santinio family. It was a short-lived venture, producing Santinio "Comets" and "Fires," because the cigars never caught on. When the business folded, Eduardo began selling cigars and smoking items to the hotels and men's clubs, and he soon started earning a good living for himself. Margarita liked New York, but she had another reason for staying there: She had stolen the love of Eduardo Delgado away from Buita, and this had caused a rift that would last for the rest of their lives. Margarita was by far the prettier and gentler of the two sisters. When Eduardo had visited their house, he was more attracted to Margarita and little by little began to spend more of his time with her. Even though he was twenty years older than she, Margarita fell in love with him. He was a kind man and very good-looking for his age. One day, when he was supposed to take Buita dancing, Eduardo confessed everything and began to court her sister openly. For years neither Buita nor Margarita spoke a word to one another. Relations eventually improved when Margarita moved to America and Buita found herself her own husband. Mercedes always told that story to explain Buita's mean streak, but there was more to it than that.

Alejo received Margarita's letters monthly and kept them in a special box, rereading them whenever he felt the desire to leave San Pedro. In her letters she tried to entice Alejo to New York with stories about the high-living Cubans he would meet there. He would have a good time with this crowd at dance halls, ballrooms, restaurants, and parties, and he would get to see something of the world. Buita had been to New York with Alberto to visit Margarita and had liked it, but Alejo had never been outside of Cuba. Next to his better-traveled sisters, he felt like a country bumpkin. Sometimes as he walked through the main plaza of San Pedro, he bemoaned his simple quiet life, wishing for more. What would he do if he remained in Cuba? He didn't want to be a farmer like his brother. That work was too hard for too little return. He had struggled with the idea of opening a store of some kind in town, but at almost thirty years of age, he realized that it might be his last chance to change, to have an adventure.

One evening Alejo went to his mother and told her that he was thinking about making a journey to America. And he did the same with family and with his friends, finding support from all except his brother Hector, who could never dream of leaving Cuba. Hector kept a farm in the countryside, lived like a nineteenth-century gentleman, raised his children strictly, and didn't care much for the modern age. He referred to America as the "machine country" and told Alejo, "You're your own man, so go if you want," but his disapproval was obvious and this made Alejo doubt his plans. Still, he decided to go.

Mercedes was secretly shocked by this decision, and she was afraid that Alejo was going to leave without her. Dwelling on this possibility, she spent many of her days with her mother and sisters, weeping and suffering from a case of racked nerves. The afternoons found her in the cemetery where her father was buried, kneeling beside his white tomb with her hands folded in prayer, whispering to him. Finally Alejo asked her to go with him. Then she was relieved and in some ways happy to be leaving Cuba on an adventure. Alejo would be removed from the influence of Buita who was a thorn in her side; Mercedes would have him for herself.

When Alejo looked into her eyes and spoke about the future in his soft voice, Mercedes believed they would be happy. But who gave thought to the fact that they spoke no English? Who considered the differences between doing business in a small Cuban town and in America? Or that they would need plans, connections...that it wouldn't be a casual little vacation voyage? Or that Mercedes would be unhappy with fear and loneliness, or that they would miss the very things that so bored them now? Alejo? He thought only that he would have more excitement and fun, perhaps more opportunity, and that he would escape the midday lethargy, the sleepiness of humid, heavy-aired, Cuban afternoons.

So one day Alejo and Mercedes received passports from a certain judge, Alfonso Alonso of Oriente Province Cuba, dated June 10, 1943.

The following week they and about ten members of their families made their way south to the bustling port of Santiago. Among the family were Luisa and Rina and their children, doñas Isabel and Maria, Buita and Concepción, and Hector. Mercedes was wearing a plain cotton dress, sunbonnet, and dark glasses. Alejo was wearing a linen suit and stood by the water's edge casually smoking American cigarettes, Lucky Strikes, "Un fumo muy bueno," as the billboard ads used to say. He passed the hour speaking quietly with his sisters, but when the boarding horn sounded and one of the crew told them to get moving, Alejo put out his cigarette and buried himself in his mother's arms.

She kept repeating: "Dios mío, I don't believe you're leaving us."

"Don't be worried, I'll come back in a short time," he told her, as if he would indeed return soon. She kept patting his back and re-assuring him that she would pray for them. Then it was time for the final embraces and all the women, including Buita, were crying. Alejo and his brother, Hector, shook hands in a manly way, but in the final moments they came together like children, patting one another's backs and kissing each other's faces, and then Mercedes did the same with her mother and sisters, and Alejo kissed his sisters and mother. Then they went up the boarding ramp and stood at the railing.

Seagulls swooped at the water which was choppy and rocking the ship. A woman's hat blew away. Mercedes kept waving down at the dock, and with the last whistle she almost leaped over the railing and ran down the ramp, but Alejo took hold of her, calmed her, and then he lit another cigarette. He waved down to his family. All waved back except Buita, who stood with her arms folded, looking sternly up at Mercedes. Then the ship pulled away from the dock and headed northeasterly toward the Windward Passages, away from the bursting sunlight on the horizon and the bending royal palms and their sweet aroma that Alejo would never smell again.

6

While Mercedes spent much of the journey by herself, Alejo passed the days under the shade of a deck umbrella, playing cards and making conversation with the other Cubans on board. These were well-bred Cubans with enough money to go on journeys whenever they liked. They came from families who had profited during times of great hardship. They were clean, well manicured, well scented, and well dressed, with soft leather shoes from Spain, linen suits, panamas. They liked Alejo because he was polite and clean-cut and spent his money buying them daiquiris and icy beers. And the waiters liked him. They came from Europe and spoke very little Spanish. They liked the way Alejo imitated the Americans who wore Stetson hats, leaving a rolled-up dollar bill under a plate, as a tip, after the morning refreshments were served. An Italian waiter would come along and slap the back of Alejo's jacket with a soft brush, for which he received a twenty-five-cent piece and a return slap on his shoulder. Alejo and the Italian treated each other like brothers. The waiter would come up on deck after working hours and sit in the dark, watching the sea, morosely silent because he had left his family in Italy. Playing the big man, Alejo bought the waiter a drink and then another, so that money flew from his pockets. Everyone had seen refugees in those days. The Cubans of coastal towns would find families of dark-eyed Europeans, dressed in black, exhausted from their journey, resting in the plazas. Alejo had seen refugees in Holguín and in the newsreels, and as he left the deck to play some rummy with the other passengers below, he considered himself a fortunate man.

Gambling, he lost money. Luck was not with him, and when he wanted more money he would send Mercedes down into their compartment below deck. She had hidden his cash inside a pair of low-heeled shoes at the bottom of their black trunk. Sighing, she would open the trunk and take out the money for him. Sometimes she slipped an extra amount into an envelope, which she hid in her dress. Saving money in that manner would become a lifelong habit. Even though they had about five thousand dollars—in those days a considerable sum—she was worried that it would suddenly disappear. Alejo always reassured her that everything would be fine. And for a long time those few words were enough for her. What was he going to do with that money? He had some kind of vague plan to double, triple, infinitely multiply it. His plan was vague, because there was no plan. Somehow he would find Cubans in New York to give him ideas, honest Cubans like his sister and her husband, to point him toward prosperity. Somehow he would triumphantly return to San Pedro with gifts of fine clothing, electrical appliances, watches, and jewelry for everyone.

Alejo was not worried. At the very least he would be able to find work in New York. As one of the Cubans on board put it, "If you're willing to kill yourself working, you'll always make money."

On the third day of the voyage Alejo was approached by a man from Havana who was returning to New York after a visit. He had heard about Alejo's ambitions and noticed his generosity. As Alejo stood by the deck railing having a smoke, this Cuban presented him with a business proposition. Then they sat on the deck chairs, talking for an hour. The man had a *negocio*, a shoe store in the Bronx, and he offered Alejo a share. He said he needed the money to bring one of his brothers up from Cuba, that he didn't have enough to do it. A little while later Alejo was rustling through the trunk in the compartment, counting out five hundred dollars.

"Alejo! What are you doing?" Mercedes pleaded. "You've been spending money like water. Are you rich?"

"It's for a friend."

"Who?"

"His name is Gregorio Cruz and he's from Havana and that's good enough for me."

Then Alejo left the compartment and went up to the deck with the money. Uncertain about the future, Mercedes sat on the bed, felt the motion of the ship, and sighed. "Ai, but I wish my father was alive," she said, as she would whenever there would be trouble later on, after she had her sons.

Trying to nap, she kept turning over in that bed. She tried to read a romance novel, but soon she put it away and decided to go up on deck. At the stern of the ship she leaned over the railing, staring into the waves and the whorls of electric eels that followed in the ship's foamy trail. She was seeing things in the water, as if there were an ocean of waving plants, sunken caravels, and mermaids under the ship. Then her eyes grew wider and she began to shiver in the breeze, as if only a few yards below she could see her father, Teodoro Sorrea, submerged and floating on his back. As she stared down into the water she was filled with her recollections of this calm, responsible, and intelligent Cuban who had made her family so happy, and of their life together in a serene Cuba she would never know again. The faces of poets who would sit in their garden with its aromatic trees came back to her, and she thought how all good things seemed to pass from this world. Then she thought of her house on Arachoa Street with her mother and sisters, and her days as a ticket girl at the Neptuna movie theater, and her romance with Alejo, and she knew that this life, so alluring and pleasant, was now being washed away forever in a trail of white foam in the choppy sea.

In the morning all the passengers rushed to the railing because the ship's whistle had sounded entry into New York harbor. New York, America. *Los Estados Unidos.* "De Junidad Stays." They saw warships, tugboats, and American flags everywhere. They saw seagulls circling over the docks. They saw the Statue of Liberty, startling as the moon. They saw buildings and marinas and countless merchant ships unloading their cargoes by crane. Hurrying down into their compartments, they returned with their bags and held one another as the ship began to dock and another whistle blew, and they went down a ramp into America, past policemen and rushing porters and messengers and sailors and dock workers. Mercedes and Alejo were happy and excited, checking through customs like a couple of rich Cuban tourists in New York for a visit.

Suddenly they heard a voice: "Alejo! Alejo!"

Behind a wire fence they saw Margarita and Eduardo Delgado.

"Here, here," Eduardo and Margarita called, waving their hands.

Eduardo was very tall but frail-looking, and he kept dabbing his mouth and nose with a blood-speckled handkerchief, his pañuelo, which he kept in his jacket pocket. Margarita looked very much like Alejo, with a long face but pretty features. Seeing her brother for the first time in seven years, Margarita started to shake and laugh and blow many smoke rings from her cigarette, and she threw her arms around Alejo and kissed him, repeating, "Alejito! Alejito!" And she was nice to Mercedes, saying, "And this is your wife? How good she seems!" Then excited talk came, convoluted like crazy speech from a speeded up phonograph record.

They were out on the street, waiting for a taxicab, when the Cuban from Havana came up to Alejo and embraced him. "We will see each other soon," he said. "This is my address in the Bronx." Alejo did not doubt Cruz for a second. Good-bye to Cruz. Good-bye to another Cuban family posing for pictures. Good-bye to the Italian waiter who was sitting on a saggy, brown leather suitcase. They drove under endless projections of metal: trestles, elevated trains, cranes, water towers, construction sites, street lamps, telephone poles, power lines, highway ramps. Mercedes was tired but excited and nervously took hold of Alejo's hand and closed her eyes as they made their way uptown to their new home in America.

America, 1944–1947

1

Their new home, the residence of Eduardo Delgado, was in upper Manhattan, squeezed between the sinister reaches of Harlem and the shadow of the University, which meant the neighborhood consisted of professors and their students, workers and their families, hoods, cops, old ladies, and whores. The college people were on top and nearly blind because the lower classes were invisible to them. Underneath were the workers—carpenters, plumbers, firemen, stokers, building superintendents, and handymen—and down below, with the hoodlums and whores, were the new people, like Alejo and Mercedes, who did not speak English.

The buildings of the neighborhood were constructed in the 1920s in a frenzy of neoclassical imitation. Everywhere stood pillared and corniced stoops with fancy ornamented colonnades and fences with cast-iron heads of the gods, Jupiter and Mercury being the most popular. There were small entrances into labyrinthine basements, and back yards that sloped like ravines and rose in the distance on huge masses of stone and hills of poison oak and thick bushes. There were old black wrought-iron light poles, and to Mercedes's delight, down the hill, a block away, was a park with wide-spreading trees and steps that followed descending terraces into central Harlem.

The very foyer of the building where Eduardo Delgado lived fascinated Mercedes because it had marble walls and steps and columns and two vast mirrors that reflected one another endlessly. When the sun spread into the hallway, it filled the mirrors with a radiant cheeriness that eventually receded into a pit of darkness. Way back in the depths, shadows entangled like forest briars and faces seemed to appear. In these mirrors Alejo would look himself over, admiring his suit and sporty shoes, whenever he went downtown in the evenings. Mercedes would look at herself making faces—smiling, frowning, showing her teeth, fluttering her Woolworth's eyelashes—Mercedes, in a fruity hat and short-sleeved dress to show off her decent figure... In these mirrors Eduardo Delgado always looked so exhausted, sometimes had his terrible coughing fits and turned blue around the eyes, and in them Margarita took hold of his arms and rapped at his back until the fits were over.

Settled in, the Santinios lived like boarders in a tiny room at the end of the hall. They had a little dresser, a radio, a crucifix, a chair, a mirror, and a bed. The hall from their room circled the apartment, so that they could pass through the kitchen, main bedroom, living room, and back again. From the living room windows they could see the street, garbage, the sidewalk, a black Victorian-looking gate into a front courtyard in which hung laundry lines, and a brick building with people in the windows. In the kitchen there was an icebox and an old gas stove with hooves. The flecked walls made noises and always threatened to fall. In the bathroom, a pull chain toilet, no shower.

For a time Mercedes and Alejo had their fun. On some days they rode around town, visiting the new Cubans they had met, or strolled through the park and down to Times Square for the war-bond shows. Alejo was patriotic and went to the hospital with Margarita every few months to give blood. He also bought some war bonds because it was for a good cause. He liked going to the big movie houses and seeing the huge department stores. He was always playing the big shot, spending money on gifts. It was like an infection: he would come home with new hats, hand mirrors, clocks, handy-dandy gadgets for the kitchen. He bought dolls and wind-up mice for the children who played in the street and hung out on the stoop and for the children of his visitors. On some nights he took Mercedes, Eduardo, Margarita, and their friends out for dinner, and afterward they went to dance clubs on Broadway, and it wasn't until early morning that they returned and made time for sleep.

The house was filled with boarders in the early days. Alejo's photographs of them hung on the living room wall. There was a photograph of Alejo with another Cuban, taken after a snowfall in Central Park. Alejo was dressed in black and proudly holding a chunk of snow—everything was so white except for a few stark trees in the background. He seemed to be floating in the air. Mercedes was sitting with Margarita on a bench not far away, freezing, with her head tilted back as if the cold air could not be swallowed. They were dressed to the hilt, real classy, with fur muffs and foxes and black mesh hats. Behind them a few pigeons walked, dazed in the snow like zombies. But Mercedes was beautiful with a bewildered, somewhere-else look. Beside Alejo was his old friend, Edelmiro, who had come up from San Pedro to visit. They had been companions since boyhood when they used to hang around the bad sections of San Pedro and go to cock fights. Edelmiro was about thirty-five at the time and unmarried. He had fought against the Fascists in Spain years before, and had lived in Paris before going back to Cuba and the university to become a banker. He often came to the apartment, sometimes lived there, and was always being whispered about by the women who tried to set him up with their female friends. But he preferred his bachelorhood and turned them down. He eventually stayed in America, moved to Chicago and then back to New York, becoming one of the first Cubans to settle down in the mysterious labyrinths of Chinatown.

In another picture Mercedes and Alejo stood posed in front of the stoop with three beautiful women, sisters whom Mercedes and Alejo knew from Holguín. The three sisters left Cuba in the 1940s because they hated the dictator Batista and his government. Batista was indirectly responsible for their brother's death. A judge who publicly opposed Batista, he had narrowly escaped assassination by machine-gun fire while calmly playing checkers with a friend on his porch in Santiago de Cuba. The friend died; the brother went into hiding for a month and then tried to flee Cuba by boat. But he was drowned in a storm, never to be seen again. Embittered by his death and harassed by the government, the three sisters came to New York and stayed in Eduardo's apartment, in the room next to Alejo and Mercedes. They were like three Rita Hayworths in the most conservative dresses, very aristocratic and deeply religious women, who would sometimes take care of Mercedes in the future, in the bad days when she would be locked out of the apartment or be beaten up by Alejo and need a place to go. They would never be married—Mercedes would one day call them the "three virgin saints"—but they knew what they wanted in life. Each took a turn working so that the others could go to school. They applied themselves to the English language, filled up notebooks with English phrases, found good jobs, and finally moved.

And there was a photograph of an older man, a professor of Classics, from Matanzas. He started coming to the apartment around the time the three sisters left. He looked like Pablo Picasso and had tiny shriveled hands. He was visiting the University as a guest lecturer, heard that some Cubans lived nearby, and showed up at the house one day. At night he would come to the apartment and cry on Alejo's shoulder, reciting endless stories about how good his childhood had been in Cuba. Alejo would tell him to find a girl and forget his troubles, but the professor would break down, saying that as a child he had always loved smooth things made of ivory and how he had gone around kissing other boys on the eyelids as they slept in the shade, to which Alejo would say, "Have some food." Happily accepting Alejo's advice, the professor would eat and drink and forget his myths of Cuba and drift into talk of the myths of ancient Greece. In time the professor moved away, but Mercedes and Alejo remained with Margarita and her poor sick husband, sharing the household with other boarders.

Eduardo Delgado, whose name would always adorn the hallway bell like the inscription on a monument, was suffering from a bad heart and chronic asthma, or tuberculosis. He was always coughing up blood and turning purple. His poor state of health was not helped by his smoking or by the fact that he killed himself for his business. He was tall and thin, with heavy eyes like Peter Lorre's, and a thick beard that he had to shave twice a day. At night the apartment re-

39

sounded with his coughing fits. Often Alejo and Mercedes would awaken because of the horrible noises and go to the bedroom to see if Eduardo and Margarita needed help. Alejo sometimes took Eduardo to the hospital, and then Mercedes would sit with Margarita, trying to calm her nerves. Poor Eduardo had already suffered two heart attacks, and no one believed he would live much past fifty. Margarita now had to watch him suffer. He was a man who had never given thought to marriage until the day he decided it was time to have a family. He may have been a virgin when he had met her, who knew? He had a simple, good nature and he seemed oblivious to the dangers of hard work. His failing health was inexplicable. Alejo would one day say, "He is getting fucked by life," knowing this would send Margarita into fits of deep weeping.

Holding her, Mercedes would whisper, "Don't be worried, this will pass. He will be fine." Stroking her hair as lovingly as a mother, she repeated, "Don't be worried, don't be worried."

At that time Eduardo Delgado decided to have a child. On a night when Eduardo Delgado suffered long, contortive pain, he exploded his sperm inside Margarita's womb, bringing into being the child who would be known as "Ki-ki" Delgado. At that time Mercedes also became pregnant with Horacio. Her insides hummed, and she dreamed about a spring garden filled with pollinating bees and large-winged butterflies. During their pregnancies, Margarita and Mercedes became inseparable companions, tending to each others needs and maintaining cheer even when Eduardo came home in the most solemn of moods.

Eduardo accepted his illness and was slowly selling off stock in the store. He had even offered Alejo a share of the business, but Alejo told him no. He was intimidated by the long lists of contacts in Cuba and America, export documents, ledgers, and bookkeeping of the kind that used to keep him away from the house in Cuba on Sundays, when his father and his brother Hector worked the accounts on a porch table. It was Alejo's first big mistake in America. He could have done well for himself with a nice little shop on Forty-third Street and Madison Avenue, where the rich executives liked their panatellas and coronas from Havana. But he associated Eduardo's poor health with that shop, and for years the very smell of tobacco reminded him of Eduardo's bloody handkerchief and the illnesses that were killing him. Eduardo did not know when he would die, but he took the money from selling shares in the shop and put it into an account for Margarita at the First National Bank, which had offices in Holguín and Santiago as well as in New York. He began to come home earlier and earlier each day, and he greeted Mercedes and Margarita with kisses, jokes, and gifts.

His son, Enrique, or Ki-ki, Delgado was born in August 1945. In October of the same year, Horacio Santinio was brought into the world. Alejo named him Horacio Wilson Santinio, the Americanizing "Wilson" after the U.S. president, whom Alejo considered to be a great man. When Horacio and Mercedes came home from the hospital Alejo threw a big party, and Cubans from all over the city showed up; wild, shaking dancers leered down into Horacio's crib with hyena and wolf smiles. For months the euphoria over the births made for a happy home. Even Eduardo's health seemed to improve. Letters to Cuba told the families about the babies. Doñas Maria and Isabel, Rina and Luisa, and all the Santinios were very happy, except for Buita. She stood out on the porch of her house in San Pedro reading the same lines of Alejo's letter over and over again: "And now we have two new little Santinios in the world. Everyone here is happy." She kept reading those lines with envy and thinking about Mercedes with a fertile belly and a little baby and about her sister Margarita, who stole Eduardo from her. But she was really incensed at Mercedes. How dare she have a child? How dare she? A baby for Mercedes when there were so many others in life who deserved it, she told herself as she stormed in circles around her house. That lunatic with a child, she cursed, hating Mercedes.

2

As in the fairy tales—and Mercedes always laughed about this—Buita was barren. It was her source of grief and shame. Years before Alberto came along, Buita had lost her first husband because she could not get pregnant. It was supposed to be a deep family secret, but everyone

41

knew. She was nineteen years old, and they were together for almost two years. He just left her, just like that, when she couldn't have a baby. She wasn't even a real woman, he told her. It left her in a bad way. Walking in San Pedro she would envy the little mulatta women who had babies at thirteen. She trusted in God but always asked: "Dios mío, why me?" Why barren when her mother, Doña Isabel, had borne thirteen children, two dying at birth? Her other sisters had children. But Buita spent her days rearranging dolls on her windowsill. She dreamed about a dried up riverbed, droughts, and ruined gardens.

What did she do? She went to church and prayed for hours on end but never became pregnant. She soured in character, complained about everything. It wouldn't have been so bad if she weren't getting older, but time was ticking by.

For a while she went to every doctor and *santera* in Cuba. Santeras were spiritists who practiced magic and were said to work miracles. She took walks into the worst barrios where those witches lived, where the ground was laden with lizard skins, bones, and dead butterflies. She took foul-tasting potions, drank holy water, smeared vegetable creams on her privates, and kept a taut rope around her waist. She was even hypnotized inside a solar tent and sent back...back...in time, finding herself in ancient Egypt, where she had drowned a cat in a river. But knowing this did not help. She was very kind to children, made them snacks, invited them into the house to look at her dolls, and always found little boys to go walking with her to the market.

And what did her husband Alberto Piñon think about the situation? Alberto whose band, Los Bufos Cubanos, was known to rumba fans everywhere? He didn't seem to care if Buita could not have children as long as he could have his afternoons in bed with her. He was a stoic who minded his own business and had seen enough of the world to know that children were not absolutely necessary to the happiness of a couple. He had women all over the place. In Europe, Mexico, America, and in Cuba. Women who made no bones about what they wanted from him. He was handsome, sharp like a *caballero* of the ballroom epoch of the 1930s, with his hair slicked down flat and parted in the middle like Rudy Vallee's and with a big flashy grin that had mesmerized Buita when he met her in Havana in 1937. There was a big fancy store called the El Encanto in those days. He was buying a pair of socks there when he saw her. It was hypnotic, the way her face, filled with longing, flashed into his eyes innumerable times as she tried on an almost weightless scarf, pink and floating like a dragonfly in the fan air of that store. Buita had her hair up in a bun and wore rouge on her cheeks, lipstick on her lips. An enormous hand seemed to push him forward so that he brashly introduced himself to her. Their courtship flourished. The respectability of the Santinio name baited him into deep romance. They were married, and the years began to pass. Alberto would return from the band's tours and find Buita at the Santinio house in San Pedro, irascible and in a state of alarm, feeling abused by fate, *jodida* or "fucked up," as they used to say, afraid of disappointing him. But he didn't care. He had put the troubles of the world completely from his mind. He existed in a realm of simple goals. Even World War II impressed him only as a series of canceled performances. The war stranded him in Morocco for three months, chased him into Italy and then to London, where he performed before the aristocracy of Europe who had fled from the Nazis. He played in halls that glittered with diamond tiaras and rings. He met the king of England, stood in a room with Winston Churchill, and rubbed shoulders with Charles de Gaulle, as they both leaned forward to fill their glasses from the punchbowl.

After the war ended Alberto started to think about a new profession. He was an intelligent man who had an interest in engineering and house construction. He saw a future in that business, and he saw that the money was in America. He knew a family of Cubans who lived in Miami, Florida, and he made a few trips there to look around. With money from the band's tours, he bought up swampland, some of which would one day be part of Northeast Miami, with houses every-where. Liking the opportunities and luxuries of America, Alberto Piñon started to think about leaving Cuba and settling in Florida.

In 1946 Alberto's band was booked into New York for a run at the Royal Palms Club on Tenth Avenue and Fifty-fifth Street. Buita and Alberto came to visit. Alberto worked at the club six nights a week. It was a huge dance joint, festooned with papier-mâché pineapples, bananas, and orchids. Its doors and windows were painted with silhouettes of bending palms. There was a long horseshoe bar and a huge bandstand where the orchestra played under a barrage of colored spotlights. They played songs like "Siboney," "El Manicero," "Malagueña," "Quiéreme Mucho," "Babalú," "Tabú," "Eclipse," and "Por Eso no Debes." Famous people went into that place. One night the actor Errol Flynn showed up with an entourage of hangers-on. Xavier Cugat came, too. He knew Alberto from a long way back. Showpeople, local politicians, gangsters, and couples from all over the city out for elegant ballroom dancing came to the Royal Palms. There were women in tight dresses with skirts slit up to their thighs and net stockings held up by flowery garters. Their breasts flowed over their dress tops and wobbled when they danced. Big asses swayed during the rumbas and as *comparsa* lines circled the floor. The women wore as much perfume as Persian princesses, and the men tended to get out of hand, drinking too much and bumping into the walls. On any given night Alejo would be out on the dance floor with Buita, and at one of the tables decorated with flowers and candles would sit Eduardo and Margarita. But where was Mercedes? She was at home in the apartment watching after little Horacio and Ki-ki, staying up in bed and praying for the day when Buita would leave.

From the first moment of her arrival Buita was a real bitch to Mercedes, assailing her with countless criticisms, treating Mercedes, who would have loved to go dancing, like a maid. Buita liked to order Mercedes around, calling her "lazy," but did not lift even one finger to help with the housework. She preferred to take little Ki-ki and Horacio down to the sunny many-terraced park for walks in the afternoons, to eat big meals, entertain countless guests, buy herself clothes, powder her cheeks a blush-red, and enjoy Mercedes's suffering. And Buita loved to flaunt her control over Alejo, who, according to Mercedes, had started treating her "bad" in those days. Buita made Mercedes jealous of her closeness to Alejo. She was always brushing Alejo's hair, smoothing out his jackets and tie with her hand, and pulling loose threads from his shirts. She would speak about their life together back in Cuba, and how, in her eyes, he would always be her little brother whom she loved very much. "Blood is thicker than water," she liked to say. And, when holding her nephew Horacio in her arms, "He's so handsome, just like you were as a baby."

Within a month of her arrival, Buita took a job as a seamstress in a factory on West Twenty-sixth Street. She liked to have extra spending money. On her days off she would organize trips around the city to places like the Statue of Liberty, the Empire State Building, and the Bronx Zoo, trips from which Mercedes was usually excluded. Buita did not like going anywhere with Mercedes and always convinced Alejo to leave her at home, alone. Dressed up on a Sunday afternoon in a pleated skirt, pearl-buttoned blouse, and big Hedda Hopper hat, Buita would lead a crowd of the family and her friends out of the apartment without so much as a word to Mercedes. On those days, and at night when they went out dancing, it was as if Mercedes, who would watch them walking down the street from her window, did not exist.

But she could do nothing to Buita. She was afraid of making trouble. So she would stay home and watch the kids, cry, listen to the radio, and curse her sister-in-law. She deferred to Buita because she was afraid of being left alone in this new country where she did not know the language. According to Buita, Mercedes owed the family gratitude for giving her a place to live when she did not even have a job. She had no right to complain about her constant cleaning, cooking, shopping. "This is not your home," Buita would tell her, "so if you complain, I'll make Margarita throw you out into the street." And she believed that Buita would do it. Alejo never said a word to defend her. She was constantly afraid of eviction from the family...from American life...from this world into the next...How could she live without Alejo, and without knowing the English language? As it was, when she went out Mercedes would go down the street quickly, afraid that someone would stop and speak to her, as if there was a law against not being able to speak English. She answered most questions with nods and a shake of her head and found her way around the neighborhood with single words: "Church?" "Store?" But that was not enough to take care of herself. She wanted to know enough English to speak to people and make new friends. At night she was always studying a notebook in which she wrote down the English phrases that were so painful to learn: *¿Qué hora es ya?* "What time is it?" *¿Dónde está* *la tienda?* "Where is the store?" *Estoy sola aquí.* "I am alone here." *Yo vengo de otro país.* "I come from another country." *Estoy perdido.* "I am lost." *¿Puedes ayudarme?* "Can you help me?" *Estoy sola y tengo miedo.* "I am alone and afraid." *Por favor, no me pegues.* "Please don't hit me." *Yo quisiera ser su amiga.* "I would like to be your friend."

She would repeat phrases like these over and over again, trying to break the monotony of her evenings, trying not to be afraid.

Asleep, she cried out in the dark from bad dreams. She prayed for her father's ghost to come to the apartment, but she prayed in vain. The only times she ever saw him, she was beginning to drift off to sleep and wasn't an adult anymore but a little girl in a bright yellow dress, standing before the fiery window of their house in Cuba, reciting a prize essay or poem for her papa. She would try to find shelter in her old dreams of Cuba, remembering only the good and rejecting the bad. She did not like to remember her father beating her with a strap for high-strung, nervous behavior—her uncontrollable "freshness" toward her elders, for lying, for seductively calling out to male passersby—she did not like to remember how she often went to sleep with her legs covered with welts and thinking that her father despised her; she did not like to remember how her mother and sisters regarded her creativity as lunacy and how her desire to be an artist in that society of the 1920s and 1930s was regarded by her family as an eccentric's joke because she was not a boy. Once I had so much promise, she would think, so much—and for what, to be meek? To stay in a dark apartment at night with children, to have a sister-in-law who would like to see me dead, to stay home while the rest of the world enjoys itself?

She would cringe, hearing Buita's laughter at night, and when she heard whispering through the door, she was convinced that it was Buita, maligning her to Alejo. She imagined Buita would be insulting her because she wasn't the best wife in the world and did not jump at Buita's orders. Buita sometimes called her *"bruja, bruja!"*—witch, witch!—when the fashionable partygoers whom they met at the club, the young Cuban dandies and their wives, came to the house with their dazzling spats and high-heeled shoes and danced to the record player.

Mercedes would go into the bedroom to be with the children, Ki-ki and Horacio, finding shelter there until the dancers spilled from the hall into the bedroom and the lights went on and the kids woke up screaming. Everyone had fun those nights except Mercedes, who didn't like some of the men because sometimes they grabbed her ass, or tried to, and because Buita barked out orders like a rabid dog: *Fill up that tray, bring more beer, cut up more chicken, cook more rice!* Seeing Mercedes's exasperation, Alejo would sit beside her and say, in his most sympathetic voice, "Don't worry, one day you'll be used to the duties of a wife."

But she never got used to those nights when she was left alone, or when she would sit quietly in the dark, afraid that Buita was going to hit her, or when the club friends came home at two in the morning and Buita ordered her around. When were they going to leave for Florida, as Alberto said they would? Why weren't they going? Mercedes showed great interest in this journey and encouraged Alberto and Buita to leave and start a new life there. But Buita would smile and say, "Go? We're not in a rush!"

The three-month gig at the Royal Palms extended with great success to a year. By then Eduardo Delgado's terrible cough had worsened. He had sold the store entirely and now passed the days deciding where he and Ki-ki and Margarita would go next. Eduardo often spoke about returning to Cuba, to his childhood town, Cienfuegos, where they could live quietly. Buita kept insisting that Eduardo and Margarita also move to Florida. She wanted to be near little Ki-ki, whom she loved very much. Because Margarita didn't want to go, she began having terrible fights with Buita. Then the old wounds were reopened.

"Go back to Cuba! Leave me!" Buita told her, screaming. "Take Eduardo and Ki-ki. Go ahead. And while you're taking them from me, why don't you take Alberto, too!"

It turned out that Buita's constant badgering finally drove Margarita from the house. One day Eduardo and Margarita announced they were leaving for Cuba. This devastated Mercedes, who regarded Margarita as an ally and didn't like the idea of being left alone with Buita. On the day in 1947 when Eduardo left with his wife and child, Mercedes wandered off with Horacio, to watch movie after movie in a Broadway theater. Then she went to another movie house. She didn't want to go home.

Where was Alejo? Alejo had found a night job as a cook. Since arriving in America he had worked in the harbor, unloading cargo—hard labor that he didn't like—and he had worked in an ice warehouse, cold as the Arctic, on Eleventh Avenue. But these were jobs without a future. He lent and invested money along with a number of Cubans whom he met through Buita, but, one by one, each of these schemes came to nothing. With the parties he paid for and the bad deals and his generosity at the dance hall, his money was disappearing. He would not let on, except to Buita who offered him the consolation of her money if he needed it. When he wrote letters to Cuba, Alejo spoke vaguely of new business prospects, and no one doubted him. He could have gone back to Cuba and worked the farm with his brother, but he liked America. "It's good here," he wrote in letters. "I'm going to stay."

When he started to run out of money, Alejo ended up working as a waiter. Someone from the Royal Palms had given him the name of the headwaiter at a big hotel. The headwaiter liked Alejo and hired him to take care of desserts. It was light work that earned him good tips. But serving others seemed humiliating, so Alejo asked the headwaiter to set him up in the kitchen assisting one of the cooks. Slowly he learned about the preparation of food. He was a vegetable slicer, a cream whipper, a peeler of potatoes. He was given a chef's hat, a white uniform, a belt with hooks for kitchen utensils. Behind the glittering kitchen with its huge ovens was a dingy passageway to the shower room, where he was given a locker. His job had its own benefits. Each night he would come home with packages of meat and poultry that he got from the butcher and boxes of pastries and slabs of dark German chocolate from the baker. And he came home with bundles of hotel silverware and with a pay envelope of forty-two dollars a week. Even though he burned his hands holding pots and tore open his palm with a knife, he was working, and the future was still before him. Now he always smelled of animal blood and meat. Mercedes often found flour in his shoes, and it sometimes mixed with the lilac lotion and caked in his hair.

While Alejo worked nights, Mercedes remained at home with Buita. They would sit in the same room for hours in complete silence. Each had her own malicious thoughts. Thoughts of fear and envy. Sometimes Buita took care of Horacio, holding him in her lap, kissing his face, smiling and whispering to him. "Your mother is a lunatic," she would say. "Wouldn't you like to come and live with me one day?"

Horacio was too young to really understand what Buita was saying. But Mercedes knew, and not liking this, she would take Horacio out of the house. Sometimes she carried him to the park, where all the old ladies and young lovers sat on the benches, or she went in the opposite direction, down the street and across the avenue to sit near one of the University fountains and stare at the immense library colonnade with its heads of Plato, Socrates, and Aristotle, names and faces she did not know. She would sit in the dark with Horacio sleeping in her arms until it was very late and she thought Buita had to be asleep. Then she would come back quietly and go to bed. In the winter she often took Horacio down Broadway to visit the three sisters from Oriente, always waiting, to their annoyance, past midnight before going home. One January night Buita stayed awake, waiting for her. She was very bold and just came out with what was on her mind.

"You know, Mercedes, sometimes I like it here very much. But there are times when I miss Cuba. Don't you, child?"

"Yes, sometimes."

"Wouldn't you like to go back?"

"Where?"

"Back to live in Holguín with your family. Ai, but your mother must miss you. It's nice and sunny there this time of year, not cold. It's horrible here when the heat doesn't work, isn't it? If you wanted to go without any trouble, you could leave little Horacio with me, and I would give him a nice home."

Mercedes could not believe what Buita was saying.

"With you? After what you've done to me? Am I stupid?" Mercedes was shaking and turning red. "Buita, if you knew how much I hate you, why you would die!"

"And if you knew my hatred for you!"

"Witch!"

"Whore!"

"Lowlife!"

"Big whore!"

"Shit!"

And they started circling one another. A pot of black bean soup was on the stove, and Mercedes grabbed it and dumped it on the floor by Buita's feet, and Buita, wanting to bang her face on the floor, grabbed Mercedes's hands and pulled her close. But Mercedes got away. So Buita pulled down a rack of plates and smashed them on the table and on the floor to make Mercedes cry, and then she threw Mercedes into the wall. Horacio began to cry because Buita now pushed Mercedes down to the floor. Mercedes got up and kicked Buita and started throwing everything in sight, bottles and forks, spoons and knives, and then Mercedes spit in Buita's face, and Buita took a broom and smashed it into Mercedes's back, chasing her down the hall and out of the apartment into the street.

At the time Mercedes was wearing only a blue cotton dress with little marigolds printed on the material. There was snow on the ground and a high wind, and she began to shiver. She went down to the basement and out into the courtyard where she called up into the bedroom window, "Buita, open the door and let me in...please." But Buita pretended not to hear. Mercedes waited in the courtyard, pleading with Buita. All of the neighbors must have heard. Some must have thought it was the "crazy woman" screaming, and they paid no attention. But one of the windows on the fourth floor opened up. A little kid looked out and got his mother, who came down the stairs with a blanket and brought Mercedes up to her apartment.

That was Mary from upstairs. She was Irish. She had no problems with Mercedes's Spanish or her broken English because she was a deaf-mute. That evening Mercedes and Mary stayed together, and while Mercedes poured her heart out, Mary nodded with all the sympathy in the world. She was a kind woman who had her own suffering. Her husband was a bartender who worked nights and was never home to watch over the kids. They ran wild in the streets. One of her daughters was mentally retarded. Mercedes and Mary both had troubles and this was enough for them to communicate.

To avoid Buita on other nights, or after they had been fighting, Mercedes would come upstairs with Horacio, sit in a red chair by the window, and speak to Mary for hours. Throughout the courtyard Mary's gagging, mangled voice would be heard, and Buita, hearing Mercedes in these "conversations," would look out of the window and shout in Spanish, "Why don't you come downstairs and clean the house?"

"And why don't you go to the moon!" Mercedes would call back, so happy because she had a friend and a place to go, away from Buita. But sooner or later, she would have to go back home, and the work and insults and fighting would begin again.

Mercedes eventually befriended almost everyone in the building. Hearing her shouting matches with Buita every night, they must have taken pity on her. No one else spoke Spanish in the building at the time, so at first she got along with just "hellos." But with the English language slowly coming to her, Mercedes soon knew everyone's story. She knew about the woman with the stuffed dogs on the first floor who used to be a writer but gave up when her husband died, and about the pretty woman on the fifth floor who had tried to kill herself and had spent time in an asylum. She knew about the little old lady on the sixth floor who lost her family to the Nazis. She knew about the drunks, the crooks, the womanizers. And she knew about the good people. By sitting on the stoop in good weather and nodding with great friendliness at neighbors and passersby, she came to know most of the people of that street. The old ladies up the hill, the wives who walked their dogs in the evenings, the young mothers with their babies in strollers. These were people who were not afraid to talk with her. Because of them, she began to feel less alone.

Unknown to Mercedes, Buita spent much of her time trying to talk Alejo into moving to Florida. She maligned the job he had found for himself and somehow blamed it on Mercedes. "That woman has dulled your sense of good and bad," Buita told him. "Come with us and buy some land and we'll help you find a decent job."

But Alejo liked his job, his friends, the city.

"Don't be a fool," she told him. "Stay here with that woman, and you'll be a cook all your life."

Such advice from his sister saddened Alejo but did not change his mind. Her opinions pushed him away from Mercedes. Almost every day, Buita had new accusations against her. She was a thief, a poor mother, a witch. "Poor Horacito," she would say about her nephew. "He would be better off with his aunt who loves him."

One day something happened that almost convinced Alejo to give Horacio to Buita. It was the afternoon. Mercedes and Horacio were in the living room. Horacio was crawling on the floor, when Mary called Mercedes to the window. Her husband was out on the sidewalk beside her.

"Hello, Mrs. Santinio, pleased to meet you." He had disappeared for a few months—had been to jail and just gotten out.

And while Mercedes was standing at the window Horacio crawled into one of the kitchen cabinets and found an open can of rat poison and drank it all down. By the time Mercedes went into the kitchen, he lay still like a blue doll in the middle of the floor.

The hospital doctors managed to revive him. They pumped his stomach and gave him blood. With Horacio's near-poisoning, Buita had a great day, accusing Mercedes of negligence and telling Alejo, "See? She's no good. No use at all. That boy's going to be crazy or hurt if he stays with her." And she added, "Give him to me."

Alejo considered it, and Mercedes felt she could hardly blame him. She knew he was starting to feel frustrated by his family predicament. He was tired of being in the middle of so many bad feelings and tired of his self-doubts, heightened by Buita's nagging. Sometimes he wanted to be rid of Mercedes just to bring peace. But he also loved her. The situation depressed him. Slowly Buita was getting to Alejo. The amazing thing was that Buita, despite her cruelty, was correct in many ways about life. There were more opportunities in Florida. It was a better place to raise a family. Sweet with flower smells and a pleasant ocean wind, it was warm like Cuba and had no harsh winters. There were palm trees and orchids everywhere. Lots all over Miami were selling cheaply. But either Alejo didn't have the money or Mercedes talked him out of it. Or he was stupid. Who knows? But he didn't take any of Buita's advice. How could Alejo know that property values would triple over the years? Why did he buy shares in a nonexistent light-bulb company? Why didn't he suspect that the fields near Buita's house would one day be a thriving mercantile district, clogged with traffic and crowds of passersby and shoppers? Why did he buy swampland in New Jersey instead, which to this day is still swampland? Why did he fail to see opportunity? Why did he believe many of the other things that Buita said, that Mercedes was no good or that she was crazy, and not believe her when she was correct? Who knows what would have happened? But one day a letter from Cuba made Buita shift her efforts.

During a rainy night in 1947, Eduardo Delgado, who had left for Cuba nine months before, suffered heart failure, leaving Margarita widowed and Ki-ki without a father. Like a saint of salvation Buita set out for Cuba. Alejo was sad about Buita's departure but Mercedes was happy, hugging Horacio and giving him kisses. She was happy helping Buita and Alberto pack and happy when they finally walked out the door. They left on a Sunday night. It had been a year and a half since Buita had come to New York, and Mercedes felt like she had been released from prison.

An Evening, 1951

1

The years passed. Mercedes was pregnant with her second child and Alejo had not become wealthy. But he had bought himself a number of sporty brown-and-white-and-tan shoes and a brown pin-stripe suit with long tails, à la the wolfish jitterbugs of the day. With his hat and shining cufflinks, he looked sharp when he went out at night. As for Horacio, Mercedes dressed him, for the most part, with neighbor's hand-me-downs and items left behind by visitors to the house. And there was always the trash space under the hallway stairwell where people left old shirts, pants, shorts, socks, dresses, and shoes that she took in for Horacio and for herself. But in her mind she devised imaginary clothing for Horacio, princely robes to fit the poetic nature that she was certain she had passed on to him. From the first days when Horacio crawled on the floor and dancers partied in the living room, she believed that he had inherited her father's and grandfather's talents. As if one man died to flow into another. "Never forget that you have aristocrat's blood," she would tell him. "You have the blood of an artist."

She would tell him these things as he played on the shredding linoleum floor.

"You can see and do anything you want, niño. Your grandfather was a poet and your great grandfather was a singer. That's why you can do what other people can't. You have Sorrea blood."

Then, looking far away, she would say, "Look what we can see, niño. Instead of seeing the street, we can see a river. Instead of the building, we have a mountain. And what do we have here?" she asked, touching his hair. "We have delicious-smelling flowers!"

"We do?"

"Oh yes, we Sorreas can see anything we want. You can have anything, niño."

"Where's Pop, Mama?"

"Dios mío, chico, he's out."

Much of the time Pop disappeared for two or three days, and Mercedes, alone with Horacio, did not always know what to do. There were long silences, Horacio looking around with his sad eyes, and Mercedes watching the street from the window. So she would tell Horacio stories. Tonight she began, "Niño, you were named after your great grandfather, Horacio Sorrea. He was a great opera singer, and his voice made him famous in all of Spain. He was an enormous man with a barrel chest and the eyes of a Caesar. He was very important and well respected, and he lived in the city of Palama on Majorca, a big island off the coast of Spain. Everything was white in that city, all the buildings, all the churches, the roads, the walls. There were statues everywhere. His house was big and white with black gates. When we came to visit, he gave me and Luisa and Rina a room with large windows and a canopy bed. At the time I was very happy. I wore a sunhat and was always getting kissed by my papa. And your great-grandpapa was good to me, too. He was always kissing me, and each night before bed, he would come into our bedroom and give all of us money so that we could buy candy the next day.

"In the evenings, before we ate dinner in a grand room set with crystal, he would sing for us, usually an aria from one of the Italian operas, and then afterward we would sit down to a huge meal and he would always say, 'We're going to the worms, so eat up,' which your grandmother, Doña Maria, didn't like to hear. She was very religious, while he was not. But she loved him just the same, and we all loved him...I was very sad when he died."

She went into the bedroom, returning with an old photograph of the first Horacio. It was taken at his deathbed. He was old with white beard and furrowed brows. His eyes were closed, his hands placed atop an open Bible.

"That was a few years later. We were back in Cuba when one night we heard your great-grandfather singing. His voice seemed to be coming out of the walls and floor. It woke everyone. My father, bless his soul, looked everywhere and spent the night on the porch. In the morning all the doors in the house opened and slammed shut three times, like they say a tomb door does when a soul rises to Heaven. Later we found out that Horacio had died in Spain that day..."

She touched Horacio's face and said, "And when he died his voice went to you."

Some neighbors now passed in the outer hallway, and from habit Mercedes went to peek through the keyhole at them. She was always spying on people: out windows, from behind curtains, shades, and venetian blinds, through cracks in doors. Horacio was looking out the window but saw only a passing car. She returned and kissed Horacio, suddenly panicking, as if she would be alone forever without him. She nervously ran her fingers over his ribs, tickling him and cackling, making a face. He would not smile. Then she didn't know what else to do.

Generally she encouraged Horacio to use his talents, as if that would provide him with some shelter in life. Sometimes in the evenings, they sang. She loved hearing him. She was proud of his voice. Nearly seven years of age, Horacio had already been singled out from his classmates by the choirmaster for free voice lessons. He practiced in school three days a week, and on Sundays Mercedes would take him to church and sit in a pew below the choir balcony, listening to Horacio sing. She would sigh, thinking of her days when she sang on Radio Holguín with her classmates. She also had a beautiful voice, pure and mellow, as if pushed through the hollow of a tree. Singing made Mercedes feel happy. She remembered many melodies, and to these she sang the lyrics in the same way that she spoke English, partially. She sang everything in *la, la, la*. That night she tried a radio jingle from years before:

56

> Lopez's furniture is the best
> Come in and give your soul a rest
> la, la, la, la, la, la, la, la, la, la
> Bring your cash, bring your cash
> and you'll sleep well at night
> la, la, la, la, la, la, la, la, la, la.

But Horacio did not feel like singing, and so she brought out a composition notebook and crayons. They drew pictures together. He made houses and figures of men, she made haggish women and flowers. (One day he would be able to draw anything. Out on the street, where the kids passed the evenings drawing with boxes of colored chalk, he would be known as "the artist," for his ease in drawing anything the older boys suggested: bosoms, nudes, cops and robbers, guns, knives, pricks.) Even as they drew, Mercedes and Horacio remained in the living room near the window, watching the street. Occasionally Horacio saw Mercedes feeling around her huge belly, and he thought she must be in pain. He grew tired of his drawing. He wanted to listen to the radio, but he couldn't because Alejo had thrown it out the window long ago in a fit of rage. And at that time they had no television.

They left the living room and went into the bedroom. In those days Mercedes didn't like to sleep by herself. She was always seeing things in the dark. Often she had a bad dream filled with sadness, about people leaving her. One second here, the next second, gone like a puff of smoke. Or she would see Buita coming at her from the shadows with a knife. When Alejo lay beside her in the big wide bed, she slept well and had beautiful dreams about Cuba. But in his absence the dark became too much for her, even if her Horacio slept by her side. Trying to sleep she kept wondering, "When is he coming home?"

She stared out the bedroom window at the dark courtyard with its one light. A roof door slammed shut with the wind, then—bang—it slammed shut again. She was thinking about a stroll with Alejo in Holguín years before, and then she thought about what Alejo did to her just a few weeks ago. She had burned up three of his shirts with an iron. He had grabbed her hard by the wrists, twisting them until she was forced down to her knees, and made her repeat, "I'm sorry, I'm sorry for being stupid." Horacio had been in the room and tried to pull Alejo off her, but he was too enormous for the little boy. Alejo had played the big man with Horacio and pushed him away. A "big man" was strong, no one was to question him, he could do as he pleased. But Alejo was not comfortable in that role. He was a Jekyll and Hyde: The next day he had been contrite and come into the apartment with a present for Mercedes and candy for Horacio. He had lightened up on Mercedes: no big abuses, just the usual giving of orders and his disappearing act.

"When you have a baby, you never know. Some people can wish you harm," she told Horacio. "So you have to be careful."

She took a deep breath and exhaled. Now she was always sleeping on her back. Horacio watched her for a time and then asked her, "Why does Pop stay away from here?"

"Ssssssssh, chico, don't ask me that."

Mercedes was thinking about Alejo's recent behavior: he had started to drink to excess. And out of nowhere, he had begun taking her to bed each night. Drink riled him up; first thing, when he came home from the hotel, he closed the French doors, pulled down the shades, and turned on the fan to drown out the bed noises. Depending on her mood, Mercedes liked it. Only when she was feeling homesick or angry with him did she not want him to have a good time with her body. What she did not like at all was the smell of his breath, like rye whiskey or rum, and how he sometimes could not even stand up straight. She could take the days of Buita's abuse and of being locked up in rooms, but the sight of Alejo falling down drunk was too much for her.

The first few times he had come home drunk, he was happy, brought her a bright, cheery scarf or another present and danced with her in the living room even though there was no music. And he had called Horacio into the living room, given him a dollar, told him to give his Pop a kiss and to buy himself a toy. And he had begun to sway, hanging onto the wall. His drunkenness struck her as funny because in Cuba he had never touched a drop of anything but Hatuey Indian Malt. Nothing more, unless there was a special occasion. And then he only had a little Spanish brandy or Cuban rum.

Alejo started out each day innocently enough, having a few drinks here and there in the hotel, where the liquor was free. Wooden cases of scotch, vodka, gin, and rum were stored behind a pair of shiny metal doors. A huge freezer and ice machine beside the liquor closet sent out chilling waves of frost into the kitchen whenever it was opened. The liquor closet was locked only with a latch and hook, so that around noon, all the men on the morning shift began to pass around shot glasses of whiskey and rum. By then the morning's preparations for the crowded businessmen's luncheons were completed, and the bar had become so busy that a bottle or two would never be missed. Then, among the sizzling and simmering pots and pans, everyone hurried to serve out the platters, each man at his post, ladle or serving fork in hand, with his little drink ready when it got too hot, and the headwaiter started shouting through the double doors for them to hurry. After the rush the cooks turned to the preparation of dinner and guzzled a few more slugs of booze here and there. By the end of the shift, the cooks and helpers were painlessly drunk and ready for the subway ride home.

This was not somber, melancholic drinking. It was the drinking of kinship. Men at work. Greek, Italian, Jew, Haitian, Latin, Negro, having a few laughs, talking about women, and teaching each other phrases in their own languages, in the long run entangling English with French and Italian and Spanish and Greek and Yiddish and jive. In the rush of good feelings from the whiskey, there was a lot of joke telling, talk of sex, gambling, and card games. Their salaries were not high, but the companionship and booze made up for it.

But a year ago, in 1950, something had happened in Cuba that made Alejo's drinking more serious. One day he received a letter from his mother and stood by the window to read it by the sunlight. The letter in his hand seemed very old, written in faded light blue ink as if from the nineteenth century. The light lit up the page and seemed to pass through his hands. He read that his brother Hector was dead.

There had been a rainstorm in Cuba and Hector, then about forty-five years old, was riding his horse home in the dark. He was drunk and riding too quickly when lightning cracked the sky. His horse bolted, throwing him headlong into a tree, and he broke his neck. If he was not already dead when he slid down into the mud, he drowned in the rainwater.

Alejo cried out: "Dios mío! I can't believe it! My brother, my brother!" He was like a wounded animal, shaking and his chest heaving, as if he were going to have a heart attack. "My brother! What can I do? Mercita tell me, what can I do?" he cried in a high-pitched voice, leaning against the wall, his head and chest ready to burst. "Dead like nothing," Alejo kept repeating.

"Don't kill yourself over this," Mercedes told him. "He was your brother, but it's not as if you have been hearing from him all this time."

What Mercedes had told him was true. After the kisses and embraces at the harbor before the journey to America there had been not another word between them, not a letter, no news, until Alejo learned that his brother, whom he loved very much, was dead.

Now Alejo would take a swig of rum, have a thought that made his eyes burn, and then bury his head in his arms. "¡Carajo!" he would say over and over again, "my brother is dead."

"Don't be a fool, that's not going to help you," Mercedes would tell him about the rum. "You're too good for that, too strong, too much of a man..."

But despite her sympathy—and she felt very bad for him—Alejo's spirit grew melancholy. He took to disappearing at night, had his way with her in bed, and tried to have a good time, as if his grief had left him. Sometimes when he was drunk and he touched Mercedes, she would run down the hall to find shelter with Horacio, and Alejo would call out, "To hell with you!"

One afternoon he just wouldn't take no. Horacio was sick with a virus, and Mercedes was tired. When Alejo began to run his hand up and down her side and then placed her hand on his sex, she pushed him away.

"Don't touch me!"

"I'm the man, I'll touch you when I please."

"No you don't, Señor. You think you can come in when you want to and do as you please. What am I, a slave? You didn't even look at me for two months and now—what happened? Did someone say that you don't sleep with your wife?"

"Mercita, come here!"

She was in the corner of the bedroom, trying to hide herself beside the closet, but he grabbed her by the wrists and threw her onto the bed.

"Take off that rag!" he said about her dress, which was like a rag. And when she hesitated, he tore it down the front and then got her into bed. She was squirming under him and pushing his face away from her. "Malo! Malo!" she kept repeating. "Bad man! Bad man!" But he had his way with her.

Now she never resisted him. Instead, when he took her to bed she allowed herself to float away. Her body was in bed, but she herself was elsewhere: in the hallway, looking down on Horacio, by the window, looking at the clouds. All he would have had to say was, "Mercita, my wife, come here... my flower..." and she would have gone willingly. No. He was determined to show her that he was the man and to break the spirit that challenged him. No wife of his was going to turn her face away from a kiss or shrink at his touch, refusing him love. No. He was the man. And he was not going to go without love just because he took a "little drink" now and then.

This evening was no different from any other since his brother's death. Where is he? Mercedes wondered. There was a noise at the door, but it was not Alejo. She sighed, and Horacio, beside her, pretended to sleep. On the bureau the Wes-clock continued to tick-tick-tick. Next to it there was a framed photograph of Alejo and Mercedes in the good days. He was wearing a guayabera and was very thin and handsome. She had her hair up in a Betty Grable coif, and her ruffled blouse with mother-of-pearl buttons and flowery embroidered vest gave her the air of a young starlet from Hollywood.

"Mama," Horacio said, "I can't sleep."

"Just have good thoughts and go to sleep."

"Mama, what are you thinking about?"

"About my family. My papa—but that's not always good. If you think too much about a dead person, he will think you are calling him."

"The dead?"

"Yes, child, like in the movies you love to watch."

Inside her belly there was a gentle kick. Horacio put his hand on her belly. Suddenly in a bad mood, Mercedes yanked it off.

"Be careful, child!"

"Did it hurt?"

"You ask too many questions. Just be careful!"

Restless, Mercedes got up. There were some voices coming from the street. She went into the living room and looked out the window: There were some drunk Irish kids passing around a bottle of beer and a soldier standing beside a car, urinating in the street.

"Psssssssh, I hate waiting every night."

2

Downtown, on Tenth Avenue, Alejo finally left the club where he had been drinking with a friend. He had been staying in Brooklyn the last two nights, going to parties thrown by new acquaintances. Each time he meant to stay only a few hours, but he would get carried away and stay until it was time to go to work. He kept a change of clothing in his locker at the hotel, but now, running out of money, he had to go home.

With another kid coming, he was going to straighten out. He had lost his temper with Horacio too many times. Sometimes he didn't want to deal with his own situation. He would have a drink and the kid would start crying. No matter how much Alejo loved the kid, he was too noisy, and so Alejo would say, *Cállate, cállate!* "Shut up! Shut up!" Not that he didn't want to pay attention to Horacio, but this was Mercedes's job. She was the woman of the house and he was the man. The man's job was to go out and work, which he did, and pay the bills, which he did. Her job was to clean the house, cook, and take care of the baby. If the baby was crying too much, then she wasn't doing everything right. In Cuba, they know how to raise children so that the man doesn't get involved, but in the small apartments of New York, you see the kids all the time. He had hit Horacio too many times, and he had tried to make it up, but it was too late. He would come home a little drunk and call Horacio over. Remembering the day before, when Alejo had slapped him for no reason, Horacio would play deaf and dumb and run down the hall, hide in his room.

That wasn't Alejo's fault: when Buita left him and Hector died in Cuba, he felt abandoned in the world. A wife cannot be pure family. You have to provide for her and prove yourself. And if you can't do that, if she doesn't respect you and calls you a drunk, then you have to go out and find people who do respect you. And pretty women to dance with you and shake their bodies for your admiration. That woman, Mercedes, was letting herself go. She was thin before, but now she was pregnant again and too fat with the baby, which filled her up. In Cuba, a man could truly have his way. Poor Hector used to have his way. He had Myra and the children at home on that farm outside San Pedro, and he had his nice little mistress in town. Papa had his little girl, too, so why couldn't he? Díos mio, how Alejo missed Hector and the rides they used to take to the broken-down part of town, with the little shacks and the dirt floors and nothing but a mattress or just piled up newspapers covered with a sheet. The girls took care of them there. They could find it anywhere, even in a cane field, should he feel bad for that?

Was it so bad to have a few drinks? So he spent money. He spent too much on entertainment, but he didn't forget the rent; he paid it with his sweat. He didn't go to loan sharks but to the union, and he paid them back the next week. Other men didn't give a fuck if their kids starved, and they kicked their wives out into the street for yelling about one little drink. So his family shouldn't look at him, at their provider, in such a way. They should have respect, and the boy should give him kisses and not run away. Do they think he doesn't deserve their love and respect? That he's supposed to beg for it? That he, Alejo Santinio, should beg for a piece of ass from his wife and for a kiss and hug from his own son, when he is the man of the household?

When the new one was born he was going to teach him respect and love. And he was going to treat him good. This one would be a good Santinio. He would know there's nothing wrong with a few drinks. He would be a boy who would love his Pop. And his name would be Hector, after Hector Santinio. And if it was a girl, they'd have another baby until a male was born and there was once again a Hector Santinio in this world.

3

It was very dark. The roof door was slamming in the wind. The slamming door, to the ear of a child trying to fall asleep, was ghostly, a result of strange forces, the kind that Mercedes always spoke of, just making life a little more difficult for uneasy sleepers. Worries became animated in the dark and slammed into the window like pounding fists, upsetting Mercedes who became more and more nervous, hitting and pushing Horacio away for no reason. The door slammed, and voices came down from the third floor. The deaf-mute speaking in her mangled vowels and her dead-drunk husband trying to explain something and giving up, repeating, "All right, all right, what doyouwant-metodo, die?" Mercedes breathed as if in pain, and electricity tightened Horacio's muscles, and for them both sleep was impossible.

Horacio kept wondering if his talents to draw and sing would help keep out the suffocating gloom he felt surrounding him. He wondered if he would ever stop hearing shouts in the dark hallways or see his Pop in the next room drinking until he fell down. But that night nothing had changed.

At the door, finally, there was the jingling of keys. The door opened and closed with a sudden, tremendous slam. Its frame was so painted over that it had to be pushed hard and always banged into the glass *armadio* in the niche in the entranceway. There was a picture of Christ with a burning heart on the door, and it fell down. Then Alejo, leaning too far forward, rushed into the armadio, things fell, and Mercedes opened her eyes.

Footsteps in the hall and then Alejo's voice: "Mercita, Mercita it's me."

She did not answer him.

"Mercedes," he called out with more force. "I'm here."

"What do you want?"

"I'm hungry, make me a steak."

"It's three in the morning."

"I don't care. I'm hungry."

"Well, I'm not your slave. Get one of your friends to make a steak."

"Mercita, Mercita, don't make me crazy now." He went into the bedroom, took hold of her wrists and started to squeeze, when he realized what he was doing.

"Please, Mercita," he said. "I'm very hungry. Cook me a steak."

"Psssssh," she said, getting up, "I am a slave."

She went into the kitchen and took a steak out of the refrigerator. There was always meat and chicken and shrimp, which Alejo would bring home once or twice a week, wrapped in freezer paper, from the hotel. As she prepared the steak, Alejo sat at the table, smoking cigarettes. She said nothing, until he went to get the whiskey bottle from the cabinet and began to pour himself a shot. Then she said, "Look at your face when you swallow that. Why?"

"Because I am the man, and if you don't like it, get out."

How many times had she heard him say that? She sighed. After she served him the steak, she went back to the bedroom, got Horacio, and they went down the hall to Horacio's room where they tried to sleep. Alejo ate his steak then went to his bedroom. Finding the bed empty, he went down the hall and pushed open Horacio's door.

"You sleep with me. Leave him here."

When Mercedes didn't answer him right away, he took hold of her and dragged her from the bed and down the hall. In their bed he smothered her with his enormous body. She tasted his salty sweat and the whiskey and steak on his tongue and mouth. The bed shook for a long time under Mercedes's and Alejo's weight. He made great breathing noises; she sighed. He ground his teeth and his face and body turned a livid red. He shouted something— She turned her face away from his and let her arms slide off his back. Tenderly, he kissed her neck and rolled off her. Then they went to sleep as best as they could. In the morning Mercedes took Horacio to church and, sitting below the balcony, listened to him sing in the choir.

A Pleasant Day, Late Spring, 1954

1

The other son, Hector Santinio, born in 1951, was now three years old. He was standing on the boardwalk with Mercedes, who was squeezing his wrists because he didn't want to come along but kept running over to Auntie Buita, up on a visit from Florida. The birth had been long and painful, and when the doctors had put Mercedes under with ether, she had lifted up into a whirl of clouds...and she had seen Heaven. As she had always claimed, Heaven was an enormous garden with flowers everywhere, and her father, Teodoro Sorrea, was sitting on a low white bench, gazing off into the distance, over valleys and a river. Flocks of birds filled the sky, and angels, followed by thousands of souls, flew upward into the sun... The doctors pulled Hector, red-faced and wailing, into the world.

Now Hector was in his sailor suit that Buita had given him—white shorts with anchor embroidery, mariner's shirt, sailor's cap—and sucking a big lollipop that Buita had bought at one of the Coney Island stands. Alejo's and Hector's godfather, Edelmiro from Cienfuegos, were walking ahead on the boardwalk, stopping to snap pictures of the group with a Kodak Brownie box camera, and then hurrying to a beer stand and returning with hot dogs and sodas and paper cones of french fries. Alejo was laughing; he really liked the amusement park with all the rides and crowds. Horacio walked with Aunt Margarita, who said little, which suited him fine. But Buita was making Mercedes jealous. She was hugging and kissing Hector and buying him every little thing that he saw on a long stick or at the end of a string: balloons, monkeys that trapezed between two pieces of wood, a whistle. He enjoyed these gifts, and that made Mercedes jealous. Look at him! and I was the one who carried him for nine months, and just look at him going after her, just because she buys him candy! she thought.

A wind kept coming off the gray Atlantic. The women held onto their hats. Mercedes could have been carried off over the railing and dropped into the silvery gray water, and Buita would have kept walking. No matter what Mercedes said or how often she called to Hector or smiled, Buita ignored her sister-in-law. "My, but you're such a good boy," she said to Hector in Spanish, touching his head and pinching his face.

Later Buita gathered everyone but Mercedes to the railing.

"Now let's take a nice picture for posterity," Buita said. Edelmiro took the shot, which included Mercedes who had joined at the last moment. She managed to smuggle herself into three or four shots but always off to the side, near the very edge of the picture. In all of the shots Buita was holding Hector in her arms and giving him kisses. Alejo seemed to have an innocent's face. Mercedes was frowning; she looked like she was being tortured.

That day Mercedes had wanted to go to the park or to visit Mary upstairs, but she went along to Coney Island to watch over Hector. She was very thin and nervous, walking along the boardwalk, straining to hear what Buita was saying to her youngest son. She always imagined the worst.

"And what does she say to Hector?" she asked Horacio, who had been walking with Buita and Hector earlier.

"Nothing, Ma."

But she knew that Buita was always talking about her.

"Oh, tell me, niño. I know you hear her."

"I don't, Ma."

"I'm your mother, tell me."

"She doesn't say anything."

"Ai, don't tell me you're on her side now?"

Horacio had not taken sides with Buita. He distrusted her. Horacio never took sides with anyone. He kept to himself and tried to get along in life without making trouble. He was not yet nine years old and already working two part-time jobs: in a stationery store, delivering papers, and in a cleaners, watching the shop for a few hours after school while the owner made his deliveries. He tried not to get hit and to be cool with the kids on the street and not to cry much. And he tried not to feel bad when Alejo took Hector places, to the store, to the park, down the street. Even when he felt like kicking his brother's ass or saw misery in Mercedes's face, he tried to walk along and enjoy himself.

"You know that woman hates me," Mercedes told him. "If she says anything, let me know."

"Sure, Mama." But he wasn't even listening to adults anymore; he only listened to himself, figuring out ways to escape.

Overhead a Sopwith biplane flew through the puffy clouds, its motor puttering. They sat on benches, watching the loops. Alejo enjoyed that sight, as mysterious as the mail planes he had sometimes seen heading north over the fields in Cuba. He leaned close to Mercedes, whispering something, his voice so quiet: "¡Qué bueno! No?" She answered him with her eyes, which darted enviously between him and Buita who was bouncing Hector on her knee.

They came to a freak show, a row of tents behind the giant ferris wheel, which featured among other attractions, "Wanda of Atlantis." She was a mermaid in a pool of water. It cost ten cents to look at her. Everything inside the tent was dark and scaly; there was netting hanging off sea-weathered beams, huge rusted hooks, sea shells, and rubber fish. There was a recording of the ocean coming in, and a woman singing in a high-pitched voice, calling for someone.

In that dark, gloomy tent, Hector's lightness stood out. With his white hands, legs, and face, and in the white sailor suit, he looked almost albino. Horacio with reddish hair and freckles, looked Irish, but Hector looked like a little German. Upper-class Cubans who visited the house always praised his fairness, calling it "Spanish, Spanish." But the poorer Cubans and Latins thought Hector's skin color was a mistake of nature. He was as fair as Mercedes but without her dark features; his skin was lighter than Alejo's. Hector was standing under an anchor, when Buita gave him a big kiss. It made Mercedes sick. "That child's always smiling for her," she complained to Alejo. Alejo, who was having a good time, put his arms around her, trying to cheer her up.

"How much longer are we going to be here?" she asked him.

"As long as we're here," he said.

When they came to the mermaid's pool, they stood at the railing looking down at her for a few minutes, until the spell was broken by Buita's remark: "How obvious."

The mermaid was a voluptuous Italian woman, about twenty-five years old, in a flimsy sea-shell bikini top and a tight skirt with phony fins sewn onto it. Mercedes was amused for a moment, but when she saw Alejo was staring at the woman, she demanded, "Let's go from this place."

Buita was holding Hector's hand, but Mercedes pulled him away, walking quickly ahead toward the rest room area. While everyone else waited, sitting on the benches by the railing, drinking their beers, she helped Hector use the sea-water toilet and used it herself. Then she leaned against the wall, suddenly faint. Hector was too young to understand what was going on, but he knew something was wrong.

"Mama?"

"That woman makes me ill."

Poor Mercedes, she had been jittery from the moment Buita came to the apartment, nearly a week ago. On the day Buita arrived Mercedes had been in the kitchen. Black beans were overrunning a pot, a suckling pig had started a grease fire in the oven, and the plantains were burning up in the pans. Hector had pissed on the floor, and his crying had pushed her nerves so far that Mercedes had given him a real slap in the face: "Now you be quiet!"

Suddenly Buita was standing at the door. There were no kisses, no hugs. "I can see that you still haven't learned how to cook yet," Buita announced, after looking into the kitchen. And then she opened her arms and gave Hector many kisses, took him into the bathroom, and cleaned him up. She hadn't even rested her feet. She was wearing rouge and perfume and sweet-smelling makeup, which Hector liked. In her arms, Hector had stopped crying.

At night, with Buita in the house, Mercedes did not get much sleep. The old knife dream returned to her and kept her awake until the early morning, when a few hours of sleep gave her some rest. In the dream her bedroom door would open and Buita would lunge at her with the knife. The floor would gradually become covered with her blood. Mercedes would gasp, awaken, and then quietly go to Buita's room to spy, wondering if she should go after Buita with a knife first. The mornings found her in a bad mood. She had to take care of the baby, cook, and clean the house. She snapped out orders to Horacio, sending him out to the store, telling him to change diapers, and hitting him if he didn't move fast enough. Her hands got nervous. It was too much, the kid crying out and Buita in the house at the same time. They wore her out, made her sluggish. She walked the hallway slowly, she wanted to be somewhere else.

Horacio was calling into the bathhouse window from the top of an upturned oil drum. "Hey, Mama, everybody's waiting," he said in Spanish. Mercedes pretended not to hear. He called again. In the saltwater bathhouse, the toilets and floors were encrusted with sand and the high windows let in streams of sunlight. Mercedes stalled for time, hoisting up Hector's shorts and combing his hair. Horacio called again. In the bathhouse a lady was changing into her sunbathing dress. She was short and fat with thin, varicosed legs and a towel wrapped around her head. "I think someone's calling ya," she said a few times.

Mercedes nodded, but didn't say anything. She was afraid of speaking in poor English and of being ridiculed.

"Lady, is there something I can do for you? You don't look so good."

"No, no, everything is good with me," she answered. "Thank you."

But she really didn't want to go back out there with the others. She didn't like the way Buita was talking about her, so rapidly in Spanish. She could hear her saying, "What is that lunatic doing? Where is she? Where is she?" She didn't like the way Buita put her fingers in Hector's curly blond hair, or for that matter, the way Alejo beamed when Buita seemed happy. And she didn't like the way Alejo and Edelmiro eyed the girls on the boardwalk, or the confusion of the passing crowds. The rides were too noisy and confused her, as did the signs that were everywhere—THIS WAY OUT, IND KEEP STRAIGHT, DO NOT STAND UP IN THE ROLLER COASTER UNLESS YOU'RE IN A RUSH—which she did not always understand. Children screaming and the crack of gallery pop guns bothered her, too, as much as Buita's pacing, which she spied through the window. But she couldn't think of anything to do, and so she finally came out, dragging Hector behind her, and the party proceeded.

While everyone went on the different rides, Mercedes sat on a bench with her hands over her lap. "If she wants to be a party-pooper and a wallflower," said Buita, "that suits me fine." As Mercedes waited on a bench they went on the Cyclone and, whirling upside down, saw the Atlantic and its thousands of swimmers, and Piper Cub airplanes in the sky with promotional trailers for suntan lotion floating among the islands of clouds, and the boardwalk going on forever and oozing with movement. The roller coaster made everything twist like a cinder-block falling down a hill, and they came out red-faced and laughing as they checked their pockets, so delighted like all the other tourists and vacationers because they had never seen a roller coaster in Cuba like that! Mercedes sat around while Buita bought Hector and Horacio American flags, the ten-cent kind, and then she watched them ride into the House of Horrors. She turned her face away—a few sailors whistled at her crossed legs—while Buita and the others rode cable-pulled carts under a balcony of ghouls and skeleton men into a lair of witches, where men with gnarled faces hung from the ceiling. Then they went on the Dragon Ride and the Whip. Soon it was getting dark, and Mercedes really wanted to go home.

But as Buita said: "Why? All the fun's just beginning."

That's when they started with all the games of chance. They went to play the wheels of fortune and won nothing. Alejo, having no patience at all, put thirty-five nickels down on a thirty-eight place board and lost every time. He thought it was stupid to put down one nickel at a time. Putting down many, he lost them quickly. He answered his losses with a shrug. "Don't worry," Alejo said to Hector. "We'll get you something here."

Buita and Margarita and Edelmiro put down their nickels, all for the two Santinio boys. And the wheels spun—and nothing! They must have stood by the booths for half an hour. Suddenly Alejo pulled Mercedes in close to the counter and gave her a nickel, which she put down on the number three, and the wheel turned and it came out number three.

"Well, you *are* good for something," Buita told her.

"Again, again," said Alejo, after the man gave them a big stuffed dog. This time she put it on the number seventeen and that also came in, another stuffed dog. The concession man frowned when she put another nickel down, saying, "Lady, you're too lucky for us." But after that she won nothing more, because the man started to work a floor pedal keeping the wheel from hitting Mercedes's number. After a few more tries, they left the booth. Mercedes was smiling and happy because she had beaten Buita at something—but "lucky"? Two stuffed dogs after so many years in this country? "Lucky," as if Hector could understand that she had won them? "Lucky," with Buita around? "It only goes to show you," said Buita to the others, "the luck of the crazy."

They continued on, ate dinner in a boardwalk restaurant. American junk, delicious and fattening: hamburgers, french fries, hot dogs, pizza, knishes, calzones, beer, Coca-Cola, candied apples, and Hershey bars. Sounds of chewing, a few smokes, an ocean breeze, yawning... Then the next stop: of course, the Guess Your Weight booth. Alejo weighed in at 240 pounds, 80 more than when he came to the States. Buita, 140. Margarita, what you would expect for the day when men liked big fat hips, 125 pounds or thereabouts. Mercedes, 100 pounds.

By that time the park was lit with little colored bulbs, as far as the eye could see, and young couples were strolling and making out on the boardwalk. A dragon of a Chinese ride was snarling red streamer fire. And Mercedes was dreaming about the old times in the park near the Neptuna...

They decided to go home but on the way to the train saw the House of Mirrors, and disappeared inside. As usual, Mercedes waited by herself on a bench outside, and a half hour passed. They did not come out. The admission price was twenty-five cents. That was exactly what Mercedes had in her dress pocket, so she went in to find them.

She bumped into mirror panes and saw herself over and over again with large eyes, boxed into corners. She followed the maze, boom! only to find herself in the same spot again, confused and looking everywhere for help, off to the right and left, following herself as she went back to the beginning and off into the center again, boom! only to find herself, all crazy and fucked up, and shaking and thinking to herself: Why am I here? Why did I carry them in my belly for so long? What if I never get out? I should have stayed home with Mary, but what do I get? My children run away from me. I love them but they look at me and think one thing, *¡qué loca! ¡qué loca!* But once I was very young and pretty and I liked to go dancing and enjoyed the kisses of handsome men, I liked to kiss and dance and go walking in the park, boom! Dios mío, Dios mío, they're going to throw me out of the country and Alejo will leave me. If he knew how some things hurt inside of me, when he looks at me with disgust but at other women with desire, wanting to touch them and not me... Pssssssh, they think I wasn't young or didn't know what it is like to have my fun! In Cuba *yo gozaba*, I had my fun and kisses... but where are they? And who are they? They don't even want to look at me! *¡Soy su mama! ¡Venga! ¡Venga! ¡Venga!*

When she finally came out, dizzy, only Margarita was waiting for her on the bench. She was smoking a cigarette, looking a little bored. Everyone else had gone home. Mercedes felt tired and confused and bad. She felt lost and stupid. It was the way she felt when she took the wrong trains after shopping in Brooklyn and could not find her way home: the way she felt when she cooked a meal that would never turn out right; the way she felt when Alejo wouldn't look at her for days on end, when she was convinced that she was ugly and so she grew even thinner and more nervous because she was too upset to eat. It was the way she felt after hearing certain words over and over again: *divorce, bills, drunkard.* It was the way she felt after hitting the baby for no reason, or protecting Horacio from getting hit by Alejo, getting hit herself, and then hitting Horacio later because her anger and frustration had no place to go. She held Margarita's hand for a moment, straightened up, raked her fingers through her frazzled hair, and went on in the dark with the strange Christmas lights everywhere, to the train and home.

Cuba, Cuba, 1954

1

It was the summertime, and Alejo Santinio had sent Mercedes and Horacio and Hector down to Cuba by airplane. Mercedes had been homesick for Holguín and wanted to see her sisters, and for them and her mother to see the children. And there had been too much fighting in the house, a situation that was forgotten during their visit in Cuba, except that regrets about her life sometimes sent Mercedes to bed at two in the afternoon. Her sisters would comfort her, send the children out to play.

Horacio thought of Cuba as a place of small towns and hick farms. He did not see it with Mercedes's romantic eyes. Romanticism existed in the distant past and died with the conquistadors, gallant caballeros, and señoritas. Almost everyone from the past time was dead, save for the ghost he saw. Most of the people he would have admired were gone, down under the ground with the worms and stone. Teodoro Sorrea, the great artist, was someone he wanted to meet. And why? In his eyes, his grandfather was a first-class hustler. Not the saint Mercedes always made him out to be, but a dude who almost made a fortune off that tax-skimming scheme. But he had stalled for too long and dropped dead too soon. Maybe he would have sent Mercedes off to the university, and she would have become a great poet. Then

Horacio would have been born in a beautiful house with much sunlight, and his head would not have been knocked around.

Horacio did not see Cuba as a place of romance. He could see under and through things. He saw Luisa's and Rina's nice houses on cobblestone streets. A farm of pigs, sheep, and flea-ridden dogs. Thick, festering bushes full of tiny, red, long-legged spiders, red ants, and thick-shelled beetles that sounded like hurled stones when they flew out and hit the walls. Termites with bodies like embers swarmed in the rotted tree stumps of the farm. And he saw aunts Rina and Luisa and their children: Paco, Rafael, and Delores, who belonged to Aunt Rina; Virginia and Maria, who were so pretty and attentive to their mother, Aunt Luisa, widowed some years before. He saw the ditches, pools of stagnant water, thick clouds of flies and mosquitoes. He saw the clogged-with-shit stone toilets that were made tolerable only by the strong fragrances of the fruit trees and blossoms. Cuba was in the nineteenth century—okay, a nice place, and not anything more. There was a lot of eating going on, some belching, food everywhere, unless you were poor and then worms grew long in your intestines.

He took trips into the country with Rina's husband, Uncle Manny. Trips to the steamy Neptuna, where the Frosty Cool Air Conditioning had broken down. He rode in the truck with Pucho, a mulatto who had been adopted by the family next door, went to Woolworths and came back and found a hacked-up iguana lying in the yard, black balls like fish larva spilling from its torn stomach.

The ghost was the only thing that really impressed Horacio. And Aunt Luisa's kisses. She was all right, good to everyone, especially to him. When they went places, whether to the beach or to the marketplace or to Rina's farm, she put her arm around him and liked to give him kisses. And with no demands! She was thin with a young face and long black hair. She and Aunt Rina had a dress shop, and in the afternoons, she paid Horacio a dollar to watch the store for an hour while she went home to take a nap. Then she would come back, and he could go off and wander around the town with its hot stone roads and square blue, pink, or white houses.

On the weekends they would go either to the beach or out to Rina's farm, about ten miles north of Holguín. This was a real farm with squealing pigs that rolled in the mud and fields of cane and fruit trees. The big event of the day was the cooking of the pig. There were three buildings on the farm: an old cool house from the days when they grew tobacco, a horse stable, and the main house. In front of the stable was a dirt road and a shallow declivity. At its bottom was a chopping block where the family cook would sit, casually hacking off the heads of hens with a machete. The hens would run a few feet spurting blood like crazy and then drop, and the blood would settle in a thick pool of feathers and chicken heads that the dogs liked to eat. Then the cook would drop the chickens into a pot of boiling water so that the feathers could be easily pulled off. Flies everywhere. But that day Uncle Manny and the farmhand dragged out an immense pig weighing about ninety pounds, beheaded it, and then cleaved it in half. Horacio was sitting beside Aunt Luisa reading a funny book—*Superman* in Spanish— when Manny, square-shouldered and robust as a bull, called him over to help take the pig away. Horacio went over, and they tied a piece of rope around the pig's hooves and then pulled him toward a barbecue pit. It was hard work. Horacio was rewarded with a Coca-Cola.

The sides of pork were lying next to the pit when an iguana came along and burrowed his way into one of the haunches. Later, when Manny discovered the iguana nestled inside, he tried to pull it loose by its tail. But with its dinosaur teeth clamped into flesh, there was no way of jerking it free. So Manny and the cook dragged the side of pork across the yard and hauled it up onto one of the lower branches of a mango tree, then built a fire of leaves and twigs and newspapers underneath. The idea was to smoke the iguana out.

Everyone waited on the porch for the iguana to run away. There were columns of black smoke, bursting of fruit skins, withering leaves...and soon it let go and fell onto the ground. But suddenly it seemed as if hundreds of black flowers started raining down from the tree. They landed and spun around, creeping like fire in all directions. In fact, they were large, ugly tarantulas. There turned out to be a huge nest of them in the tree. Falling, they scurried in all directions and some went up the porch steps, under the chairs, under skirts, and between shoes, and into the house. And soon everyone was after them with shovels and brooms and sticks. For an hour this hunt went on, and by then the sides of pork were cooking.

The meal was delicious, too greasy as always, too heavy because of the monstrous portions of black beans and starchy plantains. After dinner it was dull and relaxing to sit out on the porch listening to the "night bells," as the crickets were called, and to watch the stars rise over the field. It was boring, but at least it was peaceful.

Before they had left to visit Rina and Luisa, the apartment walls had shaken from things and people smashing into them. Alejo's fist, a chair, a bottle, Alejo pounding the wall and knocking furniture aside, while Mercedes ran in circles inside the circular apartment and visitors tried to come between them but were pushed aside. Kindly visitors, like the three sisters from Oriente, had covered up Horacio's and Hector's eyes and ears with soft delicate hands, while Mercedes fled down the hall. But Horacio had called out, "Stop, you stop, stop, stop, you stop," so much that his voice had grown hoarse. Then for days the apartment had been quiet. No one had spoken, except Alejo, who had swallowed his manly pride trying to apologize for his outbursts. He had sent Horacio and Hector and Mercedes to Cuba because he loved the family and wanted to keep the family afloat.

Besides, Mercedes had promised her mother, Doña Maria, a chance to see the children. Now, during their visit, Doña Maria often sat on the porch in a wicker chair, holding Horacio's hand and smiling at him. She was suffering from heart disease. Her hair had turned white and her hands had begun to shake. Everything she had to say was like this: "You've made an old woman very happy by your visit, Horacio."

Kisses from the aunts, reassurances from Uncle Manny...

The evenings ended around nine-thirty when yawning competed with the sounds of night. One by one, the family retired. Horacio and Hector and Luisa stayed in the same room on the second floor. The balcony of this room faced a field. The moon would rise at one side of the field just outside the window. Horacio liked to watch it, amazed that it looked the same as from New York.

They were sleeping the night Teodoro Sorrea's ghost came along. It was well after midnight. Luisa heard a noise and sat up in bed. She woke Horacio. By the balcony was Teodoro, now only a luminescence in the shape of a man, wavering like light rippling on water. "Dios mío," Luisa said, making the sign of the cross. Horacio could not believe his eyes. The ghost seemed to be spreading his arms open and sadness emanated from him. "Me estoy quemando," the ghost said. "I am burning." He stood on the balcony for a few minutes, turned away, and then disappeared. This was really the only thing about Cuba that made a lasting impression on Horacio.

2

And Hector? For him the journey was like a splintering film. He was so young, his memory had barely started. Impressions swooped upon him like the large-winged, white butterflies in the yard. There were quiet, floating dragonflies, star blossoms, hanging lianas, and orchids of sweet smells. The sunlight, *el señor sol,* a friendly character who came out each day. Nightingales, dirty hens, sparrows, doves, chicks, crows in the dark of trees. Orange-bottomed clouds shaped like orange blossoms, sun up in the sky, big hairy trees: acacia, tamarind, breadfruit, banana, mango, cinnamon, mamey. Rainbows arching between trees, prisms inside puddles... In town there were old carved church doors, Christ up to heaven, stagnant wells, a lazy turtle, the sleeping dog... bakery smells, white laundry sheets, a laundress. Taste of eating Hershey bar, taste of eating slice of pineapple, taste of eating chicken, taste of eating trees, taste of eating steak, taste of eating flowers, taste of eating sugar, taste of eating kisses, taste of eating fried sweet plantains. "Cuba, Cuba," repeated incessantly, "Cuba, Cuba..."

Then something solid happened. He was sitting in the yard, examining a flower. The flower was purple with three oval wings and long red and yellow tendrils that ended in stars. There was a dog, Poochie, licking up his face. Then Poochie rolled over and his pathetic red dick slipped out from his heaving belly. Hector petted the dog's belly, and the dog rolled around on his back. Then Hector heard a noise coming from the bushes. A bird hopped from branch to branch. Poochie, wagging his tail, happily circled the tree and started leaping up and down, anxious to eat the bird. When Hector went to pet Poochie, the dog snarled and Hector began to cry. But in those days things did not bother him for very long. He went and sat on the kitchen steps. A breeze came in across the treetops from the east, and it felt good on his face. He was in his favorite sailor suit but without shoes, so his toes could play with the ants that teemed up under the floor tiles.

"Oh Hector! Hector!"

It was Aunt Luisa. She was in the kitchen, reading the dress-shop ledger book. The light of the afternoon printed a rectangle on the table and over her soft face. "Oh Hector, come and give your auntie a kiss and you'll get a delicious treat."

He kissed her and she laughed, patting his head.

"How affectionate you are," she said and pinched his cheeks. Then he waited for the treat. He loved to eat, so much so that with each day he grew a little chubbier. His legs and belly were fat. His cheeks, so, so plump, were red. In the evenings he was always happy to sit on the floor with his female cousins, eating snacks given by Luisa. Chewing fried toast covered in sugar with his eyes closed, listening to Aunt Luisa's soft, pleasant voice as she sewed in the half-light of the room. Chewing sounds and Luisa's voice mingled with the street noises outside: clop, clop, clop of horses, insects' songs, a dog barking, the murmur of spirits in the Cuban ghost land. Taste of sugar and bread. Luisa sighed as she put aside her sewing for the moment and leaned forward to touch Hector's face. "You're such a little blondie," she said.

Aunt Luisa fixed his drink, which he slowly drank down, savoring its taste. It was so good, with nutty, deep-forest flavors, sweet but not too sweet, with just enough bitterness to fill the mouth with a yawning sensation. He asked for more. She kissed him, poured another glass, and he drank that down. It went deep into his belly but shot up again, from time to time, into his sleep, night after night, for years to come. For some reason he would remember that drink, wondering what it could be, so Cuban, so delicious. Then one day, years in the future, Luisa would come to America, and he would find out its name.

He divided his time between the two aunt's houses, eating and drinking everything in sight: caramel sweets, hard candies, plates of fried pork in rice, bananas, sweet papaya ice cream, leaves, twigs, soda crackers, honey-dipped flour balls, sour Cuban milk, Coca-Cola, and even water from a puddle. At Rina's house he would sit in a chair placed in front of Uncle Manny's workshop and eat his lunch. Uncle Manny was an enormous man with white hair and wire-rimmed glasses. He had a horse face and liked to wear khaki clothing and read newspapers in an enclosure of prickly bushes. He was a bookkeeper but kept this little workshop in the backyard in order to do some silversmithing and watch repair on the side. Luisa and Rina sent him customers from the dress shop. The workshop: a pine shed, boxes of watch gears and tiny screws, coils of soft wire, and a burner used for heating a little pot of coffee. Smell of metal, rubber, silver, talcum, eucalyptus.

Now Hector was watching him melt silver in a tiny ladle over a flame. His demitasse of coffee steamed on the wooden counter. Swirling the silver around, Manny said, "You know what this is boy? Cuban blood." Hector looked at the steaming coffee, and Manny laughed. "Not the coffee, boy, the silver. You have this in your veins." The silver swirling. "You know what you are, boy? You're Cuban. *Un Cubano*. Say it."

"*Cubano, Cubano*, Cuba, Cuba..."

Hector sat watching Manny for a long time, wondering if the demitasse was full of the exotic, delicious Cuban drink. His eyes would dart between the ladle of Cuban blood and the coffee, and noticing this, Manny let him sip the dark espresso to which he had added sugar and dark rum. Hector spit it out, and Manny laughed again.

"Don't worry, you'll like it when you're older."

But he drank many other beverages: Coca-Cola and orange juice at Aunt Rina's. In town, at the bodega, some kind of crushed ice drink mixed with pieces of fruit and syrup. All so good, but not like what Luisa gave him. And he was always drinking Cuban water, especially on those trips he and Horacio took with Manny out to the countryside. Manny sometimes did the accounting for a pal of his who worked at a pharmaceutical warehouse. His pal used to give him free bottles of medicine and aspirin, which he would give to the poor *guajiros*—"hicks."

"How they can live like that," Manny used to say, shaking his head, "how they can live like that?"

And Manny would take the family up north to Gibara to go swimming. That was where, according to Mercedes, Hector got sick.

The whole family was together: Mercedes, Luisa, and Rina, the cousins, Manny, Horacio, and Hector. All the women sat under a big umbrella, reading fashion and Hollywood magazines with actors like William Holden and Cary Grant on the cover, while the men ran in and out of the warm ocean. The current whooshed Cuban sand between their toes. There were starfish by Manny's massive feet. His strong hands took Hector aloft onto his shoulders, real high up, the way Alejo used to do, back in New York. He was so high up, he could see all the palms and the Persian-looking cabanas and the weathered boardwalk, the sea all around him, a curly blue mirror.

Breaking the waves, Manny marched out into the ocean, his great chest of white hair foaming. The skies overhead, zooming by. Manny's voice: something about Christopher Columbus and a ship with huge white sails, Indians, skeletons under the water, and the edge of the world... And he was taking Hector out deep into the Cuban sea. Hector held on for his life, his arms around Manny's bull neck, until Manny pried his hands free and let him float off.

But down he went.

"Come on, niño, try, try, try, don't be afraid."

Hector swallowed more water, went up and down.

"Come on, niño."

But Hector went down and tasted salt and his throat burned, he swallowed and coughed, so that Manny finally brought him back to shore, where Luisa cured him with kisses.

When Hector started feeling sick, Luisa gave him more of the delicious Cuban drink, so good in his belly. But sometimes a weariness confused him and he stayed up at night, listening to the Cuban ghosts walking around in the yard. Or he could hear Mercedes speaking in whispers to Luisa. Sometimes his back ached or his penis felt shot with lead, and he could be in a room, drinking his treat, when he would hurt but remain quiet. If he did cry out, Luisa or Rina cured him with kisses. Mercedes always said, "You were so good, a quiet, quiet boy. If only we knew..."

A Cuban infection of some kind entered him. In any case, that was what Mercedes always said. What had he done? Swim in the ocean? Drink from a puddle? Kiss? Maybe he hadn't said his prayers properly, or he had pissed in his pants one too many times or cried too much. Maybe God had turned the Cuban water against him and allowed the *micróbios,* as Mercedes would call them, to go inside his body. Who knew? But getting sick in Cuba confused him greatly, because he had loved Cuba so much.

3

In her way Mercedes made sense of these things. This was what she said about that journey.

"We went there to see my poor mama, bless her soul. She was viejita, viejita, so old and happy to see us. There were other reasons we went, for a vacation, you know. Alejo couldn't take that much time off, three months, so he sent us along.

"When we got to Havana we took the train east to Holguín. That was a long trip, twelve hours, but at least we got to see a little of everything: the big sugarcane plantations, the ranches, the mountains, the old colonial towns with their dusty train stations and the poor farmers going everywhere with their caged, dirty, white hens. Horacio was pressed against the window, looking at everything with big eyes, but Hector was too hot for the whole trip, inside a stuffy train. And, Dios mío, it was hot in those days. So believe me, we were happy when we finally came to Holguín.

"My sisters loved both of the boys very much, and they loved my sisters back. The boys were as happy as little mice and everything was pretty: the house, the town, and the flowers that were everywhere. I remember Manny...his children came to America last year on a boat from Mariel Harbor. He was a big man, so good, especially with the poor. He died in 1960, young, like everyone else who's any good in this world, but in those days he took us everywhere. To the movies and out to the farm and to the ocean, where maybe Hector got sick.

"I tried to be good, but it's impossible to watch the children all the time, with all the running around and playing. Horacio was good, quiet, and minding his own business, but Hector...he made me go crazy down there. We would leave him in the yard in Luisa's house, saying, Stay put, but he wouldn't do that. Running around, he got into everything. I didn't mind that, but he went around drinking water out of puddles in the yard. There was dirty water down there, filled with little micróbios, which is why he got sick. We didn't know it then. He looked healthy, mi hijito, my little son. He was nice and chubby, and, little by little, he put on more weight. Horacio put on some weight, too, all those chorizos and plátanos omelets that he liked so much. So we didn't think anything about it. We went through the days in peace, Horacio having fun and Hector so curious and happy. Who knew that he would be so sick? I didn't.

"Alejo was writing me nice letters, saying nice things in them, saying for us to have a good time. The only thing he asked us to do was to visit his great grandmother, old Concepción. That's where Horacio and Hector got their light hair. From old Concepción. A long time ago, when Concepción was a young girl, maybe seventeen or sixteen years of age, walking in Santiago de Cuba, she met an Irish sailor by the name of O'Connor. He was very light and fair, with blond hair. He had sailed around the world about five or six times and was looking for a place to settle, was swept off his feet by Concepción, and eventually married her. So her name became Concepción O'Connor, and his blood passed down quietly through the generations until my sons were born.

"In any case, we went to see her one day. She was almost one hundred years old. But she was clean and still had all her senses. Her arms were thin, like young branches, and her hair was white, white. But she had young eyes, and was so happy to see us! She always sat in one place on the patio under an umbrella so that the berries dropping from the trees wouldn't hit her in the head. She was something of a celebrity, too, having been written up in the *Sol* and *Diario de la Marina* because she was so old and not yet dead. She was very happy to meet us, and when she saw Hector's little blond head, she got all happy . . . to think that more of the sailor was around!

"And I took the boys to see my old house. It was just like it used to be, so beautiful, except that now we couldn't go inside. A government man lived there and had servants who wouldn't even let us peek around. There it was, a beautiful white house, so nice . . . the kind of house we could have all lived in if our luck was a little different, and if my poor papa did not die . . . .

"Still we had our fun. We went to the marketplace and saw a bull-fight. And then I showed Horacio and Hector where a witch lived when I was a little girl, and we would pass the time watching the farmers going by on the road. Down the way there was a blind negro, un negrito muy bueno, who played the guitar and used to sing for pennies. For hours we would stand beside him or go riding around; every one of us had fun.

"But Hector became very sick and made trouble for me. I don't know what happened. Maybe it was the drinking water there or something in the food, but he got so sick, and Alejo blamed me for it. Maybe I should have known . . . One day we were at the beach at Gibara and Manny was taking everybody into the water. Hector was having fun on top of Manny's shoulders, going deeper and deeper into the water. You know how sometimes you can think of things, they come to you in a second? I was sitting under the umbrella, because the sun was bad for my skin, when I suddenly felt like a little girl, and as I watched everyone in the water, I had the idea that something was going to get me in trouble: I didn't want it to happen but couldn't tell what it would be. Just a feeling of wanting to stop something before it started. Like knowing that there are bugs eating up your garden, but you can never find them. That was what it was like. When we left Cuba, Hector was sick but so happy and fat that we didn't know anything. He came back saying *Cuba, Cuba* and spent a lot of time with Alejo. He was a little Cuban, spouting Spanish."

The Cuban Illness, 1954–1955

1

They were in New York for a few months when the pains returned to Hector's lower back. At night he called out to Alejo and Mercedes, and they came down the hall to see what was wrong. Alejo figured that Hector was just afraid of the dark, a phase kids go through. After all, Hector was at the age when devils and shadowy animals roam wild in the mind. Horacio had screamed from nightmares at that age. Alejo used to come down the hall and, sitting on the edge of the bed, hold down Hector's hands, say, "Estoy aquí, estoy aquí," "I am here, I am here." He would sit there with a confused expression on his face until Hector went to sleep. But sometimes Hector woke from his sleep with a violent wretching inside, jumping up and screaming as if fighting someone or something in that room. This always made Alejo a little angry, that the kid could get this way, after having such a nice time in Cuba... a little kid, "my son." "But don't worry, su papá está aquí."

Other times Mercedes took care of him. She was not always as patient or as sympathetic as Alejo. Sometimes her answer to everything was an aspirin or Alka Seltzer. She'd come into the dark room, ask what was wrong, and, hearing the usual, come back with either a glass of plain or fizzling water. Horacio, who was in the very next room at the end of the hall, used to stay up listening to Hector moan. He tried

85

to understand why no one would take Hector to a doctor, but that was the way things were done in that house.

On a bad night, when Hector called out three or four times, Mercedes came down the hall, sat on the bed, and started pounding on his chest, one, two, three times.

"Now we're going to get the little devils out," she said, pounding his chest again. "You'll cry until it all comes out." Then she twisted his ears until he cried out, but the devils did not leave. Instead he heard a buzz, as if an angel was standing in the doorway with hand on chin, checking them out and saying, "Hmmmmmmmm...."

This continued for a few weeks. Then Mercedes finally decided to call a doctor uptown who knew about illnesses and fakery. He was from the Dominican Republic and was practicing medicine in the United States without a license. He came to the house with his wife. She dressed like a widow in black and was the witch part of the team. She performed everything from exorcisms to rituals that cured impotence and changed a man's luck with women. The doctor brought her along to gain credibility with the more superstitious clients who did not trust modern medicine or doctors. He examined Hector and told Mercedes that a specialist's help was in order, but she didn't want to believe him. Too much trouble, too much money. The doctor left some pills and went away.

That evening, when the screams continued, Alejo came and sat with Hector, and then Mercedes came. She was convinced that he was calling out only for attention. So she pounded his chest again and told him a story: "You know, child, if you keep complaining you'll never be able to get along in this world, like the little girl we used to hear about in Cuba. She was afraid of everything: shadows, flies, dogs, the wind, and even people in her own family. She was always standing at the window of her house looking out at the people walking by, but she wouldn't go out herself. She was so afraid, the slightest noise made her cry out for help, and someone would come along and tell her, 'You have to get along by yourself,' the way I'm telling you, child. And she said yes, but as the years went by and all her friends went to school and grew up, she never left her house. Soon she was a young woman, unmarried and without a novio. Then more years passed and she

86

became an old woman, still unmarried. But she was lonely and called for people to help her, but no one came because she had been calling out all her life. So she finally got her nerve back, and having nothing to lose, she went outside. You know what happened? When she left the house by herself, she was run over by a truck and died."

Laughing, she took hold of Hector's hands and squeezed his wrists. Pounding his chest, she said, "In the morning you're going to wake up and everything bad inside of you will have gone away." Then she left him and went back to bed.

Afraid of getting into trouble or being pounded, Hector didn't call out to her again. He tried to fall asleep. Finally, after a long time, he began to dream about the ocean and Spanish galleons with foamy decks, and he could feel the mattress under him soaked and cakey as if crystal wafers had been broken. He dreamed about the whoosh of the Cuban current, Manny's laughter, Mercedes's voice, and he touched his hands to the bed, which was all wet, and in the middle of the dream he woke up again, calling out, "Mama, Mama," but it was Horacio who came instead. And he really yelled, because Hector had been urinating blood.

In the morning Mercedes was in a panic to take Hector to the hospital. "I should've known how my luck would go," she kept saying. The kid looked sort of healthy. He was fat; his limbs and belly had bloated out, and he slept like a turtle on his back. It hurt him to move. Things were dark... His muscles really hurt, he was boneless, and he felt like soaked rags inside. Horacio tried to carry him out, but Hector was too heavy. Mercedes went to the window. There were kids playing stickball outside on the street, and she called to them, "Please get me a taxi," and they got him out into a cab.

At the hospital Mercedes and Horacio waited in the hall outside the examination room where all the complicated tests were being performed. Nurses pushed many geared machines with screens and tubes in and out of rooms. Mercedes looked down into her cupped hands, trying to have faith in science, about which she knew almost nothing. When the machines passed she looked at them in awe, as if they were saintly coffins. And she nodded to the doctors, who knew all the baffling secrets of the human body. All these machines were so new, not like what she had seen in Holguín. Medicine in Holguín was nineteenth-century medicine. People died easily. But here in America? The machines would help Hector. Miraculously, they would stop the blood, heal the broken vessels, purify the internal organs. Poor Mercedes knew practically nothing about the body, only that the heart could burst and blood was very important. And that the soul resided in the backbone and that real prayer could turn God's head so that he would squeeze out cures. She knew all kinds of old wives' tales about the curative properties of rosaries, holy water, and dreams. The power of eucalyptus, garlic, and lilies—hit-and-miss stuff that sometimes worked. Mercedes saw the body as a mystery, like a huge house with winding halls and endless rooms where food was eaten and blood pumped and where little monsters like micróbios swarmed in thick streams through the halls, a house where the walls were on the verge of collapse. She had the kind of faith in science that the ignorant have: It will do everything. She had a faith like the faith hoods with knife wounds that spill their guts have, who come to the hospitals thinking they won't die. They come walking in nonchalantly and then fall to the floor, dead.

Horacio drew pictures, and Mercedes prayed into the streams of thought that passed through her mind. She was thinking that Alejo was going to hit her, call her no good, send her away, or prove her crazy. She thought about what Buita would say, that she was not fit to be a mother. She remembered the time when Buita accused her of poisoning Horacio, and Buita's threats of sending her to the asylum. Would these things happen? No, he'll get better, don't you worry. She kept telling Horacio, "He'll get better." But after a while a doctor came out and told her bluntly, "Señora Santinio, your child is most gravely ill." For hours she remained motionless, thinking about the children she knew in Cuba who died. Tuberculosis and yellow fever were the big killers. Overnight a bad fever would bring on pneumonia, and by the morning the child would be dead. Names came to mind: poor Theodocia, poor Alphonso, poor Pedro, poor Mariaelena. For a moment, Cuba became a place of disease and death. She saw tiny coffins, cemetery stones, flowers, stoic-faced families walking through cemetery gates and down winding paths, heads bowed; she saw children crying and her mother crying. She saw her father's funeral winding through the cobblestone streets of Holguín.

Occasionally a nurse who knew Spanish came by to speak to her, but this did nothing to allay her fears. A terrible infection had spread through Hector's body. A doctor elaborated, and this was translated by the nurse: "He may have a bad inflammation of the kidneys. This condition has gone on for months. His kidneys do not work, nothing works. He cannot get the poison out of his system. He's bloated with dirty water, and it's everywhere inside him. Already the infection has spread to his liver and heart."

The doctor was holding a folder that would grow thick over the years with the bird script of specialists. Three hundred pages of blood pressure and pulse readings, diagnosis, appraisal of blood samples and urinalysis... *All from the dirty water of Cuba?*

"Just tell the Señora," the doctor said, "that we don't know what will happen."

The room was cheerless with no windows. There were two doors with wire windows. Around eight o'clock, Alejo came in. He had been at the hotel when a family friend went to get him. He looked very confused; he would not say a word to Mercedes. She called out his name, but he did not answer. He was at the desk signing papers and presenting union insurance forms and the like. There were many questions. Citizen? Yes. Occupation? Cook. Age? Forty-two. Birthplace? San Pedro, Cuba. Date? January 17, 1912. Faith? Catholic. (*Worried? Yes, yes, yes, I'll kill that witch!*)

He stood patiently by the desk, smoking one cigarette after another. He signed forms, shook his head, blew smoke from his mouth. When the nurse left, Mercedes went over to him and rested her head on his shoulders. She was waiting to be lifted away from the situation, but he told her, "This is your fault, no one else's."

Horacio was falling asleep in a chair. His eyes kept closing and opening. In his striped shirt, he looked like a tomcat having dreams. Hector was going to die. He was sure it was going to happen. Then he would sing at the funeral. In the next few days he would go to the funeral parlors with Alejo, pricing coffins. Just a few weeks before, Horacio had punched Hector around in anger. He came home, and boom! he hit Hector in the face and turned the lights off and twisted his arm. It was really nothing, but when he thought Hector might die, then every thought swirled into the fear that the dead would come back to get revenge. He did not like to think about it. He remained curled up in his seat, trying to sleep, but kept flinching each time he saw his pop's face and felt the sadness, thick in that room. He knew, too, things would explode once they got home.

Alejo sat beside Horacio, his brown felt, black-banded hat in his hands. Mercedes was beside him, but did not say a word. She kept looking off into the dark hallway, thinking about the illness. It had come almost supernaturally from the Cuban water, making her look bad before Alejo. Micróbios malos, little malicious spirits had penetrated Hector's flesh. She shook her head in confusion. The doctor said he got sick from drinking something bad. Water from the puddle? Water dripping from branches in the yard? All she could do was sit there terrified, whispering, "No me diga, no me diga"—"Don't tell me, don't tell me." She was watching the hall and Alejo's exhausted face, wishing he would move his hand a few inches closer to hers.

They remained overnight. Around two the next afternoon, a nurse led them to the room where Hector was sleeping. He was propped up, and there were needles and tubes of blood and more tubes sticking out from his nose. There was some kind of catheter shoved up his penis, and a thick tube coming out of his ass. Alejo looked him over for a moment and then left the room. Mercedes made the sign of the cross. Horacio stood, just watching. Hector seemed to him to be asleep, but he could also be near the land of the dead. A nurse called them out and said they might as well go home, and so they left the hospital.

They spent the evening with company. A Cuban family from next door brought them dinner in pots and casserole dishes, and everyone sat in the living room, eating and making small talk. Alejo disappeared. He would be gone for three days. Later, Mercedes's friend, Mary, invited Horacio upstairs to watch their television set, which he did. And Mercedes passed her time in bed, nervous and shaking, trying to sleep.

90

2

After a month they sent Hector to a hospital in Connecticut that was a terminal home for children. It was near Hartford, and there was a convenient cemetery along the way, shaded by drooping willow trees and dotted with white- and blue-streaked tombstones. The road curved into an estate of hilly greens, duck ponds, stone walks, and benches. It was very beautiful. Hector stayed in a ward at the end of a long corridor. There were two rows of simple metal beds and windows high up on the bare walls. Not one of the kids could leave the building. To get into the ward, you had to get past a guard and three double doors. Even the sunlight seemed to sneak in clandestinely, illuminating the faces of the other children like little El Dorados. The patients were innocent children. Most were filled with water and bad air and with micróbios. They came to this place from all over the East Coast, and there was even a little girl with pigtails who came from California. The children were very sick and had to take pills five times a day and were required to piss in bedpans, whose contents were examined under microscopes. Blood samples, ugly in thick hypos, were taken every week. Gas was always being administered through tubes into the noses of the children, and metallic rods were shoved up into the privates, rods so cold and violating that the children's bones would leave their bodies and walk around in the outer hall waiting for the flesh's temperature to rise again. Little adorable girls, who would have certainly grown up to be real beauties, went to sleep without a mark on their faces and woke in the morning black and blue, as if they had received the worst beatings. Then they became pale like fish and started to cry. Some crawled along the floor like lizards, while others ran wildly, banging into the walls and shaking. And when the nurses came by with their medicines, the children crawled into shelves and, wracked with pain, spoke to themselves, asking to be helped. If a beam of sunshine shot through the window, spotlighting the floor, they would crawl in it, letting it warm their insides. They would sail around the floors in their boats of light, until they could not move. The pretty girls sang until their bellies cramped and they keeled over and the crying began again. Sometimes at night two men in white hats, dressed like garbage collectors, came into the ward and would lift one of the sleeping children quietly out of bed, put him in a bag, and carry him off. In the morning one of the nurses would calmly make the bed of the missing child, without so much as a word to the kids. But they knew. Another one gone to the skeletons, vanished like so many other things: like the shaky sunlight, sucked into the mirrors and never returned, like toys and tiny shoes and dolls and mirrors, one second there and then poof! gone. Like the Superman funny books! Like Mama and Papa! Like their homes and the whole world and the sun, poof! gone so fast, pulled out from under them.

But they had their fun. They had a television set that was the greatest wonder on Earth. Howdy Doody was a mannequin and he looked just like one of them, except Howdy could still walk around. And now and then the nurse took everyone down the corridor and let them stand on a bench to look out the window, through which they sometimes could see snow falling over the meadow and the countryside.

The parents came into the hospital on visiting days. The kids who were well enough were brought down the long hallway, into a visiting room. The parents sat facing the children and did not always like what they could see. The parents had faces like rubber masks stretched out on nails. They spoke quietly and gave presents but could not kiss the kids because their kisses carried too many micróbios.

Hector was lucky. After the third or fourth month he was allowed to see Mercedes. She started to come up every couple of weeks on Sundays, with a friend from down the street who was married to a gangster, or with Mary, who had a black Oldsmobile. The nurse would come down the long hallway with Hector and put him into the room with the screen wall. Then, after a time, he was improved enough to sit face to face with her. They would sit on a bench by the window. Hector had no idea what was going on. She would hold him while he squirmed in her arms. He knew her face, recognized the jittery voice. Sometimes she didn't look him in the eyes and just started speaking her Spanish so fast, fast, while Hector wondered where the rest of his family and their friends had gone. He kept seeing Alejo in the shadows, but Alejo was never there. And when he asked Mercedes for Pop, she always grew uncomfortable, spoke about the weather, gossip, or the neighbors. Sometimes, at these moments, he noticed she had bruises under her eyes.

"Your papa," she would say in Spanish, "they won't let him in here. They say he has a cold and can't come in. He's standing outside."

Once she went so far as to show him the window facing the field and in the distance, a stark denuded tree about which she said, "See him over there, he's smoking a cigarette. They won't let him in until he's finished."

But he never finished the cigarettes and never came inside to visit Hector, who wanted to see him very much.

Hector looked everywhere for Alejo, squirming in Mercedes's arms and trying to break free from her grasp. No matter how hard Mercedes tried to take care of Hector she would always lose. Even though she often visited him, in the future Hector would swear that it was Alejo who made the trip every weekend, showering him with toys he got from a neighbor in the building. He would recall Alejo removing his hat by one of the large, arched, yellow windows in the hallway. Alejo with packages of gifts. Alejo kissing him. Alejo with the most concerned expression on his face. He swore he heard Alejo's soft voice saying, "Estoy aquí"—"I am here"—and "I nearly died when you got sick," over the hissing radiator noises. He would remember Alejo walking through the ward of the terminal home, tipping his hat to the nurses and the staff, remember looking forward to the next week, an interminable length of time, and seeing Alejo again.

"Sure, Pop came every week," he would say, years later, to Horacio.

"He never came to see you."

"Sure he did. I saw him myself."

"Listen brother, I have no reason to lie to you. He never showed up to see you even once, not even once, because he was always out on those Sundays having a good time."

"Yeah, well you're just jealous."

"Well, you take it for the truth, brother."

Hector wanted to see Alejo because he remembered the good days before the illness, how Alejo emptied rooms of their sadness and used to let him sleep beside him and brought him presents and took him walking in the park on spring days and did not once fall down. Alejo wasn't like Mercedes, who filled the house with nervousness and worry. She had the high cackling laugh, the crazy eyes, she started the arguing, and she made Alejo turn red in the face and pant.

So maybe Hector did see Alejo in the shadows or in the light that fell onto the bedsheets or onto the walls of the hospital. He believed that Alejo had shown up even though everybody in the world swore differently. (And where was Alejo? He passed his days holed up with friends, getting stewed and worrying about bills, and crying about human mortality and about his sick kid, made sick by that woman, a thorn in his side, who couldn't even take care of the boy for a few lousy months, crying about his son named after his dead brother and now ready to go into the next world, "no, that kid isn't going to go...no, give me a drink...ah, qué bueno, nothing to fill up the empty like a drink...qué bueno.")

Alejo's presence made Hector feel calm, but Mercedes's presence was a punishment. The ordeal made her overly strict and protective. The few hours she saw him, she spent reminding him about how he almost died. And then she would go away, and he would be left alone, murmuring, "Cuba, Cuba..."

And that was the other thing. The origin of the disease. Cuba, as Mercedes always said. "The water made you sick." Cuba gave the bad disease. Cuba gave the drunk father. Cuba gave the crazy mother. Years later all these would entwine to make Hector think that Cuba had something against him. That it made him sick and pale...and excluded from that life that happy Cubans were supposed to have.

"Cuba, Cuba..."

Even the nurses made something of this. Hector, being a little Cuban, didn't speak much English. The nurses figured they would help him by teaching him English. After all, he was blond and fair and didn't look Spanish. There was one nurse who took special care of him: meals, bedpans, injections, tubes.

"Do you know something," she said to him, "you're very stupid for not speaking in English. This is your country. You live here and should know the language."

To teach him English she would lock him up in a closet. He would be quiet for a while then get scared and start banging on the door. She'd say, "Not until you say, 'Please let me out!'" But he wouldn't even try. He'd pull on the door of the closet and cry out in Spanish. He was afraid: All the clothes on the shelves were haunted. They had belonged at one time or another to children now dead, and they seemed to be puffed up and to move around, as if hundreds of invisible kids had crawled into them. Dead children were like normal children except their eyes were closed. He would bang on the door and scream out in Spanish, "¡Abra la puerta! ¡Abra la puerta!"—"Open the door! Open the door! wishing in his deep dreams to open the door to Aunt Luisa's kitchen in Cuba and find a glass of the magic concoction, or to see Alejo as he went down the hall to work. He kept on saying it, in a panic, crazy, as if on fire inside. Then the voice on the other side would return, "Say it in English. *Let me out!*" Then she would shout it. "Now don't be stupid," she would tell him, "say it!"

The hours would drag and the door would not open.

Day after day, she badgered him with the same punishments and repeated phrases. In time she made him suspicious of Spanish. Spanish words drifted inside him, he dreamed in Spanish, but English began whooshing inside. English forced its way through him, splitting his skin. Sometimes he called out for Horacio and Mercedes and Alejo, Luisa and Rina, and the others, but they did not come. A few times he yelled out, "Cuba, Cuba." But no one and nothing came to save him.

Hector began to feel as if he deserved to be locked up. Each day was like the next. Vague, recent memories invaded him. He would be lifted from paradise in Cuba and dropped into a dark room. Each time he spoke Spanish and the nurse was nearby, she slapped his hands. The same nurse mocked his mother's ignorance of English. He was slowly improving, but his sentences were sprinkled with Spanish. Holding a glass of water before him, she would ask, "And how do you ask for this?"

"May I have some *agua*?"

"No! Water!"

"May I have some water?"

"Oh yes," she answered. "That's it!" And she kissed him.

In time he believed Spanish was an enemy, and when Mercedes

came to visit and told him stories about home, he remained silent, as if the nurse were watching him. Even his dreams were broken up by the static of English, like a number of wasps overcoming the corner of a garden. Suddenly he could understand what his friends were saying, "Hector, I hurt. I'm so thirsty..."

This stay in the Connecticut hospital lasted for nearly a year. Tubes went into his penis, and he listened to the kids' crying and saw them shaking in the dark and watched some of the kids who had been watching Ding Dong School and Howdy Doody with him get carried off in garbage bags. He would one day remember a little girl who was carried off. She told him a story about a dog she used to have, named Fluffy, the kind of dog you throw sticks to on a fine spring day, who goes running around and pants so happily. She told him how much she missed her dog, and she kept speaking of Fluffy running in a field, his tongue feeling so nice when he came up to lick her face. And this little girl told him she would be leaving the home to play with Fluffy, but then she disappeared in the middle of the night. He never saw her again.

One day the doctors took Hector into the examination room, and instead of pushing a tube into his body, they stuck a needle into his arm, withdrawing blood. The doctor looked at the blood through a microscope, sent it off for the tests, and that afternoon announced ecstatically, "This one will be fine."

In a week Mercedes went to see the doctor, who told her she could take Hector home. The doctor behaved like a schoolteacher that day, pointing to a chart of the human body and finding the diseased kidneys, which were shaped like the island of Cuba on maps.

"You must be careful with him, Mrs. Santinio. The kidney is a vital organ, subject to rapid and easy deterioration, and it must be treated properly. You must be attentive when administering all antibiotics and medications. He must be careful about what he eats. His diet must contain little or no salts, fats, sweets. Everything must be boiled. No fried foods, no sweets, no rich food of any kind. Recovery is rare and there is a high incidence of recurrence, but as long as you are careful and give him all the prescribed medicines, he may live for many years..."

With such happy tidings, Mercedes went into the ward to gather his things. She was nervous about taking him back into the world. As he passed down the hall with its wobbly rectangles of sunlight cast by the corridor windows, the prospect of true sunshine excited him. It was the spring, and when the door from the hospital opened, in the sky was the astonishing sun. A beautiful spring day with smell of grass and buzz of insects in the air, and with hospital attendants lounging in short-sleeved shirts on benches by a small river that passed through the grounds. But Hector was wearing a heavy coat! Mercedes did not want to risk his catching a cold. They followed a path through the high grass, past little gardens with busy dragonflies and bees, past a gazebo, a willow tree, a lily pond. Mercedes noticed that Hector was starting to perspire, melting like a snowman. So she hurried with him to the car. Behind the wheel was the gangster from down the street, chainsmoking, and beside him, his wife, and Horacio, waiting as usual, silent because strange things were going on at home. Mercedes and Hector got into the back seat. Each time Hector tried to undo the coat's buttons, Mercedes redid them. Each time he tried to roll down the window to get some fresh air, she rolled it back up. Whenever Hector tried to get close to Horacio, she pulled him back, or else Horacio moved away. Hector possessed micróbios contracted in Cuba. He would be unable to touch anyone but Alejo for years.

At home Alejo was sitting in the kitchen, pretty much as if nothing had happened. When he saw Hector, he looked at him with pity and then opened his arms, and Hector ran to him. Then he started to speak to Hector in Spanish, and Hector nodded and listened but he did not speak back. When Hector finally spoke, he used English, which surprised Alejo. Alejo asked him all kinds of ques ons, "Why don't you speak in Spanish?" and Hector, feeling ashamed and afraid, became silent. Alejo looked at Hector, wondering if this was his son. There he was, a little blondie, a sickly, fair-skinned Cuban who was not speaking Spanish. He patted the kid on the head, turned around, and took a swig of beer.

Later that night Alejo rushed down the hallway to save Hector from a bad dream. He put his big meat-smelling hands on Hector's face until the kid fell back to sleep. Then he went back into the kitchen to have a drink. He slammed doors and began swearing. He told Mercedes, "You made the boy that way. You'd better take care of him, or out you go!" In his simple way, he wanted the best for Hector, for all the family. But from now on, whenever Alejo's friends came to the house, they would look Hector over and make jokes in Spanish. They laughed, rolled their eyes, patted his head. Now he looked American and spoke mostly American. Cuba had become the mysterious and cruel phantasm standing behind the door.

Another Day, 1958

1

Alejo went down the hallway to the bathroom. He washed his face and gargled with Lavoris to get rid of the night stink. Too many cigarettes and too much whiskey and beer left a dry taste in his mouth and a mucous, unstable feeling in his stomach, as if he had mercury in his gut, a rotted digestive system, sick stomach, muy flojo, muy flojo, soft and rotted, and a headache like a fist in his brain. But what could he do? It was a sticky summer morning and he didn't want to, but he always got up. No fuckin' attitudes but responsibility, no fuck you, man but yes, sir! He always went to work and never missed a day because the men in the kitchen respected and counted on him. He was a big man around them. And besides, you always go to work, as he would say, no matter what, because the bills pile up, and you become a useless bum if you don't, and later in the day when the work is over, you have your self-respect. Work is everything . . . work was everything.

During the night Hector had screamed out because the monster was prowling in the hall. The monster was Alejo, hanging onto the walls to get from the kitchen to the bathroom, which was next to Hector's room. Hearing the screams Alejo had gone into Hector's room, looked him over, sat on the bed. He wore baggy undershorts; the flap was open and the big raw-looking penis just inside, as red as his face that stared down at Hector in the dark. Drunks who came over had the same look, as if they were falling apart, and when they pissed with the bathroom door open, each leaned one hand against the wall and held his thing in the other, completely oblivious to anyone's presence. Even when they closed the door, it mysteriously opened. Even when it was someone who knew the doors and its tricky latch, like Alejo. The door would open and Alejo would be standing there, wobbling. Sometimes he bounced into the walls as if pushed by an invisible hand, and then, holding his thing, he might accidentally piss into the tub or onto the floor. Then boom! down he would go, and Hector and Horacio would find him there and try to get him up, to move him off the floor. Taking his arms and pulling without success, Horacio would say, "We may as well leave him here," and Hector would look on, confused by seeing his Pop stretched out on the floor like a dead man, with his thing half out.

Mercedes used to tell Hector about a monster in the hall. This was intended to keep Hector from seeing things like Pop falling and grasping at the walls, Pop in that horrid state. She explained that the hallway was dark and narrow and filled with Cuban dead people and the Cuban devil whenever she wanted to cover up the screaming and the fighting. But after a few hours she would drag Hector out of his room anyway, and show him Alejo. "I want you to be a witness to this," she would say. "This is your father! Look at him lying on the floor and see what he is really like!"

Hearing this from his room, Horacio would charge into the hall. He never liked it when Mercedes carried on about Alejo. "All right, all right," he would shout. "We see him. Do you think we're fuckin' blind?"

Sometimes they could shut out Alejo. But there was nothing they could do about Mercedes, yelling at all hours. The neighbors, finally losing patience, began to lean out of the window, shouting, "You crazy down there? Be quiet or we'll call the police. We're trying to sleep!" So Hector and Horacio would leave him on the floor and go back to bed, sleeping badly and waking when Alejo got back on his feet again and the sound of his loud urination gurgled in the toilet.

While Hector slept last night, the monsters had materialized: monsters of fire, of knives, of disease, of contaminated oceans; monsters of mother's screams and brother's punches and of seeing Horacio slammed into the wall by the back of Pop's heavy, ringed hand; monsters of running, of confusion, monsters of anger and Hell, scaring him until he called out and Alejo had come to save him. His father's presence was enough to calm him down. It was all right. Alejo wasn't really stoned and so he didn't fall off the bed and onto the floor as he did some nights. Those times, Hector tried to sleep and forget that his father was near.

But, no matter what, in the morning Alejo always got up to go to work. Mercedes was in bed under a swirl of sheeting, half-asleep, and staring toward the ceiling. Then, sighing, she rose from the bed and solemnly began Alejo's breakfast. He liked his breakfast the same way each morning: a piece of toast with jelly and butter, a piece of hard cheese, two cups of strong black coffee. He ate and Mercedes gathered his things: his keys; wallet, fat with papers; his cigarettes. Then she went back to bed. The morning was a peaceful time. Flickers of light in sharp angles thrown by the window into the hall. Things so quiet.

Simply dressed, feeling sick, Alejo went down the apartment's hallway into the serene morning light coming in so thick by the window and spreading everywhere. It was like the light of Jesus's tomb, a burst of radiance. He went to the door. In his back pocket, he carried an English phrasebook and a handkerchief. On this day he had taken, of all things, a blue penny-collector's book with round slots for the differently minted pennies: Lincoln, Denver 1922; Lincoln, Denver 1922a; and so on. He liked collecting these. At the hotel he always went through boxes of change from the bar, looking for pennies he needed. He secretly believed he was accumulating a small fortune. He came by other coins as well: an old, old, black Roman coin from the time of Marcus Aurelius, which he later lost in the Bronx; a few Confederate coins; a coin from the old, old Cuba bearing the image of King Philip of Spain. What else did he carry? Little penny boxes of Chiclets, the popular chewing gum.

Horacio, who delivered newspapers early in the morning for the stationery store, saw Alejo in the hallway. He didn't say too much, especially since Alejo had wrecked him the night before. Horacio would hurry to work at the stationery store down on the avenue, a few blocks away. He didn't like going there because the owner was a miserly workhorse who used to have fistfights with thirteen- and fourteen-year-olds to show them how tough he could be. But they were robbing him of cigarettes and toys and comic books and pink Spauldings. With delivery tips, the job paid all right. Seeing Alejo, Horacio was quiet. Alejo said, "A nice day, huh?" in an apologetic, noncommittal way, as if the man from the night before lived in another apartment.

On this particular summer day Horacio was taking a towel and bathing suit with him. After delivering the papers he would help out behind the breakfast counter for a few hours. Around eleven, when he left work at the store, Horacio and some of the neighborhood guys were going to Rockaway Beach. They would meet on the corner and play around, throwing their sailor hats down and jumping on parked cars, sounding on cops. Then they would go down to the subway, just like in the Bowery boys' movies.

"Hey Horacio, be careful," Alejo called after Horacio as he headed for the door.

No answer. The slamming of the door.

Then Alejo left. Outside on the stoop, in front of the pillars, he met Mr. Kent from upstairs. Mr. Kent worked as a motorman for the Long Island Railroad and was from the Midwest and passed his evenings in the living room beside his wife, reading pioneer, wildlife, and fishing novels. In the morning, walking to the trains, he often liked to discuss the books with Alejo, who was a very good listener. They had met in the very first days after Alejo's arrival and had always been good, quiet friends. Mr. Kent liked to wear checkered short-sleeved shirts and tennis shoes on his days off, a style Alejo also liked. They were very similar in demeanor: both quiet, low-keyed. They met and would meet every workday morning for twenty-five years, cross the avenue, cross the University campus and descend into the subway kiosk, catch a train, and finally part at Fifty-ninth Street, where Mr. Kent switched to another line.

Alejo traveled on to Times Square, to the shuttle and north through Grand Central Terminal, to the hotel. He went in through a side entrance, changed at a locker, and finally came out into the kitchen around six or six-fifteen to start chopping the carrots and onions and celery necessary for the day's salads and soup. Alejo was hungover and moved around slowly, as if through water. He was ready for the first cigarette of the day that would make him feel sick for a half an hour and then pep him up, helped by three more cups of strong black coffee. The early morning was the worst part of the day for Alejo. Waves of moroseness would sweep through him unless he avoided thoughts of Cuba and his family and his position in life. But he was always cheered by the happy singing of Umberto, the maître d'. Umberto always sang, unless someone had died. Usually he sang corny popular songs like "That's Amore" ("When the moon hits the sky like a great pizza pie, that's amore…"). Umberto was one of those immigrants who is eternally grateful to America. He would declare: "This is a great country. Here you don't starve." He gave Alejo Italian words like *bambino* and *fongul* and introduced him to hot Italian sausages, which were like timid but delicious cousins to greasy chorizos. He and Alejo were good friends. The first hour the maître d' would sit talking to Alejo, telling him stories and singing. And Alejo would listen and nod as he went on cutting and chopping on a thick wood block. A little while later, the others would begin to come in. All pals: the Dominican, Puerto Rican, Haitian, Negro; cooks, waiters, and cooks' helpers. A kitchen staff of refugees, getting on with the business of the day. Donning their waiter's and cook's outfits, tying on aprons, and attending to the schedules Umberto set up, they readied utensil trays and ovens, pots of stew and soup.

Alejo worked, chopping vegetables and throwing them into the huge gleaming pots. Then he hurried between his worktable and the big closet where all the condiments were stored. He set these up for the waiters. Sometimes he went into the meat freezer, large as a truck garage, with hooks and hanging animals as far back as he could see. He helped the butcher haul out beef slabs, whose frozen blood chipped off and splintered into Alejo's palms, staining his apron and giving his clothing the blood smell. Big and strong, Alejo left the Arctic coolness and set the beef down under an electric saw and sat there pushing the beef into the blade.

* * *

Around eight, Mercedes woke, fresh from her dreams. Hector was in the kitchen. She came out wearing a beltless robe that sometimes opened. "Now let's get dressed," she said to Hector. Sighing, she took him by the hand into the bathroom. "Don't be so slow!" There were micróbios all around, so she scrubbed him hard with a brush. She pushed and pulled him by the back of his pants. A day of responsibilities lay ahead of them. She went into the bedroom to get dressed. She was disorganized. On her way to the bedroom, she started making breakfast, boiling water in a pot for eggs, and then she forgot about it. She half dressed, in clothes that a friend had given her. She came out and gave Hector a glass of orange juice. There was a waterbug or cockroach with black cellophane-looking wings floating in the middle of the orange juice. She picked it out and put the glass down before him. The water in the pot had boiled down and so she added more water. Then she put in the eggs. Later Hector ate the boiled eggs and drank the orange juice. He did everything Mercedes told him. He didn't touch a lot of things. He didn't go outside without her. He didn't eat the delicious ham and sausages and turkey and chocolate that Alejo brought home from the hotel. There was a cloud inside his brain. He didn't lift a finger around the house. He just listened to Mercedes: "What a life we have. We have nothing, but Cubans who came here yesterday own houses and cars. They come here and call your papa and ask him for help. He gives them money and feeds them, but as soon as they come up in the world they forget about us. They go up in the world and we stay the same. What are we? Nothing but poor people. Psssht, we never hear from these Cubans until they need something from your papa. They have their own house but call your papa at work to ask him if some friend just in from Cuba can stay with us. Never in their own homes, but with us, as if we run a hotel!" She picked up a knife and placed it on top of the refrigerator. It would stay there for days. "Remember Edelmiro? When do we see him? He doesn't come here anymore. Only for your birthday, and that's all. He lived here, he should remember us, know that we are good people." She put the dishes into the sink and started to clean.

No matter how often she swept the floors, they always needed more.

Stopping after twenty minutes, she would go back to the original corner and begin to sweep again. "I should have stayed in Cuba. Then I wouldn't have so much trouble in this life. In Cuba, you could always find some poor unhappy person who could clean a house." Finished with her cleaning, the house still needed cleaning. But she put away her broom. Now came out the packets of medicine, the vitamins and pills that Hector had to take each day. He sat at the table and took everything.

"We have to go to the clinic today."

"No!"

"Well, I don't want to go, but if you don't go, you could die."

So he got himself ready to go to the clinic. He didn't like being pulled around, the overcrowded waiting room, the waiting. Thick hypos sucked blood from his arms. He would have preferred to stay in his room, playing with comic books and soldiers.

"Do we have to go, Ma?" he asked.

"Oh yes, now we have to go."

Mercedes was bored and worried. She spent a long time looking at herself in the bedroom mirror. She thought of a story she would tell him later, while they were waiting to see one of the doctors. She would tell him how they used to go to a private specialist who worked for next to nothing, "a true humanitarian," as Mercedes used to call her. But the doctor went to Africa on a foundation grant and was never seen again. So now they were limited to the clinic of public health, a dive, and to the old family doctor, on 110th Street, who did not always know what he was doing.

"I'm getting old," she said, looking up from the mirror. There were two Chinese bud vases on the dresser, with rubber roses in them. There was also a picture of Alejo and Mercedes as a gorgeous couple on the roof of their house in Cuba back in 1941, looking off into the future. She looked at the photograph, looked at herself, touched her face. "Ai, how ugly I've become."

She came out. Hector was playing on the living room floor. He had Civil War soldiers that his godfather, Edelmiro, had given him for Christmas. The toy soldiers fought in the American Civil War and sometimes he pretended they were fighting a war in Cuba. He was attacking when suddenly he heard something in the kitchen: like arms hitting the table. He played on, heard a groan.

"Help me! Help me!"

In the kitchen Mercedes was sprawled over the table, gasping for air. Her eyes were turned up and she kept repeating, "Help me! Help me!" Hector went to her, held her head up, and she said: "Water... water...."

He ran around the kitchen, found a glass, and filled it with water. Then he held her up and put the glass to her mouth. She did not move. He shook her a little bit and said loudly, "Mommy, please"...but nothing. She looked very pale, and so he pressed the glass to her lips. He was looking at her closely for signs of life when a large moonlike smile came over her face. She sat up and started laughing, "Ai, I wanted to see if you would let your poor mama die! You didn't. You were afraid. Ai, but you love me! You didn't want me to die! You were afraid!"

It was so funny that he wanted to go deaf and dumb, like Mary from upstairs. Mercedes was speaking to him and laughing, but he didn't hear her. Her jittery Spanish flew like pins into his side. Down the hallway and into the bathroom, Hector went, to urinate. He was thinking about staying away from clinics, about going to a nice place like Pop's kitchen. Once he had gone there with Horacio, and the men in the kitchen gave them everything they wanted. Hector sat on a high stool and consumed huge quantities of food usually forbidden to him. He had a chocolate fudge sundae with fresh whipped cream and strawberries. He ate bacon and lettuce with mayonnaise on toast. Then ham and turkey on rye with caraway seeds. The men in the kitchen huddled around him, patting his head. Then the Negro cook, who had a burn scar on his face, gave him a Donald Duck comic book that some kid had left in the restaurant. A little later, Diego, Alejo's Lon Chaney-looking best friend, asked Horacio and Hector to pick out three numbers for the weekly pari-mutuel game. They picked the numbers and then drank some Coca-Colas.

Alejo had taken Horacio and Hector out into the restaurant and showed them the table where Joe Dimaggio usually sat and ate his lunch. And there was the table where Harry Truman once had feasted on a cake in the shape of an American flag. At another table, close to the horseshoe bar, was where the writer Ernest Hemingway, who spoke good Cuban Spanish, would sometimes sit and drink daiquiris. He was a good tipper.

They had seen the dark locker room: a wall of big-titted, pink-nippled pin-up girls, a rack of light green Coca-Cola bottles, shower stalls and water cooler, slow-turning overhead fan, coils of rope in dark corners. A man with big, floppy testicles in the shower. Alejo had gone to get something from his locker. They had looked inside. There was an old Cuban cigar box, left over from the days of Eduardo Delgado, stuffed with receipts from playing numbers, old bills, faded addresses, letters, loose playing cards...a few "dirty" man-with-woman circa 1930s pictures. Alejo had brought out a glossy eight-by-ten black-and-white photograph of himself and Diego in the kitchen. He was wearing an immaculately white uniform and high cook's hat. He was proudly holding a ladle.

"And who is that?" he had asked Hector.

"You, Pop!"

"And who is the man?"

"You, Pop!"

Hector was impressed by Alejo and his kitchen. He liked the freedom of being with Alejo and the kindly treatment he had received from his kitchen friends. He liked the photograph and the touch of Alejo's hand on his face, Alejo's hand smelling of meat and blood, and hard with calluses.

"Hector! Hector!" Now Mercedes was at the door to his room. She had his jacket. He was looking out the window at the alleycats. "Hector, we have to go now!"

So they left, down the dark hallway and out.

On the street the kids he couldn't play with were in the middle of a game called Three Steps to Germany. Others down the street were climbing up a fire escape ladder. Others were sitting on cars, laughing. Someone's pants had been stolen and how hung from the top of an old wrought-iron lamppost. The guy in his underpants was circling the pole. Everyone laughed, even the cops. Passing the kids, Hector was silent. He had a friend across the way who he played with from his window, but the others, infested with micróbios, did not know him. When he walked by, the kids called to him, "Faggot, faggot!" Some of the bigger kids, seeing him in tow, threw pebbles at his feet.

At the bottom of the hill Mercedes and Hector came to a heap of boxes piled outside a basement entrance.

"Oh, we have to look," Mercedes said, lifting up the covers. In the past she had come across perfectly good appliances, such as a toaster that almost burned down the house, a radio with frayed wires—junk, near junk. Hector watched the kids. He wanted to run away, but if he stepped as much as a foot off the curb, she attacked him, smacked his face, and pulled him back by the ears. They went by the Jew's window. He had a brain embolism. Everyone knew about it. He had a bubble that was going to explode any second. His family, dressed in black, took him from place to place secretly. His wigged mother told him never to wave to the gentiles, but he always waved to Hector. He was retarded because of the bubble. Hector would never get to know him; in a year the bubble would explode and he would be dead.

They went by the German's window. He lived with seven sisters. He never wore regular streetclothes but only a pair of pajamas all day long, all year around. The kids often stood in front of his window chanting, "Heil Hitler, Heil Hitler." The German would come to the window, screaming with a booming voice, "You lousy swine! You bastards! You bastards!"

They went by a whore's window. She fucked everything in a pair of pants. She waved hello to Mercedes.

They went to the corner. There was the drugstore, where they made phone calls to Cuba.

Walking...walking, past the shoe store with its smell of leather and its 1905 McKay Company chain-stitch sewing machine visible through the doorway. There was the shoemaker's cute little blond daughter who would show off her wares for five cents. You gave her a nickel and she went down into the basement, pulled off her underpanties, and exposed her fleshy slit. There was the gangster and Markowitz, owner of the delicatessen.

They came to the beauty salon. Mercedes's best friend, Paula, worked here. She was inside the shop, washing a lady's hair in a sink.

When Hector and Mercedes came by, she rushed out, towel in hand, saying, "Oh, you have to come over later, Mercita, I've met another man." She was so beautiful, no man could resist her. She had been married three or four times already. All the husbands had dropped dead. "And you come along too, sweetheart," she said, pinching Hector's chin. She had a big rumba ass and used to parade around her apartment in frilly slips or in just a brassiere and panties. "You're going to come, aren't you?"

"Oh yes," he answered happily.

But that was the end of the "happily." At the intersection of 125th Street and Amsterdam, at the bus stop, they waited for the bus. Hot asphalt, suffocation. Hector wanted to feel cool ocean water on his face, like when Alejo took him down to the beach. He and Mercedes always fought about that. She didn't like the idea of Hector swimming in the germ-ridden water of Coney Island or Rockaway. Everything was a threat. There were micróbios everywhere.

On the bus, to pass the time, Mercedes told him a story about obedience.

"When I was a little girl in Cuba, there was a witch who lived down the way. She had a mischievous daughter who was always playing with her potions and spells. One day, when the mother went away, the daughter drank a potion that turned her into a loaf of black bread. When the husband of the witch came home, he found the bread and made a sandwich, ate it, and then left the rest for a friend who was a fisherman. His friend went out to sea, and broke the little witch into pieces and fed her to the gulls which followed the boat."

Hector looked out the window, heard her laughter, did not say a word.

At the health clinic almost everyone but Hector was dark. The room was crowded with row after row of mothers and children. They were crammed together, treated like cheap merchandise. The kids would hear Mercedes speaking Spanish and then look at Hector.

"You Spanish, man? Shit you don't look it. Say something, man."

"Oh, he doesn't speak too much. He was sick," Mercedes would tell them.

Hector closed his eyes and tried to sleep, but there was too much

109

commotion and Mercedes constantly talked. She always found some-one else from Cuba. "You're from Oriente? Do you know the Cruzes of Holguín? Yes? Do you remember their white house? I would go visiting there. That was when Cuba was Cuba." She nodded. "And what do you make of things there now? All the fighting. Well, maybe it will soon be over.... Yes, this is my boy, he nearly died, so I have to bring him here every month. Sometimes twice. They look at his blood and his urine."

"Oh, he looks healthy. So Americano."

"Yes, but he was very sick."

She went on for a long time, talk about the price of food being a crime and the way some parts of the city were going to the dogs. "Too many Negros," she would say, leaning close so that none of the people around could hear. All around them, noises: a deep-voiced nurse mispronouncing Spanish names: Ortiz, Rodriguez, Valenzuela. The woman's name was called. Alone again. Mercedes turned to Hector, "Do you want me to read to you?"

"No." He didn't like the way her voice sounded trying to pronounce English.

"Then what do you want?"

"Nothing."

Maybe it was the way Hector looked at her, with half-sleepy eyes, but Mercedes was feeling angry. Her expression had changed. More names were announced on the speaker. Not hearing "Santinio," she got up and went over to the desk. The nurse gave her a hard time. Mercedes returned. "You tell them how long you wait and they laugh!" And she stood up, as if to carry on the former conversation. "And I know plenty of English! Plenty of English!"

All around them people were making crazy signs with their fingers. Some drunk old black woman sitting in front of them laughed. Mer-cedes shouted something else and another woman said, "Lady, you hurting my ear. Now shut up and siddown..."

In another hour the name Santinio was finally called. Then they waited in another area. Half an hour. It was nearly one o'clock. A nurse announced "Santinio" again. Hector went inside with Mercedes.

A thick needle went into his arm. The hypo filled with blood. Then they took the urine. Gave him a pill. In and out, fifteen minutes.

2

Later the numbers man came into the hotel kitchen to pick up the weekly slips. Alejo played about a dollar a week with a numbers man in the neighborhood, and another two dollars in the hotel. The hotel numbers man was a nice fellow up from Haiti, who took over when the Italian retired and sold him the route for a thousand dollars. A few of the guys in the kitchen had hit the Saratoga number. They had made one thousand dollars each. That's what the insurance policy would have paid if Hector had died when he should have died. On hearing the figure one thousand dollars, Alejo remembered pricing coffins. Then more coffins came to mind. "Let's have a little drink," he said. Diego passed another cup full of whiskey to Alejo. They toasted. *¡Salud!* Down the hatch—ai, but it burns.

Outside, in the restaurant, the cashier girl was half in tears because her mother was sick. Now and then Alejo used to spy on her through the door window. She wore a brown uniform with flowery embroidery and had a very pretty face. An Italian girl. She was morose, sad-faced. He wanted to seduce her, but she always treated him like one of the nice guys at the job. When he saw her so sad, he left the kitchen, went to talk with her.

"What's wrong?"

"Nothing."

"Something must be wrong, a pretty woman like you shouldn't be so sad."

"It's money..."

"Ah, si," he nodded.

She told him her story, hard luck about a sick mother, and soon Alejo was inside the kitchen rounding up some money, passing the hat around and coming up with almost forty dollars from seven of the workers. He was so happy, coming out with the hat. Happy that he

111

could do her the favor. Her face beamed and she didn't seem as sad. Her smile was so pretty Alejo started thinking about ways to lure her somewhere, but she was a nice girl and where would they go? Well, Martinez had a little rotting apartment in the West Fifties, which he used for gambling parties. Maybe he could ask Martinez? Ladling bubbly fat off the top of a pot of chicken soup, Alejo kept looking out the little square window in the door to see if she was looking at him. She wasn't. Just busy counting out more receipts.

Down on the beach, Horacio and his friends were busy drowning each other in the attempt to impress some chubby Irish broads who had been watching them. Among the group were Peter, Dennis, Daniel, and the seven-foot-tall Tom, who was known as the Giant. Horacio's best friend, Daniel, a Puerto Rican, kept pulling his thing, which the water had frozen and turned into a thick nub inside his trunks. He pulled it to bring it back into shape, so that when he approached the girls they would have something to look at. Coming out of the water, the guys fell on the blankets like dead men, fought with their towels, and then guzzled down beers. Then Horacio, who was starting to build a sand sculpture, got hit by Daniel: "Time to rap, man, maybe we can get them to suck our cocks under the boardwalk." "Irish girls? Oh Lordy! Mother Mary full of grace, forget it." "Listen, they all ain't corpses! Come on let's go." "All right, all right." And then, while the others watched, Horacio and Daniel walked over and, kneeling down, asked the Mary Doyles if they would like some beer.

"Sure," the girls said. They came over, sat at the edge of the blankets. The rap went very well. Things were romantic and feeling good: the ocean with its soothing roll, the sun up high, "Little Star" by the Elegants on the radio.

"I went to Sacred Heart of Mary High School," one of the girls said.

"Oh yeah? I go to Bishop Dubois myself," said Daniel.

"Oh, do you believe in God?"

"Definitely."

The Irish girls liked Horacio, because he looked so Irish but treated them well, and they liked Daniel, Mr. Athletic with his little gold crucifix.

"You live around here?"

"I live over there."

"Yeah? Your mother home?"

"Naah, she's working."

Good. Good. Good.

Mercedes and Hector walked into yet another store. The word *Bargain* had lured her off the bus. They were standing in a stifling room, surrounded by tables and tables of haphazardly strewn socks and shoes, T-shirts and pants. It was hard to move. Human breath was thick in the air. Women kept pushing at each other to get a hand on a few lousy items on the table, pushing to find a bargain.

"You come with me," Mercedes told Hector, pulling him into the crowd. She had to shove her way past a fat black woman, whose kids seemed in a state of permanent shock. Dazed, they moved easily aside, but there was a crush of more bodies, in a wave, because someone else in the next aisle wanted more room and jammed out an elbow and kicked into the crowd. Mercedes was pinned to the table, reaching into the center where there were twenty-five cent socks and underwear.

"Look for your size," she told him, throwing him a handful of underpants.

He looked and looked, elbows hit his head, arms pulled him aside. There were those expressions that said, "What are you doing here, white boy?" He wanted to go under one of the tables, but someone had pushed Mercedes away from the table, and another salesperson, carrying a big cardboard box of factory "seconds," dumped them down on the table. Some people were animals, as the salesperson called them, but they were mostly people desperate to get a good deal, and that desperation made them buy things they didn't need. To get a good deal, pushing, to get a good deal, going in blind, to get a good deal. "Mama, let's go." But she didn't hear him, she was fighting with a black woman who accused her of stomping on her foot.

"Why, you caint even talk English. Why don't you go back where you come from?"

"Oh yes? I don't have to go anywhere," Mercedes told the black woman. "You should go somewhere...." Hector tugged at her arm and pulled her away. He wanted to go home to play with his soldiers. Or to read some comic books. Or they could go see Paula at the beauty parlor. That would be good. Anywhere but that store.

They went out into the street. Down the block was a bus stop. They did not stop there. Up ahead, along 125th Street, was a huge Korvettes, where the crowds were always terrible. And before that the electric company building. They went into the electric company offices. They waited in another line, ten minutes. Came to the window. Everything was done by hand in those days; there were ledger books everywhere. When it was her turn by the window, Mercedes became nervous and jittery. The bill was in the name Delgado, after Eduardo Delgado, who had been dead for twelve years...a ghost's name.

"Stamp paid, paid," she insisted. Once, years before, a company official had pocketed the money and given her phony receipts. The electric company turned off the electricity, and Alejo almost threw her out into the street. So when she paid bills or the rent, Mercedes wanted everything in perfect order: PAID in big letters. Everything paid for in cash, the jittery hands, the nervousness...she didn't want to be kicked out of the country for some infraction; that fear was in her eyes.

"Are we going home now?" Hector asked.

"Yes, yes after Korvettes."

When it got too hot in the kitchen, the men would go down the wooden stairway to the locker room where the walls were cool stone. There were huge sinks and faucets with spray heads for cooling off their faces. When it got unbearable, they would go down there and spend a long time dousing themselves and looking into the old speckled mirrors. There was little turnover in those jobs. Only the very ambitious got ahead, the guys who kissed the boss's ass. Alejo always stepped aside. Need a cook for the big restaurant upstairs. The big restaurant with the potted palms and the arabesque tiles and the strolling violinists. Pays fifteen dollars more per week. Union dues are the same. It is Class A. No, no, Alejo always said no, and let the other guy take it. Nice guy, that Alejo. But still making fifteen dollars a week less. He wouldn't leave his friends. He was comfortable. He had his friend Diego. They drank together. They had their pictures taken together. Alejo wouldn't desert him. He had even saved Diego's life. A heavy ballroom lighting fixture had snapped loose from the ceiling, hitting Diego and caving in his chest. People had left him for dead, but Alejo took care of him, sent for a doctor. Diego was grateful, respectful to Alejo. How could he leave that? They washed up together. In the late afternoon, at the end of the shift, they took their showers at the same time, trying to get the grease and food smells off.

Alejo was washing his face when Diego tugged at his elbow. When he turned around, Mr. Wagner, the boss of the hotel's restaurant was standing there.

"Oh hello, Mr. Wagner. How are you, sir?"

"Fine, fine." But he was walking around, sizing things up. His presence upstairs spread through the kitchen in a shock wave. Everyone was trying to act sober.

"Slow now?" the boss asked.

"I burned my hands with a pot." Alejo held out his hands. There were many burn scars all over them. Mr. Wagner did not seem impressed. Alejo was holding in his breath, because he didn't want the liquor smell to get out. Mr. Wagner was looking around for evidence of pilfering; silverware was always disappearing. And food. He knew about the food, but the silverware was more expensive and harder to replace. Each piece was imprinted with the hotel coat of arms. The Santinio kitchen drawers were filled with them.

"I have to go upstairs, sir. Let me know if I can do anything for you."

"Sure, sure, go ahead."

Upstairs, everyone was acting busy, chopping vegetables, shoving steak into meat grinders, cleaning ovens, making pie crusts. All afraid of losing their jobs. Alejo was thinking: I've been here for fourteen years. He caught us. I won't have a job. He kept looking over at Diego; he was morose, everyone was morose. He didn't take any of the other jobs because he wanted to be nice, but underneath that he didn't think he would be good enough, and underneath that he didn't want to go away from the bar. And these guys were his friends. Ah Diego, *un amigo bueno*, a good friend.

Outside, the boss was flirting with the cashier. He said something that made her blush and laugh. The boss looked her over, tipped his hat, and then left. The black cook went out, came back in, saying, "Mr. Wagner's gone." Then, with relief, they gathered around the table and had some more drinks, whiskey or rum. Someone had brought in a bottle from the bar. Shots down, they all felt better. It was around three o'clock.

The bedroom of one of the Mary Doyles was covered with flowered wallpaper. Daniel was inside, writhing like a snake on the bed with one of the girls, who refused to take off her bathing suit. Outside, in the parlor, Horacio was making polite conversation with the other girls. It was steaming hot in the house, but they sat around waiting because Daniel was dying to get off on one of the girls. Horacio was pissed off because the others wouldn't do anything unless you got them drunk, and they had chugged down all the beer, and they still weren't drunk enough. In the liquor cabinet there was only sweet wine. So the scheming amounted to figuring out ways to get more beer. After a while the Giant and Dennis went out to find some beer. From the bedroom was all this *No, no, no*. No French kissie. No, no, no, no tongue.... This was making everyone sick. They wanted to go to the beach.

"Maybe we should go. I'll get my friend," Horacio said. But Daniel was making progress. It got quiet in the room, and when Horacio opened the door, Daniel had his hand down the front of the girl's bathing suit, and he wasn't about to go anywhere.

So they waited. Soon the Giant and Dennis returned with beer. They all sat drinking. They had pulled down the window shades and closed the door, and so it got even hotter. Their bodies were glistening with sweat. Then there was someone at the door. Frantic noises from the bedroom.

"Oh, if it's my grandmother, I'll be in bad trouble..."

But it wasn't a grandmother. It was a cousin, about fourteen years old, like Horacio. She lived in Manhattan, way uptown. Her father was a cop. She was thin and demure with large eyes. Her name was Kathleen. She must have liked Horacio because she sat down near him on the couch and started making Catholic girl school talk. He got her phone number.

116

* * *

Finally free of the stores, Mercedes and Hector made their way back up the hill. In those days everyone hung around. Kids on the corners shouted, "Faggot, faggot. Look at the little queer with his mommy. Hey, no spicky English." Mercedes pulled him along, not paying any attention. She came to more boxes piled up, searched through them. Hector knew that everyone was watching, or he believed it to be so. He wanted to run out into the street. Some old ladies came along. They lived at the top of the hill. They were each one hundred years old. They had been stars of the theater. They started out as chorus girls and made it on Broadway with leading roles in musicals. No one remembered their names. They were both good to Mercedes. Always had stories. Gave her recipes. Gave Hector a nickel each time they saw him. They giggled, pinching his cheeks. They looked like they were going to die soon, but they lived on and on, hurrying everywhere, energetic despite their canes.

Mr. Hess, the super, was throwing out garbage. He had given Hector his rifle from the First World War. Its barrel had been stuffed with woodshavings and glue. He was German and resembled Oscar Homolka, the movie actor. During the First World War, he had defended a mountain pass single-handedly against twenty French troops and was awarded an Iron Cross. He always told this story. Horacio knew it, Hector knew it, and so did Alejo. Sometimes Mr. Hess and Alejo drank together. Alejo spoke about the mountains in Cuba and his job as a postal carrier. Mr. Hess spoke about his mountains in Germany. Aware of the illness from Cuba that nearly killed Hector, Mr. Hess always made a point of saying the kid looked well. That day he said, "Ah, what red cheeks! He's got the Cuban sun in his face."

His assistant, the porter named Popeye, hauled up the bags. He was an Irish drunk who worked around the buildings. He was always doing favors for Mercedes. He had rigged the basement washing machine to work for free whenever she wanted to use it. And he was always bringing her old *tarecos*, junk, appliances and such, for which she paid him a few dollars. He was scruffy, bad tempered, always chasing after kids who played down in the basement. His hands were always black from stoking coal into the boiler. At night he would get drunk and disappear into the Harlem park with his vicious-looking German shepherd. In the mornings he would sweep the halls and whistle.

They went back to the apartment. Even though it was summer, Hector had to study with Mercedes. She was so afraid that the other kids would infect him that she had not enrolled him in school. Instead of relying on the nuns' teaching, she sat him down and tried to teach him mathematics and reading herself. She read English like a third-grader, so she was more advanced than he but not by much. The books she read she had found discarded under the hallway stairs. She was not selective. They read whatever she found. A book on American agriculture. Another on Victorian England. Books on Martians and the songs of the planets. Books on dogs, books on saints. She would move her fingers slowly under the words. She'd read comic books about funny animals, prayer pamphlets, anything. She strained, reading English, as if some words hurt her, but became very happy when she suddenly understood a word. And the words forced their way into Hector's head. English words, not those in Spanish. English words from books, English words from the street, from opened windows, from stores. Fuck you, suck my cock! Good morning! Be quiet down there! How many? English words were long lists of medicines and snippets of books that added up to confusion. She taught him, but without any sense of order, priorities. And Spanish? Spanish was the language of memory, of violence and sadness. ¡Callate! ¡Callate! ¡No me toques! Mi papá esta muerto. Yo sufro mucho!

That day the lesson lasted an hour, and then it was time for his medicines. That made him sleepy, which was fine, because even though she stayed beside him, sharing the bed, he could drift away . . . .

Now Alejo was taking his shower. His nerves were still bad because of the boss coming around. He dressed, went up to the bar. Alfonso, the butcher, found him there. He said, "Your package is in the freezer." Every day the butcher left Alejo a package of chicken or meat or shrimp. Alejo would pay him once a week. Five dollars.

"Let me have a whiskey," he told the bartender. Free whiskey, but he left fifty cents there. On the way out he stopped to talk with the cashier girl and then made his way into the dirty heat of Madison Avenue.

In Grand Central Terminal he stopped at the main newsstand. He purchased an English-language newspaper and a Spanish-language newspaper. The English paper headlined a visit by Eisenhower to the United Nations. Some kind of important address. In a week his limousine would speed down the avenue at the bottom of the hill from the Santinio house, and everyone would be there. Ike, speeding by, would wave and nod his head. In the Spanish newspaper the headline was about Cuba: CASTRO FORCES MOVING WEST TO HAVANA. Alejo bought some Chiclets, which he liked so much, and then asked the vendor for a comic book to bring home to Hector. He put the comic in his pocket. He knew that Hector, hearing him at the door, would rush to him, kiss his face, and then look in his pocket. Then a game would be played. With his hands out innocently, Alejo would say: "I have nothing," and then finally convincing Hector of this, he would take out the comic. Every day he brought something home for the kid.

Tired after so much drinking and the heat of the day, Horacio yawned. He had been watching the Giant and Dennis having a towel fight at the end of the subway car and thinking about demure Kathleen, how to fuck her, when the subway stopped at a station and about twenty or thirty "Paddyboys" rushed into the car. Their leader looked around and seeing Daniel, all smiles since he got his fingers wet, announced, "We gonna kick any fuckin' spic ass." Just like that, and then he charged at Daniel and slammed his face with a chain. The Giant, who was not a spic, left the car. Peter and Dennis were shoved out of the doors, leaving Horacio and Daniel to get kicked and punched. But they weren't touching Horacio because he didn't look spic. They cornered Daniel, taking turns punching his head around, and then they dragged him into the middle of the car and took turns kicking his balls in. Then the leader said, "Any more spics?" at which point Horacio screamed, "I'm a fuckin' spic man, come fuck with me!"

119

and they charged at him, surprised because he looked so Irish, and he jumped into the melee, yanked a chain away from one of the attackers and started to beat them hard.

3

Alejo ran into his friend Gonzales on Broadway, just as he was leaving the subway kiosk. They often went to Gonzales's apartment, which was in the basement of the building at the top of the hill, three buildings away from where Alejo lived. Gonzales was married to an old woman who, unlike Mercedes, spent most of her time in the kitchen, cooking. When they were together, Alejo and Gonzales always talked about going into some negocio together, a little grocery store. The one on the corner was run by Markowitz. Alejo had approached him a few times and made offers, but Markowitz was not ready to sell. But this day Alejo told Gonzales about the boss coming around, that he was worried about losing his job. "I work hard, but that's not always enough," he said. "I never miss a day, but they don't consider that."

It was in his mind, the fears. Everyone, including management, liked him at the hotel. They didn't pay him much, but they liked him—as if that were compensation. In fact, to Alejo, it was. To be liked was enough. As Horacio would say, "He was a nice...chump."

But Alejo always worried.

"They could fire me like that, Louie," he told Gonzales. It was only a fear. At his wages they would let him work there forever.

"Don't think about it, Alejo. The boss is always that way. He likes to keep the workers worried..."

They had a drink. Mrs. Gonzales was cooking plantain fritters and she set down a platter of them for the two men to eat as they belted down their whiskey.

"Come on, Alejo, stay for one more," Gonzales said, pouring out another with his shaky hand.

A few hours later it was dark and Alejo was not yet home. So Mercedes sent Hector to bed and went to sit by the window and wait.

Hector could not sleep. The wall plastering was saggy and uneven. He kept seeing things in relief on the walls. In one patch he saw thorny flowers. In another he saw a speeding truck. A sick child. The devil. A woman with a knife, like Mama said she saw in dreams about Buita. These things had lives of their own; they were moving around on the wall. Something else was moving. It was inside the closet. A bird with evil eyes and withered feathers was crouching in the corner on a pile of clothes . . . and worst of all was *her* voice, Mercedes's voice, calling him, "Hector, Hector," but all the way in the back of his head. "Hector, Hector," along with her laughter. And he would remember what she had once told him: "When I was a little girl in Cuba, I was a half medium. All little girls were like that. We could look into the future and hear people's thoughts. So don't ever lie to me." That did not help him. He tried to sleep, rolled on his stomach, felt like pissing, turned on his back. He was an insomniac.

For an hour Mercedes hung out the window, looking for Alejo. She passed the time gossiping with the women who stopped by, after walking their dogs in the park. She knew everyone and all their secrets. In the evenings, she was a gossip. She was always at the window, looking, looking.

Hector stirred, hearing a noise. A pebble against the window, and then a hard rap, against the windowpane. It was Horacio trying to get in from the backyard. The window was just above a backyard wooden stairway that led into the building hallway. Hector opened the window, and Horacio started to climb in. "Turn on the light, but keep quiet," Horacio told him.

Horacio sat on the bed. There were lumps and bad bruises all over his face, but worse than these was the long slash down his leg. After the fight during which they were almost killed, they had gone chasing after the Giant for running out on them. And then they had bought some more beer, gone up to Daniel's house, and started to drink. One of the Irish punks had slashed Horacio's leg as a parting gesture.

"Don't just stand there like a little fairy, get me something."

But Hector did not move. He was afraid of the dark hallway.

"Come on, brother, help me," Horacio said.

"I can't."

121

"Well, fuck you, you can't help me," and wham, he slapped Hector's face. "Now go and get me a towel and the red bottle in the bathroom cabinet."

Hector went into the hall, trying to be as quiet as possible. He went into the bathroom and returned with a towel and the bottle of disinfectant. They had put on a small lamp. The lamp head was broken so that it dangled from the lamp casing. The disinfectant crackled on Horacio's leg. Hector nervously passed the towel over the wound, and felt it filling with jelly-pus. Horacio hissed with pain, sucked in air. He poured more disinfectant, more crackling and pink vapors rising from the fissures in his skin. "Wipe it up again," he told Hector. When this was done, he said, "Now get me some bandages."

That was when Hector blew it. He opened the bathroom cabinet, and a bottle of Lavoris and another of rubbing alcohol came crashing down. Glass was everywhere.

In the room, Horacio could hear everything.

"What are you doing?" Mercedes called out as she walked down the hall.

"Nothing!"

"Why are you in here?"

"No reason!"

She pulled him from the bathroom out into the hallway and then dragged him down to his room. She shoved the door open, turned on the ceiling light, and saw Horacio, the gash, the blood on the towel. Then she started speaking a-thousand-words-a-minute Spanish: "How could you do that? You know he was sick? You know how I suffer for him? How could you do that! You'll give him micróbios! Do you want him to get sick again! You want him to die? Your father will hear about this. Don't worry! Ai, Dios mío, how could you come in here with the micróbios! Never, never again! You hear me!"

She left the bedroom, went into the kitchen, and returned with a broom. She started hitting Horacio in the face, the belly, the groin. Horacio would have hit her if she were a man, but all he could do was try to cover up and repeat, "I didn't mean anything by it! Don't hit me!" But now that she had started, nothing could calm her down. Swinging at him, sometimes missing, sometimes hitting him, she screamed in Spanish very fast. Upstairs, windows slammed shut and the big fans turned on. In another apartment a record player went on.

When Alejo came home, he tried to compose himself, play authority figure, patrón. He was a little wobbly and didn't really seem to give a damn one way or the other about a few little micróbios. But he listened to Mercedes. Waving her arms wildly, Mercedes told him, "You're the man, now do something. He's your son, do something! You're always talking about being the man!"

Reluctantly, Alejo removed his belt and started to beat Horacio. In his room, Hector could hear the leather hitting and Horacio crying out, "No Poppy, Poppy!" And he could hear Mercedes repeating, "Be the man! Be the man!" She was watching the beating from the hallway. Her artist! Her choir boy, cringing each time the belt slapped his skin. Her son, trying to cover up without a hope in the world, as Alejo put the belt aside and threw him against the wall.

"I don't want to hurt you any more, boy. Just tell your mother you'll never do it again—whatever it is that you did." And Horacio did so, and finally it was quiet for almost a half hour.

Then Hector was awakened again. Maybe Alejo had been trying to have sex with Mercedes, or she had started calling him a drunkard, or she had made some remark while he leaned against the bathroom wall urinating, with his thing in his hand. Now she was tormenting him by repeating something that got him mad, or pushing him away, or calling Buita a whore, or laughing and calling him the King of the Puerto Ricans or simply a failure.

Horacio, 1962

1

At seventeen, Horacio continued to be in love with Kathleen. Their romance had flowered in the last few years. He was always pissed off about his life, but she would take it, and stand behind him in a sort of demure, humble Irish way. He was one of the slicker guys of the neighborhood. Some of the guys had women, whores in the park, but regular stuff was rare. Horacio used to hump Kathleen every chance he could get.

He would take her behind the church after choir practice and have her on a mattress in the alley. The nuns' apartments were above the church, and their windows looked right down into the alley. Maybe they never looked out. At least they never said anything about Horacio and his girl. The Bing Crosby–looking priest thought the mattress was for the Boy Scouts to take naps on, and the janitor sometimes slept on it on lazy spring afternoons. Horacio would take Kathleen to the mattress after choir practice or Mass. He was quite a singer. He knew his Bach oratorios, his Schütz, his Palestrina, his Handel. He had a deep liking for Gregorian chants, with their solemnity that seemed to fit his moods. The music was dark and hopeless, claustrophobic in its range.

Things went like that for him. Kathleen was a good girl, but everything else was shit. His education foundered. He started out wanting to go to Music and Art, but everyone told him to go to Catholic school. He went to Catholic school, and it closed down at the end of the first year, and because he had screwed off, no one else wanted him. He went to public high school. A "stiletto" school. Short Irish detectives used to come up every week with their black-taped blackjacks to bring back order and to shake down the JDs. Everyone was fighting everyone else, and after a while, Horacio just didn't show up.

He went home and couldn't stand that either. Horacio was tired of hearing how poor the family was. Mercedes's fears drove him up the walls, and when Pop got drunk and wanted to fight, he would disappear for two, three days. One day he decided to quit school. Hearing about how hard success is to attain, and "failure, failure" about Pop all the time, snapped his self-confidence. Besides the school wasn't teaching him anything of value. Instead of going to school, he worked, and when he was not working he lured Kathleen away from her neighborhood, screwed her in a wheelbarrow in the basement, standing up against boiler-room walls, or in friends' apartments.

Horacio did always show up for choir practice. The choirmaster was a great teacher and a kindly man. It was a great honor to sing with him. Radio stations made it a practice to tape and broadcast his concerts. He treated everyone well and with dignity. He was a white-haired, roundish Welshman with a lump on his forehead. The younger kids used to make jokes about this mysterious lump, and when Horacio sang, he had the desire to touch it. The choirmaster considered Horacio one of his more talented pupils, and he could have gone into voice seriously if that wasn't "something for faggots," as the guys called it. The choirmaster was one of the few people who could make Horacio work hard without pissing him off. He was an infinitely patient man of culture, a civilized man, and he would die soon because of the lump that had grown on his head.

Horacio used to stay out all night with Daniel and Peter, doing as they pleased: drinking down in the railyards, joyriding down the West Side Highway, swimming in the river at night when drunk, and always getting into fights. Horacio liked to stab things. He owned a speargun and would fire it into a wooden board on which he had drawn the figure of a man. He stabbed knives into walls, and once jammed a serving fork into a friend's ass. He passed his time playing nickel-and-dime poker on the stoops and by harmonizing melodies with street friends. He sang songs like "The Ten Commandments of Love" by the Moonglows, and got into fights. He wanted to hit all the time, and when he couldn't hit someone else, he almost wanted to hit himself. He almost wanted to die.

Maybe feeling close to death was why he went to work for the undertaker. His interest in such work began while he was attending the public high school. There was a hospital morgue about four blocks away. Horacio had a friend who worked there, and they would sit around in rooms filled with stiffs, drinking beer. Looking at dead bodies held some kind of fascination for Horacio, possibly because Mercedes was always talking about the dead as weightless spirits; but the real corpses were thick-skinned dolls filled with sawdust. He liked the dead enough to take a job with a mortician. For months he told people he was going to be a mortician. He loved to frighten Hector with descriptions of the place: "You'd love it, brother. There are hooks on the walls and corpses hanging off them with their mouths open and their puffy tongues sticking out." He thought there was something tough in being around the dead.

"You should get a regular job," Kathleen said, "and then we can get married."

"You don't like it?" he answered. "Then leave me."

But Kathleen was in love with Horacio and wouldn't leave him, no matter how bad things got. As it stood he had to sneak around her neighborhood, go from place to place over rooftops, climbing down the sides of buildings on fire escapes to her window. Her father and brothers were cops and hated his guts because he didn't respect them. And on top of that, he was Cuban. He couldn't show up at the door and ask her out. He had to sneak in when no one but Kathleen was at home. Her whole family hated him.

One day after work he met Kathleen and she told him that she was pregnant. What to do? He took to disappearing for days at a time because her cop brothers and father had started looking for him. Cruising around in their green-and-white police cars, coming to the door, scaring Mercedes half to death. Humbly and in a meek voice, Mercedes would answer the door and tell the cops that Horacio had run away from home.

"When you see him, tell him we're looking for him," the father cop warned.

"Oh yes. Don't you worry."

Horacio stayed with friends across the street and in basements and sometimes upstairs, in Mary's apartment. One evening he came home and asked Alejo for advice. Alejo wasn't drunk; he was sober and seemed very concerned. He thought over Horacio's dilemma. "It's not a good enough reason to get married," Alejo finally said. "You're too young and you don't have any schooling. If you get married now and have no trade, you'll end up a dishwasher or an elevator operator. If I were you, I would get lost for a while."

Taking Alejo's advice, Horacio went down Broadway one day, ate pizza and drank a soda, and worked up the nerve to go into the enlistment center that had caught his eye a few days before. In the window there were posters of four handsome young servicemen—in Navy, Air Force, Army, and Marine dress uniforms marching off into a sunblazened distance—and it put into his mind that he could leave the Santinio house and see something of the world. He went in and enlisted in the Air Force. Within a month, after passing his physical exams, he would be going away.

In the meantime he wanted to help Hector gain some freedom. It always made him angry to see the way Mercedes dragged Hector down the street, never letting him go anywhere alone, and he took it upon himself to free him. He couldn't stand to hear the kids calling Hector names, sounding on him, humiliating him not ten feet from the window. Mercedes was always watching Hector and would get hysterical if he went near the curb. Hector was so controlled he didn't dare step into the street where everyone played, or go to the basements, roofs, or alleys. Kids down the way were riding the backs of buses, and some of the Ricans had knives. But Hector couldn't put a foot into the street. No matter what his tormenters did to him, even if they threw shit into his face, he would stand frozen at the curb, trying to figure out what was going on.

It made Horacio sick. He wanted to toughen up Hector. He knew that Hector could take beatings. He used to come over with his friends and play torture games with Hector, holding him down and beating his stomach and chest, trying to make Hector cry or give up. But Hector never did. They would beat his sickly weak flesh until their fists ached, and he would go off into his room, confused because he was hit for nothing; and this confusion churned inside him like a wild animal ready to burst out.

Being treated like a freak bothered Hector, but he would not show it. Instead he let it eat him up and laughed when they taunted him, so afraid of exploding and getting crazy the way people did in the house. His isolation was a state that he understood. Being separated from things was normal for him: from children, from Cubanness, from health. He heard things, they hurt inside, he said nothing, did nothing, he went to spend his time alone.

One day two brothers approached Hector and said, "Go home and tell your mother she's a cocksucker." In his ignorance of the world he thought it was some kind of compliment, and at dinner with Horacio and Mercedes he said, "Hey Mama, some guys said you were a cocksucker."

Not knowing what it meant, she laughed, "Ohhhh?" and nodded her head, but Horacio took a butter knife and stabbed Hector in the shoulder with it. Then he punched his head and knocked him to the floor.

"Where did you hear that? Who told you that?"

He pulled Hector down the hall by the ears, took him to the window. A lot of kids were out on the street. Hector pointed out the brothers.

"You're going to kick their asses for that."

"Me?"

"Yeah, you."

Mercedes ran into the living room.

"Where are you going? Where are you going?" she kept repeating. "He can't go out."

"He's going out."

The two brothers were sitting on the stoop across the street, all sweaty from playing. They were big guys with bandannas around their foreheads. One of them looked like a raccoon with dark, pouty eyes, and the other, the biggest one, resembled that movie actor, Curly of the Three Stooges.

"Kick their asses, or I'll kill you," Horacio told him.

They were across the street from the brothers, by the curb. Hector had never fought with anyone, had not so much as stepped off the sidewalk. He was worried, lame with self-doubt.

"What are you waiting for?" Then Horacio took his arm and started twisting it. "Go, go."

The street was like a river of all the things he could not do. He thought he would step out on it and drown. Inside, his muscles were fluttering, his bones seemed fragile. The tip of his prick seemed to fill with lead or mercury, as if he had to take a nervous piss. "I can't go," he was thinking, and he turned and saw Mercedes watching horrified from the window. She was flailing her arms and calling out, "Come back in here! Come back!" but he couldn't hear her. He was hearing his heart and his stomach, and then he felt Horacio's hand smacking the back of his head, and suddenly he started to charge across the street, screaming, "I'm going to kill you, I'm going to kill you!" And once he got across the street, he started swinging wildly at their heads, smashing them into the pillars, one head and then the next, so quickly that he went to punch them again and missed, cutting his fists against the stone, but then he smashed their noses and made them bleed so that they sunk off the steps in astonishment, which he could not see, because the thrill of running and hitting back and screaming took him off the ground into another world, where everything passed by in brilliant flashes of red and azure and he didn't feel helpless. He felt a power streaming from him, such a pleasure that it made him afraid. He punched until some of the other kids pulled him away.

"That was good brother," Horacio said proudly, but Hector didn't like it.

Around that time Horacio was having a feud with the Giant. He had never forgotten how the Giant had deserted him like a coward that day when the Irish beat him and Daniel on their return from Coney Island. Since then, he had wanted to get even.

He had had small revenges: Once, when he had gotten into trouble with a Puerto Rican girl whom he saw on the side, her brother's gang came down into the neighborhood, looking for him. They only knew they wanted a dude named Pinky, as Horacio was sometimes called. They came across him as he was leaving choir practice. "Your name Pinky?" they asked. "Nah, that's him down there." Horacio pointed in the direction of the Giant. They went after the Giant, beat him, and dumped him into a basement among the cats and spilled garbage cans. But the Giant later took his own revenge. One night when Horacio and Kathleen were on the roof, making out, the Giant came up. He was drunk and put his hands all over Kathleen. So Horacio fought the Giant, who outweighed him by about 150 pounds. The Giant beat him and almost threw him off the roof, and since then there had been a standoff, with Horacio dumping garbage off rooftops onto the Giant's head and the Giant trying to blind Horacio with a BB gun that he carried around.

One day Hector and Horacio were out on the street. Horacio thought it would be good for Hector to see a girl going at it with a guy. There was a neighborhood girl with a withered leg who screwed guys at the bottom of the stairs to the Harlem park, if you asked her nice. Horacio fixed it up for Hector to go down and watch, while he stayed on the lookout for Mercedes or Alejo. Hector went down the stairs in the dark and waited around in the bushes for the girl to come along, but she never showed up, so he decided to go home. He was going up the steps when he heard noises in the bushes. Then he turned around and saw the Giant standing before him. Hector called up, "Horacio, Horacio," but Horacio had gone across the street to get a smoke and was playing cards.

The Giant was looking at Hector with hatred, but suddenly he started to play around with his pants and pulled out his penis.

"You ever seen something like this?"

When Hector did not answer, he put his massive hands around Hector's neck and squeezed until Hector was down on his knees, and he said, "You know I can do anything I want with you, right?"

Hector did not move.

"If I wanted to, I could piss on you because you are a piece of shit." And then he asked, "Do you want to touch it?" and when Hector said no, the Giant pushed him down the steps, saying, "You little faggot." But then he felt bad and called Hector over and dropped a dime by his feet.

"I'll forget everything if you pick that dime up for me."

And when Hector went to pick it up, the Giant brought his weight down on Hector's hand.

"Go tell your fuckin' brother I'm gonna do that to his head," and he went away.

When Hector came up the stairs, he let out a scream. Soon he was surrounded by some guys, including Horacio. The Giant had continued down into the park.

But two days later, when the Giant was walking up the street, eating a pound of potato salad with the container lid, Horacio and Hector jumped him. Horacio smashed his head with a baseball bat and then took hold of his arms behind his back. He was laughing and telling Hector, "Huevos, huevos," Spanish slang for testicles. Hector took the bat and started to pound the Giant's lower region, swinging with all his might. The Giant let out horrible screams. All the people on the street came to watch, while Hector kept hitting the Giant until he closed his eyes from the pain and slumped in Horacio's arms.

Settling that score left Horacio in great spirits for his going-away party. Everyone but everyone turned up. The deaf mute's son, Daniel, Peter, many neighborhood friends, fellow choirboys, high school friends, a pal from the mortician's parlor. Alejo had gone all out for the party. He had borrowed a fancy record player. "West Side Story" was the big record of that night, then Cal Tjader jazz, Latin, and rock 'n' roll. Grind records. There was a table holding a mountain of ham and turkey and cheese sandwiches. Alejo had purchased about twenty cases of beer, and many guests brought their own. There was liquor everywhere, smoke, girls getting pinched, throw-up in the bathroom. It was a great party, lasting until seven in the morning.

Alejo spent the time in the kitchen with a friend. They were completely drunk. The room was swirling around them. Alejo was fat, sloppy-looking in a T-shirt, but he was good to the young guys who went in to get more beer from the sink, which was filled with ice. He flirted with the girls, gave out cigarettes, told a few corny jokes. They loved him. "Hey Horacio, man, your father's all right. He's a cool dude," even if he was melting like a wax man. There was so much food, nothing to be embarrassed about, except for Hector, who was like a miniature Alejo. Not drunk but fat and sloppy in a T-shirt and oversize pants, a freaky-looking brother, fairylike, scared. Setting Hector loose had not been enough. Now he was even more afraid of exploding. He became more gentle, more passive, a little passive clown, like Alejo in the throes of melancholia. Even the Puerto Rican dudes gave him a hard time. "That's your brother?" It really embarrassed Horacio to introduce Hector around, he was so many things Horacio did not like. What he was leaving became clear to him: the drunk in the kitchen, the lunatic mother in the back room lying in the bed in the dark, the fucked-up brother.

But the party was good. Even Hector was having a good time, until he had to bed in the back room with Mercedes. She was there, waiting for him. "See how they treat me?" she said. "See what they do? I should have stayed in Cuba." Hector had to stay with her, with the ghosts, and the muffled voices beyond the door, her cold hands on him.

What was going to happen? Horacio was really going to vanish like one of the kids from the hospital, like all of Cuba. It was that way. The things he wanted to remain vanished, the things he wanted to vanish remained. Before Hector's eyes, Horacio dissolved and became a few lines of scribble on blue airmail paper, first from Biloxi, Mississippi, and then from London, England.

Alejo Santinio, 1962–1963

1

A few months after Horacio disappeared, Alejo became ill. He worked too much, partied too much. He was obese, and his temper and melancholy sent blood rushing to his head, so that it seemed ready to burst. He would come home and eat and eat and eat.

Mercedes rushed around the kitchen cooking for hours. The stove sang with sizzling pans, and the aromas of bubbling pots hovered in the air like hummingbirds. Men in the house, Alejo's friends, hung desperately onto walls as if on turning, rolling ships. Pieces of chicken in the teeth. Sucking air in through the teeth. Digestion of pork, turkey, lamb chops, rice and chicken, olives, nougat; siren fish, shrimp, candied yams, plantains, black bean soup, avocado salad, picadillo, rice, flan, guava paste, hard cheese. Puerto Rican friends brought over *pasteles*, paper-wrapped concoctions of mashed plantains, potatoes, pork, sausage and who knew what else; so soft to the touch, like a wrapped intestine ready to be dropped into a pot, boiled for an hour, and then eaten. Soft and viscous like digestive systems, filled with lard and *fritos*, so delicious, like insides eaten over again. The men drank and ate so much that their skin began to smell like food and wine. Faces plump and red, walking bellies eating until not another morsel could be eaten, until all was filled and the insides were spongy from the endless quantities of alcohol-soaked food. Eating and eating even when the stomach, like the head, like the intestines, like the tongue, like the ass, were all ready to burst; the mouth craving, taking in drink: beer, wine, whiskey, rum for friends, vodka and gin for upstairs neighbors, absorbing endlessly as if life could be stored. Eating and drinking voraciously like babies suckling breasts, men fucking women. Food went into Alejo's mouth and became rivers of digestion inside so that his breathing grew heavy, his eyes rolled and he could hardly move. Food from the hotel and from stores: fried, broiled, cold, sizzling, into the stomach and out again.

In time a succession of such meals made Alejo so fat he had to sidle through the doorways. When he and Hector walked down the streets, jokes about cows flew around them. Hector, too, was layered with fat. Between them, they must have weighed five hundred pounds. They looked like two overfed Persian princes who had opted for the allurements of the kitchen instead of the harem. They were like twins, separated by age, with the same eyes, faces, bodies. Except Alejo was from another world—*Cubano, Cubano.* They wore matching shoes, matching pants, matching shirts. And when he ate, Hector matched his father mouthful for mouthful. Together they grew so fat, it was a neighborhood joke.

Then one day—it was snowing—Alejo tried to get out of bed but could not move. It was as if a pile of stones had been dropped on top of him. He tried to turn over and nearly fell off the bed, but the pain was acute and he did not turn his body again. He pulled himself over to the side of the bed and fell to the floor with a great bang. Then he forced himself up, put on his slippers, and went into the kitchen for coffee. Time for work! Mercedes was in the doorway watching him, as she did every morning.

"Ai, Dios mío," he said rubbing his stomach. "My stomach hurts."

"Then take some Alka Seltzer," Mercedes told him.

He did so but the pain did not go away.

"Take the day off," she said to him.

"I don't like to."

"Don't be stupid. You're never sick."

The pain spread from his stomach to his chest, and so he decided not to go to work. He went down to the corner, called the hotel, came back home. Then he and Hector set off for the doctor's office. There were mountains of snow blocking the streets. No buses came, so they walked for twenty-five blocks in the snow. The old doctor tottered out of his office, rubbing his hands because the heat in that place was very bad. Many people were waiting. They waited for an hour, reading magazines, and then the doctor looked at them, one by one, administering a pulmonary exam—the flu was going around. When he had finished listening to Alejo's chest through the stethoscope, he gave him a box of tiny pills and said, "Don't go to work, you have a very bad infection."

Alejo had trouble sleeping that night. The pain did not go away. He spent the night sighing, as if touching a beautiful woman's hair, and looking around, as if he could see things. He was sweating and breathing heavily, gasping for air. Two days passed in this fashion and he was not getting better, and it was then that Mercedes, in a panic, called another doctor who examined Alejo and asked, "How long has he been like this?"

"Three days."

"Well, then he should be dead."

Alejo's heart had constricted. A heart attack. Cubans were always dropping dead from heart attacks, but Alejo was too strong. "It's a miracle," they said about him, as they had said about Hector when he was ill. "You should have been dead."

He was in the hospital for a month, at home for two. The attack transformed him into a saint. He even went to church one Sunday, did not smoke or drink excessively. He lost one hundred pounds and began to look twenty years younger. The only problem was money. He had some benefits from his union but not enough.

Mercedes began to refer to the family as "very poor." She pleaded with all the markets and stores to give her special bargains and she got them. The delicatessen owner gave them free bread and milk, and bruised fruit for almost nothing. They had unlimited credit, which Mercedes made sure not to abuse. And sometimes someone from the hotel would come around with a little package, but not too often. The neighbors helped out, bringing food and useful household items.

But Mercedes went even further; she would keep the lights turned off during the day to save a few pennies, and she did not spend a cent for clothing or for repairs. Things broke and she fixed them herself. She took a job scrubbing floors and cleaning up in a nearby school, a joke because she didn't know how to clean. There was a piano in the classroom, and she would sit for a half an hour picking out tunes and singing to herself. Hector would sit by her, watching her hands on the keyboard, and then they would both remember Alejo and return home.

There was peace in the house for the months Alejo rested. Mercedes exaggerated the importance of rest and tried to keep him in bed. But loving the springtime, Alejo often went out for walks in the park, excursions to the fruit market, down to union headquarters for some measly disability check. Eventually the tranquillity vanished into bad dreams. He couldn't sleep well at night, and he would wake up suddenly in a cold sweat, frightened half to death by thoughts of his dead brother and the other dead in the world, his heart palpitating and hands shaking. Twinges of fear did not let him sleep.

These times Mercedes would hold him and say, "Oh, you won't die. It isn't like that. A beautiful garden awaits us. At worst you'll be a ghost. And you remember the ghosts in Cuba; they exist," as if that would calm him.

No, he would get up. Worry about his health. Worry about his job. Pacing the halls, he would hear Hector's nightmares and go rushing to help him. Then back into the halls and into the kitchen, looking everywhere, in the cabinets and under the sink, for something to drink. Mercedes had thrown out all the booze and she kept out his friends who drank. He missed them and missed his whiskey.

Then one day he got an idea. Sitting at the table, he wrote a note and gave it to Hector. It was the afternoon, around three o'clock. Alejo spoke in a whisper, patted Hector's back, and gave him a dime for his trouble. The liquor store was three blocks away, next to a bar and a big bodega. Hector gave the owner of the liquor store the note: "Please, you sell whiskey to my son, Hector. Thank you, Alejo."

The owner usually didn't sell whiskey to children, but knowing Hector and Alejo, he made an exception, and soon Hector came home with a fifth of whiskey. Then he sat at the table and watched Alejo drink two glasses. Alejo sighed with satisfaction, the taste of whiskey was so good, and he patted Hector's head: "You're a good boy." But the whiskey ran out within the week, so Hector got more for Alejo. Then, when Mercedes started to notice Alejo's drinking, he didn't even try to hide it. He went to the store himself. He had started working again and the first thing he would do when he got home was to have another drink.

"You're going to die," Mercedes told him. "You're going to be in a grave if you keep up like that."

"Leave me alone."

"Not until you use your brains. Look at you, smoking and eating again like a pig."

"I do as I please."

"And for who? Your friends? Are they going to pay for your funeral? Are they going to cry for you when you're dead?"

"Leave me alone," he said, finishing his whiskey and taking some beer after it.

"You're going to die because of stupidity. So don't cry for yourself or for your dead brother or anyone in the family. Be stupid and die."

She spoke to him this way, and accused him of drunkenness even when he came home sober. He took to sitting at the kitchen table with his hands covering his ears, repeating, "Shut up! Shut up!" Then she would leave the apartment and visit one of her friends, Paula or Mary. The echoes of her accusations remained inside the apartment.

He would whisper to himself, as if to an invisible being, "I came to this country in 1943.... I am the man.... I take care of everyone...." Then sometimes he would look around and find Hector watching him from the hall.

"Come in boy," he would say. "I want to tell you something."

He would take Hector's arm and sit him down beside him. Alejo leaning close, Hector pulling away from the Cuban smell of booze. "She doesn't understand, no one understands, but you..." He would stick a cigarette in his mouth. It would take him many matches to line the cigarette up with the flame.

2

Mercedes gave up, became resigned to the situation. She grew thin and pale from worry and then lost her spirit. She did not speak to Alejo or sleep with him. She couldn't stand to see him as he was, so she behaved like a widow, saying little and going through her days as if out of duty. She never went anywhere with Alejo, if she could help it, and if they did go out together, say, to visit some Cuban friends, they would have big fights and friends would have to separate them. Her voice would go on and on for hours: "You're going to die, if you keep this up." And he did as he pleased.

One summer vacation, Alejo asked Mercedes to go to the beach, Coney Island, and of course she refused. He was even fatter, his body was going to burst, and when it burst, she did not want to be there. Even though it was hard to believe it would happen, Hector, who went everywhere with his father, waited for the bursting.

Alejo was no sickly, pale child like those Hector had known in the Connecticut hospital and still saw in his sleep. And he wasn't a "flower," as Mercedes had earlier described him in poems. He was enormous: a size forty-six pants with big muscles. His biceps were like stone in his arms. He was a big Cuban man who was never going to die, even if he said so. Alejo's body could not be frail, not as weak as sickly children or as weak as Hector himself.

The years of seeing micróbios everywhere and those injections and medications had turned Hector into something of a paranoid. He would hear about travelers and could not imagine going anywhere himself; people or micróbios would hurt him. When letters from Horacio arrived, postmarked *London*, where he was stationed, he read his brother's descriptions of the damp, grand, old city with neatly laid out gardens and parks, musty palaces and castle keeps, and marveled that his brother had not fallen ill or been harmed in some mysterious way. And when he described the forming of luminous cloudbanks over a French valley or the great icy lakes of Austria, Hector came to think of him as a kind of superman, impervious to harm. He marveled in the same way at stories about cousins who escaped from Cuba to Morocco in a little dinghy, or about family friends who went to Puerto Rico or Illinois or Disneyland, as did Aunt Buita and Uncle Alberto on a brave cross-country drive from Florida.

So he went everywhere with the same confused resignation. Aware of how easily the body could be penetrated, like algae into rock, or a worm into a piece of salt-eaten driftwood, Hector went around expecting the micróbios to go inside him, make him ill, kill him. Shouldn't he remain at home like Mercedes, spending the hours in bed, waiting?

It was the summer. Alejo and Hector stepped down off the boardwalk at Coney Island onto the crowded beach. The usual loud partiers were drunk and stumbling all around them, and there were radios blasting Spanish and some blasting soul music. There were black dancers with gray sunburned bodies. Hector and Alejo went close to the shore, where the muddy sand bubbled with hidden life underneath. Children were hacking up crabs; in the distance was the world-famous parachute ride, like an Eiffel tower dropping white orchids into the sea. Musclemen and sand artists, sick-looking birds, vendors. Looking around, Alejo took a deep breath of the ocean air and declared, "It smells just like Cuba, huh?"

No, but Alejo spread out the blanket anyway, disrobed and stretched himself out on the sand. With his head on his hands, he watched the bathers, his eyes squinting. What was he thinking? About Mama? Horacio? Was he thinking about death, about his dead brother or dead parents, or about the way cemeteries looked in Cuba with nice white Grecian tombs?

"Boy, but I'm hungry. Hector, give me a sandwich."

They ate, salami on a roll with mayonnaise and pieces of pickle.

"Ah, qué bueno, no?" Alejo was happy, content, sleepy, listening to the surf and watching people going by, until it got too hot and then they both ran in, breaking the biggest waves. Alejo was as happy as a five-year-old, splashing himself and Hector with water. He was not a good swimmer and paddled around like a dog in circles. Then he stopped and bobbed up and down with the waves as he watched the women bathers and the white caps of water breaking against their luscious bodies.

When they returned to their spot on the beach, they noticed a woman had spread a blanket nearby. She was Spanish, about forty years old, with frizzed, sunburned, reddish hair and a pretty face. She was well preserved; when she stood up, pulling down on her bathing suit, the sun forced out the voluptuousness of her body. It wafted into their senses like a wind. Then she sat down.

Alejo looked over, nodded, and smiled, saying, "It's a beautiful day, isn't it?"

"Yes, it is," she said. And then she smiled and lay back on the blanket. Mercedes was not on Alejo's mind. He just kept looking at the woman and smiling. When she started to sweat in the heat, she got up and went galloping into the ocean. Alejo turned to Hector and said, "She's pretty nice, huh?"

Hector nodded. She was like all the women he had heard about— the "others" in Mercedes's accusations, who were like ghosts because they materialized in another world that he could not see. She was like the women Mercedes claimed wrote Alejo secret letters that were also invisible. Hector had never believed they existed, but this woman with big tits was bending down in the water and splashing around like a mermaid. And Alejo looked hungry, watching her.

"Va-va-boom," he said, mimicking Ralph Kramden of the "Honeymooners" television show.

Back from the water, her bathing suit rippled and glittered with tiny salt stars, her large brown nipples showed through the fabric. Her pubic hair showed in long mysterious strands as she stretched her tremendous body and dried herself with a towel. "My, but it's warm today," she said.

"Yes, very warm," said Alejo, nodding. He had taken out a plastic jug filled with pineapple-orange juice and rum. "Would you like something to drink?"

"Oh yes," she said and joined them on their blanket. She drank down a Dixie cup of the concoction, and when she finished, Alejo filled the Dixie cup again and raised his cup in a toast:

"Salud."

"Salud."

They became friendlier.

"I'm from Santo Domingo," she said.

"I came from Cuba."

"How long ago?"

He laughed. "A long time ago, and you?"

"I came here ten years ago," she told him. "I came here with my husband, but he ran off when things got too hard. And you, are you married, Señor?"

"I have my family. Sons."

"And a wife?"

"I have someone, but...she doesn't care what I do."

"You're lucky. My husband used to beat me if I looked at someone else." She laughed. "Now I don't care."

They sat drinking together for a few hours. Alejo was amicable, gallant, and endearing in an Oliver Hardy way, listening intently to all her troubles, smiling and filling up her Dixie cup. Her son was in and out of jail, and he hated her for having married her bum husband in the first place. And at the factory where she worked the foreman wanted to screw her and couldn't keep his hands off her...This list went on and on, not enough money...bills, bills...Alejo nodding.

Hector had been sitting off to the side. Now and then he went down to the water, stood watching the bathers, and then he swam. Children ran around him in wild herds. Spanish kids charged at the water, and he followed in from a distance. Big waves caught him, he swallowed the dirty seawater with its salt and piss. Winds swept in from the east and made him shiver; he kept looking over at their blanket. One moment Alejo was filling her cup, the next he was listening to the woman, his hand on the small of her back. What was going to happen? That kept bothering him. He liked to look at women with Alejo. Big asses appealed to him, as they did to Alejo, and the beach was swarming with them. And he was at the age when curious admiration turned into something else—a passing wave of heat, bodily hunger for another body, a throbbing prick with an independent will. There were women everywhere with glittering sweaty bodies and thick wet hair.

But then "Hector! Hector!" came from the anonymous drift of beach voices all around. "Hector! Hector!" Mercedes's voice from afar. He imagined that confounded voice. Horacio used to hear it as well when he would stay out all night, escaping Mercedes and that household, until he would fall asleep and her voice would disrupt his dreams. They both heard it, and it made them feel superstitious. Hector looked around. Her voice came again from the swarm of voices all around, "Hector Hector!" But worse were the two last words: "*help me.*" He imagined Mercedes resting in bed, in the dark of the bedroom on that steamy day, staring at the ceiling. Up ahead in the water a woman with large breasts kept getting smacked by waves that threatened to tear off her bikini top. He edged up to watch, stood there, pretending to mind his own business. Boom, the water turned her over and she came up topbare, her tits plump and strikingly white.

He was thinking about breasts, when he returned to the blanket. The woman was speaking in a low voice to Alejo. Hector could not help looking down at her legs. She noticed this and said, "He's got bug eyes like you."

Alejo pretended not to hear that, but to gain the attention of them both, the woman squirmed around on the blanket as if trying to trap something in her navel.

Her grinding was quite tempting. Alejo took another drink and the woman said, "So this is your boy?"

"Yes, he's the youngest."

"He looks like you, but he's so light."

"People say that."

"He doesn't say very much. Doesn't he speak Spanish?"

"He was sick."

She nodded as if that would be an adequate explanation for his silence and then sat up and took hold of Hector's chin, saying, "Well, he looks good to me."

They remained on the beach until about five o'clock. By then Alejo and the woman were drunk. Napping, Hector had dreams. Among them: Mercedes in bed, trying to sleep; the woman of the beach standing naked in one of the sunny rooms of Cuba; the smell of the ground after it had rained as he touched the woman's flesh and hair. Thinking of fondling her gave him an erection. And the erection made him forget micróbios, medicines, and injections, and brought pleasant sleep until the weight against his stomach became more of a pain,

142

and Mercedes's voice returned and opened up Coney Island again.

Dressing. Packing things. Soon they were up on the boardwalk. The woman, Alejo, and Hector at Alejo's side, feigning obliviousness to the situation as he would during similar walks in the future. Not with the same woman but different women. Not on the boardwalk but down Webster Avenue in the Bronx, Saxon Street in Brooklyn, or Fifty-fifth Avenue in Queens. Alejo always with the same story: "I became very ill and realized I was working too hard in this life ... I love my wife but she doesn't understand me ... Nobody understands me." Always with his generosity, his loneliness, his need to be loved, his desire to forget his body through other bodies.

They walked into the amusement area, past the Monster House, the Death-whirl, the House of Mirrors where Mercedes had been lost years before. Wherever beer was sold they stopped to have beers. Alejo kept sending Hector off on rides, and while Hector spun in circles or was slammed into the air, Alejo and the woman sat on benches, drinking and holding one another. Already Alejo was making promises to help her with a little money, food from the hotel, and maybe he could help her get a new job. Probably she would see Alejo on and off for three or four years, but Hector would never see her again. She would become invisible, a part of another world.

They walked to the subway. The woman's pink slacks were too tight. Her blouse kept opening so that her oily, hot breasts burst out. On the subway she rode most of the way to her home, in Brooklyn, with her head against Alejo's chest, but then later her head slipped down to rest in his lap. He did not say a word on the train to Hector except, "Don't tell anyone about this. It is our secret, man to man."

Around seven they came to her street. A 1940s street with cobblestones, low subway trestles, sewer smells, coaldust. The building was like so many other buildings they would see: a walkup with fans in the windows and the doors of the apartments kept open, so everyone knew everyone. The voices of gamblers and numbers runners, kids getting high, kids on the street playing ball, ladies gossiping out their windows in Spanish and Haitian, laundry on lines, garbage, little girls playing jumprope in the hall. Apartments filled with clothing racks and electrical appliances, players of dominoes or rummy, talk of the lottery, smell of beer, smell of urine, smell of dogs. Latin music, smell of fritters, good smell of perfume, food.

The woman's apartment was on the third floor, facing the street. Plastic everywhere: linoleum floors, Formica tables, the sticky, plastic-covered furniture. A television with a phony three-tone "color TV" contact sheet. Contact paper on the walls, covering holes. Statues of the saints, Jesus big everywhere. A squat pink bed, a dresser with a picture of family in the old world, an open drawer showing a douche bag, rosaries, a tin of prophylactics. Refrigerator with gummy door hinges. Oven with animal feet. Dominican flag on bedroom doorway, mirror, dressy dolls, ashtrays full of butts everywhere.

Alejo had bought groceries for her: hot chorizo sausages, chicken, rice, bologna, beer. He started cooking up dinner in the kitchen. She got undressed with the bedroom door open. She stripped down to nothing, brushed beach sand from her legs, picked it out from her hair, and then went to the bathroom to sponge herself off in the sink. She took her drink with her. Alejo sent Hector into the living room to watch TV. He saw "Gunsmoke" and "Have Gun Will Travel."

During the dinner, the woman spoke about her son. "He's a devil, as bad as his father—you know what happens." She sighed. "A bad boy, not quiet like yours. He's had some trouble with the police, but it's not his fault. He does it to annoy me, he's not good like your son." She pinched Hector's cheek, and Hector smiled even though looking at her repulsed him. He was pissed off by what was going on and by what would happen. But it also made him hard, as he spied on them. "If you meet him, Alejo, keep in mind that he's crazy, and humor him. He'll leave you alone."

Hector didn't complain. He watched more TV and pretended to mind his own business. Alejo and the woman disappeared for about an hour. Then they came into the living room, played the phono-graph, and danced. Some kind of word got around in the building because one of the woman's neighbors rapped on the door and came inside and sat down on the couch, and then a few other people came up, and then others, so soon it was a regular party.

Alejo was wearing dark green glasses to hide his eyes, and sometimes had to hang onto the walls because the floors became slippery from drink. The living room was crowded: big asses everywhere, men and women twirling around, kids running wild in the apartment. Hector watched all the dancers. He hated dancing because Alejo used to make him dance in front of drunks, and he hated the way Alejo looked at the woman and the way they danced close together, sad and deep and then happy, by turns. He passed the time ignoring everything. He watched the street from the window until it occurred to him that Alejo might suddenly "burst," as he had from his heart attack, and he wanted Alejo to stop.

But he was too afraid to say anything. Then, out of nowhere, the woman took hold of Hector's hand and pulled him onto the dance floor, cha-cha-cha, around and around, swaying hips, tight dress, swinging him around. Hector looked at her breasts and then at Alejo, exhausted and out of breath, sitting on the sofa. Hector heard Mercedes's voice, saying "Hector! Hector!" and he wanted to go.

Even though he was dead drunk, the woman looked admiringly, even amorously at Alejo. Other women looked at him that way, too, with wide eyes and smiles. What was the inherent quality that drew everyone to him? The sadness? The soft-spokenness? His physical immensity? Or was it his Cubanness? Or his essential kindness, always there, even when he pounded the walls and acted like a bull?

"Hector! Hector!" Mercedes's voice sounded in the back of his mind.

It was around one in the morning when the trouble started. The woman's son showed up. He was standing at the doorway looking at everyone as if they were worthless garbage. He was big, tall, broad-shouldered. When he saw Alejo dancing with his mother, he pulled her away, took his mother into the kitchen, and closed the door. Even though the party was still going on, his voice could be heard over the music: "Who the fuck are you to bring some man home? You ain't no fuckin' whore! Right?" Then slap noises and more yelling in Spanish, so that soon people started to leave.

Later the woman came out and most apologetically asked Alejo to leave. She had been crying and was afraid of her son, who was making himself a sandwich from the cold cuts the woman had left out on the table. Hector was watching him, and when their eyes met the son said,

"What the fuck are you looking at?" So at almost two in the morning Alejo and Hector had to leave. Down on the stoop, the woman told Alejo that her son was not always so angry with her and that she hoped to see Alejo again, and then she went upstairs to join her son, if indeed he was her son.

When they arrived home, Mercedes was sleeping in the living room. She had spent hours staring out the window. At first passersby had stopped to chat with her, but later there was only the moon and little else; street noises. She fell asleep and dreamed, something about Cuba, heard a noise, got up to see who was there. No one.

In the dream she had had a memory of Cuba. She had gone sailing with her father, Teodoro Sorrea. They were going north on a boat to Key West and drifted in shallow water under the hanging vinery of trees, and under willows, into a grotto as beautiful as an enormous opened blossom. He had told his daughters that they were going to a circus, but the real purpose of the journey was to secure arms for a politician friend. They saw no circus. Instead they were holed up in a little cottage for two days, dancing and listening to a music box in the evenings. They were supposed to stay near the cottage, never to go too far, but getting curious, Mercedes and her sisters Rina and Luisa, went for a walk and followed a path into the woods; then they came to a cave with a floor of polished stones that led to a stream of clear water. Following a path they came to a spot where they could look down very far into the deep water, and there they saw a ledge of stone, with bushes of ivory, and, sprinkled through it, pieces of gold. In the dream in the living room in New York, Mercedes made the very same journey again, but instead of finding gold, she found a skeleton entangled in seaweed, embracing another skeleton.

When Alejo and Hector came into the living room, Mercedes was sitting up on the sofa with her eyes closed, her arms folded in front of her, sleeping. Hector went down the hall to his room. Alejo went into his bedroom to undress. He tried to be quiet, but the movement of things on his bureau awakened her. And soon she was asking him, "Where were you?"

"We fell asleep at the beach."

"You got drunk," she said, circling him.

"I do as I please."

"Yes? Then die, because that's what will happen to you."

And Hector went to sleep, or tried to sleep. Their arguing voices continued until it was light. *Death* was a repeated word. *Leave me. Divorce. Woman!* All repetitions: on that night, on nights six months from that day, on nights three years from that day, on and on.

3

Other fathers in the neighborhood were, without exception, drunkards. In some households drunkenness was passed on to the children. Hector at twelve years of age would get drunk at a friend's house, feel the poisons of sweet fruity brandies oozing into his system and infecting his kidneys. Friends got drunk all over the place—in the park, down in the basements, under the railroad trestles—while their fathers went to the bar and rolled their eyes around. Hector would drink sweet wine, beer, whiskey, gin, and vodka until the world started to spin. He liked being drunk because it lifted him out of his own body. It made him feel the way a ghost must feel, amused or outraged by everything. Drunk he could tolerate anything—his sense of doom, the micróbios that were everywhere, and Mercedes, who had grasped at him too much, warned him about illness too often, called him through "whispers" too frequently, to the point where these prevented his sleep. And Hector had heard Alejo say "That woman is killing me" once too often, and was tired of the yelling and the weeping in the house. He was tired of being afraid of the world.

Mercedes suspected Hector was drinking because he would come home off the streets and go to bed early. One night Hector was in bed, stone drunk, with the covers pulled up over his mouth. He had been dreaming about women, and then he dreamed about doing as he pleased and living to be an old man. Then he dreamed about Cuba and the delicious Cuban concoction and Aunt Luisa's kisses and about going to church and being locked up in the confessional. Then the room started to spin, and he thought he was going up in a rocketship. And when he heard Mercedes knocking on the door, he said, "What are you doing?" but heard his words coming out sideways from his mouth as, "Waaayooo dooing?" like the deaf mute Mary would have said it if she could talk. Then he saw Mercedes standing over him in the dark, and he said, "Wass isss it, nosings wrong?" and she sniffed his breath and she said, "Ai, just like your father." And she slapped him and pulled his hair, screaming hysterically. Then she said, "Wait until your father gets home."

Alejo came home drunk and pushed open the door to Hector's room. He was leaning there and said, "Was did I hear about jew?"

"Nothing, Pop, I swear on it."

"Bullshit." Alejo turned on the light and took Hector by the shirt collar and threw him into the wall. "You never get drunk again," he said and punched him and then took out his belt and beat his legs, leaving them covered with welts.

But at other times Alejo could not lift a hand against Hector without suffering himself. Instead, to prove his manhood, he would chase Hector down the hallway; Hector would lean against the door to his room, and Alejo would break through it with one shove. He would pull Hector to the side and raise his hand to hit him. But then something would happen. His arms would start shaking, his face would get all red. "I don't want to hit you. Never make me hit you," he would say, turning away and leaving Hector alone in the room.

In a way Hector actually preferred to be hit, rather than see Alejo sitting at the table with his head drooping between his hands and his voice declaring, "My family has deserted me...I'm going to die." He preferred it when the door burst open and Alejo's strong arms pushed him aside like a piece of rag, when he heard Alejo's voice boom: "Now you respect this household!" He didn't like having to struggle to straighten up Alejo in a chair or help him to get his pants off at night, only to have him reel back and nearly fall down, or to hear his melancholy voice saying, "You know who loves me, boy? Not you, not your mother, not even Horacito, but you know who? My sister Buita, and you know the last time I saw her? Ten years ago. Do you know why? Because of your mother. Now I have no family, I am a man to myself, and I do what I have to do. I have my little drinks because I have to do what I have to do . . . and sometimes you can't help yourself to be who you are . . ." On and on, with sadness deepening in his expression. "You have to be strong, and you need love. No one can live without love . . . and that is something no one can change . . ."

Hector would sit near Alejo, watching him for hours, puzzled over how melancholy seemed to drain Alejo of his strength. Alejo's flesh would sag around him, as if he had relinquished control over bone and muscle to sadness, never moving except to flinch whenever a prickly housefly landed on his hot, moist skin. Soft to the touch, Alejo's body weakened as if its strength had spilled out of it like rum. "My flesh is your flesh," Hector had heard Alejo repeat many times, and remembering this, Hector felt contempt for his own body, as if it, too, was the product of Alejo's melancholia.

He sent away for a Charles Atlas body-building course and began to hang out with a friend from school, Georgie, whose family had just come up from Cuba. Georgie was a physical fitness fanatic who believed he could do anything. He memorized huge sections of Homer's *Iliad* and sometimes spoke English in that kind of verse. He would lift weights with Hector and did one hundred pushups at a time. He and Hector went to the park together to get into shape. Georgie wanted to be ready for the reinvasion of Cuba. Hector wanted to be stronger than his father. Run around the tree twenty times. Crawl up the hill and back on your knees. One hundred situps. Sweat dripping off the chin, the eyes bulging. The teeth aching. Balls aching. Situps with twenty-five and then forty pounds of weight. Clings and jerks. Shoulder press. Back lift! Knee bends with one hundred pounds! Down with Castro! Up with freedom! Hector became stronger. He could lift two hundred pounds, worked to lift two hundred and fifty.

"You, boy, come here," Alejo said to him one evening.

"Yeah, Pop."

"I'm going to tell you something. You listening?"

"Yeah, Pop."

"I don't think I'm long for this world, and love and family is every-

149

thing. I don't know if you understand me, what I'm trying to say. We are blood and the same, you and me. You understand?"

"Yeah."

"So we are inseparable. What she says isn't true. You are good and I'm good, so you don't want me to die."

"No, Pop."

"Then you know what I want? You love me, right?"

"Yeah."

"Tell me."

"Come on, Pop."

"You can't say it?"

"Come on, Pop."

"When I'm dead, you'll see."

"Yeah, Pop?"

"You'll see. You don't believe me?"

"No, Pop."

"It's true, I swear to you I'm going to die."

"You promise me that?"

"Oh, go to hell, you!"

"You go to hell."

"Forget it, sit here."

"I can't, Pop, I gotta go."

"No, you stay here and respect me."

"Oh fuck you."

"What?" and Alejo got red in the face and pushed Hector who went running down the hall to his room where he held the door against Alejo. Alejo kept asking, "Who's the man? Who do you respect?" but he got no answer and then added, "You know I'm going to die." "Then die," Hector said. And so Alejo pushed, but this time he could not move the door because Hector was holding it with all his strength. The harder Alejo pushed, the harder Hector held the door. "Please, son, open the door. I'm your father." But Hector held on while Alejo's face turned redder and he slumped down to the floor and fell to his knees. Then it was very quiet, and after a time Hector opened the door and found Alejo sprawled out on the floor. Hector said, "Come on,

150

Pop, you're the man, not me. You can hit me, Pop! Come on, hit! Please, Pop!" But his father just remained on the floor, crying.

Later Hector heard Alejo reeling against the walls in the hallway, as he struggled to make his way back to his own bedroom. He fell about four or five more times, called out to Hector to help him up each time. Hector, sitting on his bed, in the dark, chose not to move.

Visitors, 1965

1

Down in the cool basement of the hotel restaurant, Alejo Santinio looked over a yellowed newspaper clipping dating back to 1961. He had not looked at it recently, although in the past had always been proud to show it to visitors. And why? Because it was a brief moment of glory. In the newspaper picture Alejo and his friend Diego were in their best dress whites standing before a glittering cart of desserts. Beside them was a fat, cheery beaming face, the Soviet premier Nikita Khrushchev, who was attending a luncheon in his honor at the hotel.

Alejo always told the story: The governor and mayor were there with the premier, who had "great big ears and a bright red nose." The premier had dined on a five-course meal. The waiters and cooks, all nervous wrecks, had fumbled around in the kitchen getting things into order. But outside they managed an orderly composed appearance. After the meal had been served, the cooks drew lots to see who would wheel out the dessert tray. Diego and Alejo won.

Alejo put on his best white uniform and apron and waited in the foyer, chainsmoking nervously, while, outside, news reporters fired off their cameras and bodyguards stood against the walls, watching. Alejo and Diego did not say anything. Alejo was bewildered by the situation: Only in America could a worker get so close to a fat little guy with enormous power. These were the days of the new technology: mushroom-cloud bombs and satellites and missiles. And there he was, a hick from a small town in Cuba, slicked up by America, thinking, "If only my old compañeros could see me now! and my sisters and Mercedes."

When the time came, they went to the freezer, filled up shiny bowls with ice cream, brought out the sauces and hot fudge, and loaded them all onto a dessert cart. Alejo was in charge of cherries. They went out behind the maître d' and stood before the premier's table. They humbly waited as the smiling premier looked over the different cakes, tarts, pies, fruits, sauces, and ice creams. Through a translator the premier asked for a bowl of chocolate and apricot ice cream topped with hot fudge, cocoanut, and a high swirl of fresh whipped cream. This being served, Alejo picked out the plumpest cherry from a bowl and nimbly placed it atop the dessert.

Delighted, the premier whispered to the translator, who said, "The premier wishes to thank you for this masterpiece."

As Diego and Alejo bowed, lightbulbs and cameras flashed all around them. They were ready to wheel the cart back when the premier rose from the table to shake Diego's and Alejo's hands. Then through the translator he asked a few questions. To Alejo: "And where do you come from?"

"Cuba," Alejo answered in a soft voice.

"Oh yes, Cuba," the premier said in halting English. "I would like to go there one day. Cuba." And he smiled and patted Alejo's back and then rejoined the table. A pianist, a violinist, and a cellist played a Viennese waltz.

Afterward reporters came back into the kitchen to interview the two cooks, and the next morning the *Daily News* carried a picture of Alejo, Diego, and Khrushchev with a caption that read: DESSERT CHEFS CALL RUSKY PREMIER HEAP BIG EATER! It made them into celebrities for a few weeks. People recognized Alejo on the street and stopped to talk with him. He even went on a radio show in the Bronx. The hotel gave him a five-dollar weekly raise, and for a while Alejo felt important, and then it played itself out and became the yellowed clipping, stained by grease on the basement kitchen wall.

In Alejo's locker Khrushchev turned up again, on the cover of a *Life* magazine. He was posed, cheek against cheek, with the bearded Cuban premier Fidel Castro. "What was going to happen in Cuba?" Alejo wondered. He shook his head. "How could Cuba have gone 'red'?" It had been more than six years since the fall of Batista on New Year's Eve, 1958, the year of getting rid of the evil in Cuba, and now Alejo and Mercedes were going to sponsor the arrival of Aunt Luisa, her daughters, and a son-in-law, Pedro. They were coming to the United States via *un vuelo de la libertad,* or freedom flight, as the U.S. military airplane trips from Havana to Miami were called. Khrushchev was going to eat up Cuba like an ice cream sundae. Things had gotten out of hand, bad enough for Luisa, who had loved her life in Holguín, to leave. Gone were the days of the happy-go-lucky Cubans who went on jaunts to Miami and New York to have a high time ballroom hopping; gone were the days when Cubans came to the States to make money and see more of the world. Now Cubans were leaving because of Khrushchev's new pal, Fidel Castro, the Shit, as some Cubans called him.

2

Alejo had supported Castro during the days of the revolution. He had raised money for the pro-Castro Cubans in Miami by hawking copies of the *Sierra Maestra* magazine to pals on the street. This magazine was printed in Miami by pro-Castro Cubans and was filled with pictures of tortured heroes left on the streets or lying in the lightless mortuary rooms with their throats cut and their heads blood-splattered. They were victims of the crooked Batista regime, and now it was time for Batista and his henchmen to go! Alejo was not a political creature, but he supported the cause, of course, to end the injustices of Batista's rule. When someone brought him a box of Cuban magazines to sell, Alejo went down on Amsterdam Avenue and sold them to friends. Alejo always carried one of those magazines in his pocket, and he was persuasive, selling them. In his soft calm voice he would say, "Come on, it's only a dollar and for the cause of your countrymen's freedom!"

And soon he would find himself inviting all the buyers back to his apartment, where they sat in the kitchen drinking and talking about what would save the world: "An honest man with a good heart, out of greed's reach," was the usual consensus. Political talk about Cuba always led to nostalgic talk, and soon Alejo's friends would soften up and bend like orchid vines, glorying in the lost joys of childhood. Their loves and regrets thickened in the room in waves, until they began singing along with their drinking and falling down. With their arms around each other and glasses raised, they toasted Fidel as "the hope for the future."

Alejo and Mercedes had been happy with the success of the revolution. The day Castro entered Havana they threw a party with so much food and drink that the next morning people had to cross into the street to get around the stacks of garbage bags piled on the sidewalk in front of the building. Inside, people were sprawled around everywhere. There were sleepers in the kitchen and in the hall, sleepers in the closet. There was a *dudduhduh* of a skipping needle over a phonograph record. A cat that had come in through the window from the alley was going around eating leftover scraps of food.

Soon the papers printed that famous picture of Castro entering Havana with his cowboy-looking friend, Camilio Cienfuegos, on a tank. They were like Jesus and John the Baptist in a Roman epic movie. The *Sierra Maestra* magazine would later feature a centerfold of Castro as Jesus Christ with his hair long and golden brown, almost fiery in a halo of light. And for the longest time Cubans, Alejo and Mercedes among them, referred to Castro with great reverence and love, as if he were a saint.

In a few years, however, kids in the street started to write slogans like *Castro eats big bananas!* The New York press ran stories about the Castro visit to New York. Alejo and Hector stood on the corner one afternoon, watching his motorcade speed uptown to a Harlem hotel. There, the press said, Castro's men killed their own chickens and ate them raw. Castro even came to give a talk at the university. Alejo and Hector were among a crowd of admirers that clustered around him to get a look. Castro was very tall for a Cuban, six-feet-two. He was wearing a long raincoat and took sips from a bottle of

Pepsi-Cola. He listened to questions intently, liked to smile, and kept reaching out to shake hands. He also signed an occasional autograph. He was, the newspapers said, unyielding in his support of the principles of freedom.

In time Castro announced the revolutionary program. Alejo read the *El Diario* accounts intently while Mercedes wandered around the apartment asking, "What's going to happen to my sisters?" By 1962, after the Bay of Pigs invasion and the beginning of the Cuban ration-card programs, an answer to her question came in the form of letters. Standing by the window Mercedes would read the same letter over and over again, sighing and saying out loud, "Oh my Lord! They are so unhappy!"

"Ma, what's going on?" Hector would ask her.

"Things are very bad. The Communists are very bad people. Your aunts have nothing to eat, no clothes to wear, no medicine. The Communists go around taking things away from people! And if you say anything they put you in jail!"

Mercedes's stories about the new life in Cuba made Hector think of a house of horrors. In his sleep he pictured faceless, cowled abductors roaming the streets of Holguín in search of victims to send to brain-washing camps. He pictured the ransacking of old mansions, the burning of churches, deaths by firing squads. He remembered back many years and saw the door of Aunt Luisa's house on Arachoa Street, and then he imagined guards smashing that door open to search Luisa's home.

All the news that came into the house in those letters fed such visions: "Ai, Hector, do you remember your cousin Paco? He has been sent to prison for a year, and all he did was get caught with a pound of sugar under his shirt!" A year later: "Oh your poor cousin Paco! He just came out of prison and now my sister can hardly recognize him. Listen to what Luisa says: 'He has lost most of his hair and is as thin as a skeleton with yellowed, jaundiced skin. He has aged twenty years in one.'" Another letter: "Dear sister, the headaches continue. Everything is upside down. You can't even go to church these days without someone asking, 'Where are you going?' Everyone in the barrio watches where you go. No one has any privacy. If you are not in the Party then you're no good. Many of them are Negroes, and now that they have the power, they are very bad to us. I don't know how long we can endure these humiliations. We hope for Castro's fall." Another letter: "Dear sister, last week your niece Maria was kicked out of dental school, and do you know what for? Because she wouldn't recite 'Hail Lenin!' in the mornings with the other students! I went to argue with the headmaster of the school, but there was nothing I could do. On top of that, poor Rina's roof was hit by lightning but she can't get the materials to fix it. When it rains the floors are flooded—all because she is not in the Party.... As usual I ask for your prayers and to send us whatever you can by way of clothing, food and medicine. Aspirins and penicillin are almost impossible to find these days, as are most other things. I know I'm complaining to you, but if you were here, you would understand. With much love, Luisa."

To help her sisters, Mercedes went from apartment to apartment asking neighbors for any clothing they might not need. These clothes were packed into boxes and sent down to Cuba at a cost of fifty dollars each. Mercedes paid for this out of her own pocket. She had been working at night cleaning in a nursery school since the days of Alejo's illness. Alejo too contributed. He came home with boxes of canned goods and soap and toothpaste from the hotel and he bought such items as rubbing alcohol, aspirins, mercurochrome, iodine, Tampax, Q-Tips, cotton, and toilet paper to send to Cuba.

"The world is going to the devil," Mercedes would say to Alejo as she packed one of the boxes. "Imagine having to use old newspapers for toilet paper! The Russians are the new masters, they have everything, but what do Luisa and Rina have? Nothing!"

Of the family, Mercedes was the most outspoken about the revolution. Alejo was very quiet in his views. He didn't like Castro, or, for that matter, Khrushchev. But he would never argue with a friend about politics. He was always more concerned about keeping his friendships cordial. To please two different sets of neighbors he subscribed to both the *Daily Worker* and to the *Republican Eagle*. He read neither of them, but still would nod emphatically whenever he came upon these neighbors in the hallway and they bombarded him with their philosophies. "Certainly," Alejo would say to them, "why don't you come inside and have a drink with me?" When there was a gathering of visitors with different points of view, Alejo used liquor to keep the wagging tongues in line. Get them drunk and make them happy, was his motto.

But Mercedes didn't want to hear about Fidel Castro from anyone, not even from Señor Lopez, a union organizer and good friend of the family who lived in the building. He would come to the apartment to recount the declines in illiteracy, prostitution, and malnutrition in Cuba. "No more of this!" he would declare, showing Mercedes and Alejo and Hector a picture from *La Bohemia* of a decrepit old Negro man dying in bed, with bloated stomach, festering sores on his limbs, and a long gray worm literally oozing out of his navel. "You won't see this anymore now that Castro is in power!"

"And what about the decent people who supported Castro in the first place, and who now have nothing but troubles?" she would ask.

"Mercita, the revolution is the will of the majority of the Cuban people!"

"You mean the people who were the good-for-nothings?"

"No, the people who had nothing because they were allowed nothing."

"Oh yes? And what about my family?"

"Mercita, use your brains. I don't like to put it this way, but as the saying goes, 'To make an omelet you have to break a few eggs.'"

"My family are not eggs! If you like eggs so much, why don't you go down to Cuba and live there? Chickens have more to eat than what you would get. Go there and see what freedom is like!"

By 1965 it was becoming clear that Castro was not going to fall from power. Cubans who had been hoping for a counterrevolution were now growing desperate to leave. Luisa and her family were among them. One evening an errand boy from the corner drugstore knocked at the door. There was a call from Cuba. Mercedes and Hector hurried down the hill. The caller was Aunt Luisa. Her sad voice was so far away, interrupted by sonic hums and clicking static echoes. It sounded like the voices of hens reciting numbers in Spanish. With the jukebox going, it was a wonder that Luisa's voice could be heard over mountains and rivers and across the ocean.

"How is it over there now?" Mercedes asked.

"It's getting worse here. There are too many headaches. We want to leave. Pedro, Virginia's husband, lost his mechanic's shop. There is no point in our staying."

"Who wants to come?"

"Me, Pedro, Virginia, and Maria."

"And what about Rina?"

"She is going to stay for the time being with Delores and her husband." Delores was Rina's daughter. She had a doctorate in pedagogy that made her a valuable commodity in those days of literacy programs. "Delores has been appointed to a government post and she is too afraid to refuse the Party, for fear they will do something to Rina or to her husband. But we will come. I have the address of the place where you must write for the sponsorship papers. We've already put our name on the government waiting list. When our name reaches the top of the list we'll be able to go."

The only other way was to fly either to Mexico or Spain, but at a cost of two thousand dollars per person to Mexico, three thousand dollars per person to Spain. The family did not have that kind of money.

Mercedes then gave Hector the telephone. He listened to his aunt's soft voice, saying, "We will be with you soon, and you will know your family again. Pray for us so that we will be safe." Her voice sounded weak. There was clicking, like a plug being pulled. Perhaps someone was listening in the courthouse, where the call was being made.

Luisa spoke with Mercedes for another minute, and then their time was up and Mercedes and Hector returned home.

Alejo took care of the paperwork. He wrote to immigration authorities in Miami for their visas and for the special forms that would be mailed out by him, approved by the U.S. Immigration Department, and sent to Cuba.

In February 1966 Luisa and her daughters and son-in-law left Cuba. First they waited in front of the house on Arachoa Street in Holguín, where they had all been living, for the army bus that would take them on the ten-hour journey west to Havana. When they arrived at the José Marti Airport, they waited in a wire-fenced compound. A Cuban

159

official went over their papers and had them stand in line for hours before they boarded the military transport jet to America.

On the day that Alejo looked at the clipping of Khrushchev again, they received word that Luisa and her daughters and a son-in-law were coming, and a sort of shock wave of apprehension and hope passed through them.

3

For Hector the prospect of Aunt Luisa's arrival stirred up memories. He began to make a conscious effort to be "Cuban," and yet the very idea of *Cubanness* inspired fear in him as if he would grow ill from it, as if micróbios would be transmitted by the very mention of the word *Cuba*. He was a little perplexed because he also loved the notion of Cuba to an extreme. In Cuba there were so many pleasant fragrances, like the smell of Luisa's hair and the damp clay ground of the early morning. Cuba was where Mercedes had once lived a life of style and dignity and happiness. And it was the land of happy courtship with Alejo and the land where men did not fall down. Hector was tired of seeing Mercedes cry and yell. He was tired of her moroseness and wanted the sadness to go away. He wanted the apartment to be filled with beams of sunlight, like in the dream house of Cuba.

He was sick at heart for being so Americanized, which he equated with being fearful and lonely. His Spanish was unpracticed, practically nonexistent. He had a stutter, and saying a Spanish word made him think of drunkenness. A Spanish sentence wrapped around his face, threatened to peel off his skin and send him falling to the floor like Alejo. He avoided Spanish even though that was all he heard at home. He read it, understood it, but he grew paralyzed by the prospect of the slightest conversation.

"Hablame en espanol!" Alejo's drunken friends would challenge him. But Hector always refused and got lost in his bedroom, read *Flash* comic books. And when he was around the street Ricans, they didn't want to talk Spanish with Whitey anyway, especially since he was not getting high with them, just getting drunk now and then, and did not look like a hood but more like a goody-goody, round-faced, mama's boy: a dark dude, as they used to say in those days.

Even Horacio had contempt for Hector. Knowing that Hector was nervous in the company of visitors, he would instigate long conversations in Spanish. When visiting men would sit in the kitchen speaking about politics, family, and Cuba, Horacio would play the patrón and join them, relegating Hector to the side, with the women. He had disdain for his brother and for the ignorance Hector represented. He was now interested in "culture." He had returned from England a complete European who listened to Mozart instead of diddy-bop music. His hair was styled as carefully as Beau Brummell's. His wardrobe consisted of English tweed jackets and fine Spanish shoes; his jewelry, his watches, his cologne, everything was very European and very far from the gutter and the insecurity he had left behind. As he put it, "I'm never going to be fuckin' poor again."

He went around criticizing the way Mercedes kept house and cooked, the way Alejo managed his money (buying everything with cash and never on credit) and the amounts of booze Alejo drank. But mostly he criticized Hector. The day he arrived home from the Air Force and saw Hector for the first time in years, his face turned red. He could not believe his eyes. Hector was so fat that his clothes were bursting at the seams, and when Hector embraced him, Horacio shook his head and said, "Man, I can't believe this is my brother."

And now the real Cubans, Luisa and her daughters and son-in-law, were coming to find out what a false life Hector led. Hector could not sleep at night, thinking of it. He tried to remember his Spanish, but instead of sentences, pictures of Cuba entered into his mind. But he did not fight this. He fantasized about Cuba. He wanted the pictures to enter him, as if memory and imagination would make him more of a man, a Cuban man.

The day before Luisa arrived he suddenly remembered his trip to Cuba with Mercedes and Horacio in 1954. He remembered looking out the window of the plane and seeing fire spewing from the engines on the wing. To Cuba. To Cuba. Mercedes was telling him a story when the plane abruptly plunged down through some clouds and came out into the night air again. Looking out the window he saw pearls in the ocean and the reflection of the moon in the water. For a moment he saw a line of three ships, caravels with big white sails like Columbus's ships, and he tugged at Mercedes's arm. She looked but did not see them. And when he looked again, they were gone.

Hector tried again for a genuine memory. Now he saw Luisa's house on Arachoa Street, the sun a haze bursting through the trees.

"Do you remember a cat with one eye in Cuba?" he asked Horacio, who was across the room reading *Playboy* magazine.

"What?" he said with annoyance.

"In Cuba, wasn't there a little cat who used to go in and out of the shadows and bump into things? You know, into the steps and into the walls, because it only had one eye. And then Luisa would come out and feed it bits of meat?"

"You can't remember anything. Don't fool yourself," he replied.

But Hector could not stop himself. He remembered bulldozers tearing up the street and that sunlight again, filtering through the flower heads, and flamingos of light on the walls of the house. He remembered the dog with the pathetic red dick running across the yard. Then he remembered holding an enormous, trembling white sunhat. His grandmother, Doña Maria, was sitting nearby in a blue-and-white dotted dress, and he took the sunhat to show her. But it wasn't a sunhat. It was an immense white butterfly. "¡Ai, que linda!" Doña Maria said. "It's so pretty, but maybe we should let the poor thing go." And so Hector released the butterfly and watched it rise over the house and float silently away.

Then he saw Doña Maria, now dead, framed by a wreath of orchids in the yard, kissing him—so many kisses, squirming kisses—and giving advice. She never got over leaving Spain for Cuba and would always remain a proud Spaniard. "Remember," she had told Hector. "You're Spanish first and then Cuban."

He remembered sitting on the cool steps to Luisa's kitchen and watching the road where the bulldozers worked. A turtle was crawling across the yard, and iguanas were licking up the sticky juice on the kitchen steps. Then he heard Luisa's voice: "Come along, child," she called. "I have something for you." And he could see her face again through the screen door, long and wistful.

162

Inside, she had patted Hector's head and poured him a glass of milk. Cuban milk alone was sour on the tongues of children, but with the Cuban magic potion, which she added, it was the most delicious drink Hector ever tasted. With deep chocolate and nut flavors and traces of orange and mango, the bitter with the sweet, the liquid went down his throat, so delicious. "No child, drink that milk," Luisa said. "Don't forget your *tia*. She loves you."

Then a bam! bam! came from the television and Hector could hear voices of neighbors out in the hallway. No, he wasn't used to hearing Luisa's niceties anymore, and he couldn't remember what was in the milk, except that it was Cuban, and then he wondered what he would say to his aunt and cousins, whether he would smile and nod his head or hide as much as possible, like a turtle on a hot day.

4

It was late night when a van pulled up to the building and its four exhausted passengers stepped onto the sidewalk. Seeing the arrival from the window, Mercedes was in a trance for a moment and then removed her apron and ran out, almost falling down the front steps, waving her arms and calling, "Aaaaiiii, aaaaiiii, aaaaiiii! Oh my God! My God! My God," and giving many kisses. Alejo followed and hugged Pedro. The female cousins waited humbly, and then they began kissing Mercedes and Alejo and Hector and Horacio, their hats coming off and teeth chattering and hair getting all snarled like ivy on an old church...kisses, kisses, kisses...into the warm lobby with its deep, endless mirrors and the mailbox marked *Delgado/Santinio*. The female cousins, like china dolls, were incredibly beautiful, but struck dumb by the snow and the new world, silent because there was something dreary about the surroundings. They were thinking Alejo had been in this country for twenty years, and yet what did he have? But no one said this. They just put hands on hands and gave many kisses and said, "I can't believe I'm seeing you here." They were all so skinny and exhausted-looking, Luisa, Virginia, Maria, and Pedro. They came holding cloth bags with all their worldly possessions: a few crucifixes, a change of clothing, aspirins given to them at the airport, an album of old photographs, prayer medals, a Bible, a few Cuban coins from the old days, and a throat-lozenge tin filled with some soil from Holguín, Oriente province, Cuba.

After kissing and hugging them Alejo took them into the kitchen where they almost died: There was so much of everything! Milk and wine and beer, steaks and rice and chicken and sausages and ham and plantains and ice cream and black bean soup and Pepsi-Cola and Hershey chocolate bars and almond nougat, and popcorn and Wise potato chips and Jiffy peanut butter, and rum and whiskey, marshmallows, spaghetti, flan and pasteles and chocolate cake and pie, more than enough to make them delirious. And even though the walls were cracked and it was dark, there was a television set and a radio and lightbulbs and toilet paper and pictures of the family and crucifixes and toothpaste and soap and more.

It was "Thank God for freedom and bless my family" from Luisa's mouth, but her daughters were more cautious. Distrusting the world, they approached everything timidly. In the food-filled kitchen Alejo told them how happy he was to have them in his house, and they were happy because the old misery was over, but they were still without a home and in a strange world. Uncertainty showed in their faces.

Pedro, Virginia's husband, managed to be the most cheerful. He smoked and talked up a storm about the conditions in Cuba and the few choices the Castro government had left to them. Smoking thick, black cigars, Horacio and Alejo nodded and agreed, and the conversation went back and forth and always ended with "What are you going to do?"

"Work until I have something," was Pedro's simple answer.

It was such a strong thing to say that Hector, watching from the doorway, wanted to be like Pedro. And from time to time, Pedro would look over and wink and flash his Victor Mature teeth.

Pedro was about thirty years old and had been through very bad times, including the struggle in 1957 and 1958 to get Castro into power. But wanting to impress Hector with his cheeriness, Pedro kept saying things in English to Hector like, "I remember Elvis Presley records. Do you know *You're My Angel Baby?*" And Hector would not even answer that. But Pedro would speak on, about the brave Cubans who got out of Cuba in the strangest ways. His buddy back in Holguín stole a small airplane with a few friends and flew west to Mexico, where they crash-landed their plane on a dirt road in the Yucatán. He ended up in Mexico City, where he found work in the construction business. He was due in America soon and would one day marry Maria, who wanted a brave man. These stories only made Hector more and more silent.

As for his female cousins, all they said to him was: "Do you want to eat?" or "Why are you so quiet?" And sometimes Horacio answered for him, saying: "He's just dumb when it comes to being Cuban."

Aunt Luisa, with her good heart, really didn't care what Hector said or didn't say. Each time she encountered him in the morning or the afternoons, she would take his face between her hands and say, "Give me a kiss and say 'Tia, I love you.'" And not in the way Alejo used to, falling off a chair and with his eyes desperate, but sweetly. Hector liked to be near Luisa with her sweet angelic face.

He felt comfortable enough around Aunt Luisa to begin speaking to her. He wasn't afraid because she overflowed with warmth. One day while Aunt Luisa was washing dishes, Hector started to think of her kitchen in Cuba. He remembered the magic Cuban drink.

"Auntie," he asked her. "Do you remember a drink that you used to make for me in the afternoons in Cuba? What was it? It was the most delicious chocolate but with Cuban spices."

She thought about it. "Chocolate drink in the afternoon? Let me see..." She wiped a plate clean in the sink. She seemed perplexed and asked, "And it was chocolate?"

"It was Cuban chocolate. What was it?"

She thought on it again and her eyes grew big and she laughed, slapping her knee. "Ai, bobo. It was Hershey syrup and milk!"

After that he didn't ask her any more questions. He just sat in the living room listening to her tell Mercedes about her impressions of the United States. For example, after she had sat out on the stoop or gazed out the window for a time, she would make a blunt declaration: "There are a lot of airplanes in the sky." But usually when Mercedes and Luisa got to talking, they drifted toward the subject of spirits and ghosts. When they were little girls spiritualism was very popular in Cuba. All the little girls were half mediums, in those days. And remembering this with great laughter, Luisa would say, "If only we could have seen what would happen to Papa! Or that Castro would turn out to be so bad!"

"Yes, Papa, that would have been something," Mercedes answered with wide hopeful eyes. "But Castro is something else. What could a few people do about him?"

"Imagine if you're dead in Cuba," said Luisa, "and you wake up to that mess. What would you do?"

"I would go to Miami, or somewhere like that."

"Yes, and you would go on angel wings."

It was Luisa's ambition to ignore America and the reality of her situation completely. So she kept taking Mercedes back to the old days: "You were such a prankster, so mischievous! You couldn't sit down for a moment without being up to something. Poor Papa! What he had to do with you!" And then, turning to Hector, she would add, "Look at your Mama. This innocent over here was the fright of us all. She was always imagining things. Iguanas, even little baby iguanas, were dragons. A rustle in the bushes was ghosts of fierce Indians looking for their bones!" She laughed. "There are ghosts, but not as many as she saw. She was always in trouble with Papa. He was very good to her but also strict. But his punishments never stopped your mother. My, but she was a fresh girl!"

When she wasn't talking to Mercedes, Luisa watched the Spanish channel on the television, or ate, or prayed. Pedro went out with Alejo and Horacio, looking for work. Maria and Virginia helped with the housecleaning and the cooking, and then they studied their books. They were very quiet, like felines, moving from one spot to another without a sound. Sometimes everyone went out to the movies; Alejo paid for it. Or they all went downtown to the department stores to buy clothing and other things they needed. Again, Alejo paid for everything, angering Mercedes, for whom he bought nothing.

"I know you're trying to be nice to my family, but remember we don't have money."

Still, he was generous with them, as if desperate to keep Luisa and her daughters in the apartment. Their company made him as calm and happy as a mouse. Nothing pleased Alejo more than sitting at the head of the dinner table, relishing the obvious affection that Luisa and her daughters and son-in-law felt for him. At meals Alejo would make toast after toast to their good health and long life, drink down his glass of rum or whiskey quickly, and then fill another and drink that and more. Mercedes always sat quietly wondering, "What does my sister really think of me for marrying him?" while Hector waited for Alejo suddenly to fall off his chair, finally showing his aunt and cousins just who the Santinios really were.

One night Alejo fell against the table and knocked down a big stack of plates. The plates smashed all around Alejo, who was on the floor. Hector scrambled to correct everything before Virginia and Maria and Pedro came to look. He scrambled to get Alejo up before they saw him. He pulled with all his strength, the way he and Horacio used to, but Alejo weighed nearly three hundred pounds. As the cousins watched in silence, Hector wished he could walk through the walls and fly away. He thought that now they would know one of his secrets, that the son is like the father. He tried again to pull Alejo up and had nearly succeeded when Pedro appeared and, with amazing strength, wrapped his arms around Alejo's torso and heaved him onto a chair with one pull.

Hector hadn't wanted them to see this, because then they might want to leave and the apartment would be empty of Pedro and Luisa and her daughters, those fabulous beings. He didn't want them to see the dingy furniture and the cracking walls and the cheap decorative art, plaster statues, and mass-produced paintings. He didn't want them to see that he was an element in this world, only as good as the things around him. He wanted to be somewhere else, be someone else, a Cuban ... And he didn't want the family perceived as the poor relations with the drunk father. So he tried to laugh about Alejo and eventually went to bed, leaving Luisa and Pedro and his cousins still standing in the hall. Eventually, they did move away. Virginia and Maria found work in a factory in Jersey City, and Pedro came home one evening with news that he had landed a freight dispatcher's job in an airport. Just like that. He had brought home a big box of pastries, sweet cakes with super-sweet cream, chocolate eclairs, honey-drenched cookies with maraschino cherries in their centers.

As Alejo devoured some of these, he said to Pedro, "Well, that's good. You're lucky to have such good friends here. Does it pay you well?"

Pedro nodded slightly and said, "I don't know, it starts out at seven thousand dollars a year, but it will get better."

Alejo also nodded, but he was sick because after twenty years in the same job he did not make that much, and this brought down his head and made him yawn. He got up and went to his bedroom where he fell asleep.

A few months later, they were ready to rent a house in a nice neighborhood in Jersey. The government had helped them out with some emergency funds. ("We never asked the government for even a penny," Mercedes kept saying to Alejo.) Everyone but Luisa was bringing home money. They used that money to buy furniture and to send Virginia to night computer school taught by Spanish instructors. Instead of being cramped up in someone else's apartment with rattling pipes and damp plaster walls that seemed ready to fall in, they had a three-story house with a little yard and lived near many Cubans who kept the sidewalks clean and worked hard, so their sick hearts would have an easier time of it.

Hector was bereft at their leaving, but more than that he was astounded by how easily they established themselves. One day Pedro said, "I just bought a car." On another, "I just got a color TV." In time they would be able to buy an even larger house. The house would be filled with possessions: a dishwasher, a washing machine, radios, a big stereo console, plastic-covered velour couches and chairs, electric clocks, fans, air conditioners, hair dryers, statues, crucifixes, lamps and electric-candle chandeliers, and more. One day they would have enough money to move again, to sell the house at a huge profit and travel down to Miami to buy another house there. They would work like dogs, raise children, prosper. They did not allow the old world, the past, to hinder them. They did not cry but walked straight ahead. They drank but did not fall down. Pedro even started a candy and cigarette business to keep him busy in the evenings, earning enough money to buy himself a truck.

"Qué bueno," Alejo would say.

"This country's wonderful to new Cubans," Mercedes kept repeating. But then she added, "They're going to have everything, and we...what will we have?" And she would go about sweeping the floor or preparing chicken for dinner. She would say to Alejo, "Doesn't it hurt you inside?"

Alejo shrugged. "No, because they have suffered in Cuba."

He never backed off from that position and always remained generous to them, even after their visits became less frequent, even when they came only once a year. And when Pedro tried to repay the loans, Alejo always waved the money away. By this time Virginia was pregnant, so Alejo said, "Keep it for the baby."

"You don't want the money?"

"Only when you don't need it. It's important for you to have certain things now."

But Mercedes stalked around the apartment, screaming, "What about the pennies I saved? What about us?"

Dark Ignorance, 1967–1969

1

After her sister's departure Mercedes went through a long period of bitterness. "You work so hard, and for what?" That was her response to everything those days. Every night Alejo would come home and find her in a mood of deep moroseness, and he would attempt to soothe her. Miraculously, he was trying to be better to her, but she would not accept him. When he put his arms around her, she would move away.

"Why do you do that?"

"Because of what you did to me!"

She reminded him of how he ran around, playing the big man, spending their money, and of how he let Buita treat her like a slave.

"I didn't want to be that way," he said. "But sometimes a man does what he does."

"You didn't? Pssssh, but you did. You were bad to me, all for that woman Buita!" And then she would shout Buita's name so that it was heard a thousand times in one night. Her eyes would get big, her hands would shake, and as she stormed around the house, Alejo tried to have a soothing little drink. She calmed down when his friends showed up, but if he ordered her to cook a meal at midnight, as he often did, then she started again, shouting until two or three in the morning, so that no one in the apartment could sleep.

For that reason, Horacio found himself a woman in an East Side discotheque and moved out. They lived together for a time until it seemed certain Horacio would soon be married. This excited Alejo; he went out and bought himself a very handsome blue suit that showed off his most gentlemanly qualities. But it turned out that Horacio, wishing to avoid the troubles of a big wedding, eloped with his young bride one day, and that was the end of that. The suit went into the closet.

And because of his parents' shouting, Hector tuned out of the situation. He remained silent, he would go to a friend's apartment, get drunk, and find shelter in feeling dizzy.

Sometimes there was peace, a calmness that was hard to trust. But sometimes that calmness remained. Alejo would come home and sit in a nice comfortable easy chair with its reclining back. He had his beer and a bowl of fruit or a tray of food, and he sat watching cowboy programs on television, the *vaqueros* zooming across the plains and shooting it up. He seemed so calm, with the light flickering in his face, almost like a little boy in a shoddy movie house in Cuba, watching Hoot Gibson, a little kid who wanted adventures and to live a long, wild life. Alejo liked to watch "Sugarfoot," "Rawhide," "Gunsmoke." Maybe at one time he had been a Cuban cowboy. He had been a farmer, Hector knew, and there were cattle on the farms of Oriente, miles and miles of grazing land. Sometimes when Hector passed through the living room on his way out, Alejo tried to speak to him, but by then the conversations went like this:

"Hector, come here, I want to talk to you."

"What is it?"

"Nothing, just want to know how you are."

"Yeah, yeah. Well, I'm all right. See you."

And Hector would leave, without saying a word more, not even telling him where.

One day during a period of calm, Alejo came home and began discussing with Mercedes the idea of opening a little general store in the country outside of New York. He was starting to think about leaving the hotel. After listening, Mercedes replied, "And where are you going to get the money? From the clouds?"

"From credit."

She laughed. "They won't give credit to a cook. Ask your million-aire friends who are leeches on you. Go ask for all the money you liked to give away."

But Alejo continued to talk about opening a store. It would be a little general store where the local people would come by and chat with him and have something to eat and drink. He would find a small town with calm afternoons. The work would not be hard or rushed, and he could watch television. It would be, except for television, just like Cuba of the old days. Down there, bars were found only in the big cities. In the small towns all the drinking went on in the general stores. Out front were the meats and canned goods and barrels of rice and herbs and candies, and in the back there was a little counter that could be lifted up from the wall, when the owner wanted to leave. Behind the counter there was a bucket of ice for Hatuey Indian Malts and other beers, and behind that, a rack for bottles of rum and whiskey. Then maybe a coffeepot, and some kind of steamer to make café con leche. On the way home from work or on an empty afternoon friends and neighbors gathered, could have a few laughs. On the street there might be a cock fight or an animal auction. In any case, it could be viewed from the counter, as people had their little drinks, or good, icy-sweet malts, a guanábana batida, a Coca-Cola. In San Pedro there was such a place near the church, and Alejo used to go there as a young man and talk over his plans to come to the United States.

One afternoon Alejo returned from work with an armful of pam-phlets and brochures on properties for sale in the country. He got them from a friend whose brother was a real estate agent. Sitting at the kitchen table, he looked over these brochures and set three aside, ate dinner, examined them again, and then was left with two brochures of interest. One was of a retirement community with swimming pools and tennis courts. He may have chosen it because, in one of the tiny pictures, there was a blue-green meadow like the Viñales Valley in Cuba, with horses galloping through clusters of trees. And on the cover there was a fine brunette in a bathing suit sitting by the pool, looking up and smiling at him. The price of a house in this com-munity was twenty-five thousand dollars down. That was too much.

However, the other brochure was really just a mimeographed sheet with the following description: "House and storefront, 1/4 acre of land. $15,000." This excited him. He carried the sheet around and looked at it in the evenings, conferred with friends, asking their advice.

Another day he came home with a brochure on bank mortgages, and the same evening an old friend, Eliseo Hernandez, came around to the house to explain the many intricacies of such purchases and the responsibilities of running a business, which Alejo had avoided since the days of Eduardo Delgado, when he had once had a chance to own the tobacco shop. Eliseo had come from Cuba in the mid-1950s. Alejo had put him up and lent him money. Over the years Eliseo had prospered and now he owned a number of apartment buildings in the Bronx. He told Alejo, "I'll lend you some money if you're serious about this thing."

Alejo began to plan.

This consisted of going out and looking at the property in question with Eliseo, meeting with the owners, and making contact with food suppliers in the Bronx. The only problem was the timing. Although Alejo was not ready to retire for another five years, he wanted to go through with the deal now. Thinking it was all a dream, Mercedes told him he would be crazy to leave his job for so uncertain a venture. Wanting peace and tired of her doubts, one evening he told her, "I'm the man, and I'll do as I want!"

And he might have bought the property if he had not had his accident. It happened one early morning. In the hotel kitchen there was a huge kettle ready to be moved from the stove, and being strong, Alejo was sent by the head chef to get it. The kettle was very heavy, and giving it a yank, Alejo lifted it and carried it across the room to another table; then he sat down because something had pulled loose inside his stomach and it was painful for him to walk. He worked the whole day, and the next morning he went to see a doctor who informed him that he had ruptured himself.

In a few weeks he went to Flower Memorial Hospital where he was put in a room with a tremendous, sunny view of Central Park. During his stay the doctors conducted the usual examinations and were amazed how battered his heart, liver, and lungs had become. The hernia was secondary; suddenly he had to lose seventy-five pounds! And no smoking! And no salty or fried foods! And no sweets! And no drinking! They cut him open, retied certain muscles, and left him in that sunny room to recuperate and memorize the lists and lists of requirements they had set for him.

During the hospital stay, which lasted six weeks, Alejo lost interest in buying the general store. The suddenness of his hospitalization with all its costly bills reminded him how much he needed his union insurance benefits. There was also a pension he could look forward to, and social security if he remained working at the hotel for another five years. Above all, he would miss his friends from the hotel. Cooped up in the hospital room he grew nostalgic for work and his pals. Suddenly the idea of being away from them, and for that matter from his friends in the neighborhood, made a move from the city to buy a store seem unpleasant. One afternoon when Eliseo called to say that the real estate manager had found another interested buyer, Alejo acted as if the store had not meant that much to begin with, and told Eliseo to forget about it.

Alejo spent his time watching TV, reading hot Spanish girly magazines like *Pimienta*, flirting with the nurses, and seeing visitors. Everyone in the family visited him. Horacio and his wife saw him one evening, Mercedes and a friend on another, Hector in the early morning, before he went to school. After two weeks in the hospital, Alejo looked great. There was redness in his cheeks and he had lost twenty pounds. He still looked enormous as he sat up bare-chested and hairy in the hospital bed, his lower abdomen covered with thick bandages. He was happy as a mouse when Hector came into the room carrying a bag of candy, but Hector was cold, aloof.

Alejo was laughing. "You know what the doctor told me?"

Hector shook his head.

"He told me no more fooling around!"

"How do you feel?"

"Good, but it hurts like a burn."

And then he motioned Hector closer and peeled down some of the top bandages to show him where the doctors had cut. There were two deep, dark-red ridges coming up to his navel, all stitched up. "Pssssssh, but it hurts. Me duele mucho."

"Well, it'll go away," Hector told him. And then, as Alejo asked him about school and life at home and Mercedes, Hector went deaf. No matter what he was asked, Hector answered "Fine," and then he said, "Look, I gotta go. See you later, all right?" And then, as he was about to leave the room, Alejo said, "Chico, aren't you going to give me a besito? For your Pop!" Hector came over and gave Alejo a light, cautious kiss on the neck and didn't like it or trust the situation, as if Alejo's calmness was a trap and he was suddenly going to blow up or see ghosts or cry and slam him into the wall. Alejo took hold of Hector's arms, but Hector found himself saying, "Ah come on, Pop, enough is enough," and he left right after that. It was his one visit and it was enough.

2

Hector was tired, tired of being a Cuban cook's son and hearing people say, "Oh you look just like Alejo!" Look like Alejo? It made him cringe. He felt like a freak, a hunchback, a man with a deformed face. Like Alejo? At least Alejo had his people, the Cubans, his brothers, but Hector was out in the twilight zone, trying to crawl out of his skin and go somewhere else, be someone else. But he could do nothing to change himself to his own satisfaction. Anything he did, like growing his hair long or dressing like a hippy, was an affectation, layered over his true skin like hospital tape. Hector always felt as if he were in costume, his true nature unknown to others and perhaps even to himself. He was part "Pop," part Mercedes; part Cuban, part American—all wrapped tightly inside a skin in which he sometimes could not move.

He would go and get lost. Sometimes down to the rich neighborhoods, West End Avenue and Riverside Drive, and down to the park where he sometimes went with a red-sunburst, cowboy-looking guitar that he had stolen out of a music store window. He had just pulled the guitar off its stand and gone running off with it. If he had been caught, he would have gone to reform school like the deaf mute Mary's kids, but he didn't get caught.

One day, when he was sitting in the park under a tree, strumming a chord, some rich kids who were high on acid came by and asked him if he wanted to come to a party with them, and he said yes. They always had parties when their parents went away on weekends, they said. They would take LSD and eat opium and swallow pills. Hector went into various apartments, with white bearskin rugs, books everywhere, African instruments on the walls, color TVs, and big mirrors at the ends of halls, two bathrooms, maids trying to ignore everything. He took drugs with the others in order to be a friend. Young pretty girls turned into wild flowers and cats. They pulled down their panties and hopped on top of pianos, shook their loins and showed off their parts, while the piano strings hummed up their long slender legs into a softness that gave off scents like perfume from another world. They made him insatiably hungry, until he wanted to eat and taste them, all the beautiful flower children kissing and fucking and eating grapes and ice cream and brownies in the kitchen and in the closets. Fine and naked zombies walking around and fluttering their hands like butterflies. Girls in the corner, naked, braiding their long hair and moaning each time the sunshine warmed their necks and the smalls of their backs.

And Hector would sit there trying to maintain his cool, but all around him corpses were hiding in the closets, their eyes looking out from the dark. He could always hear Mercedes's high pitched voice calling him: "Hector! Hector!" And he would swear that Alejo was in the next room, even though he was far away. Then there was the problem of his own body, the Cuban-diseased body with its micróbios and a heart thumping loudly, ready to burst. Looking in a mirror, he would see Alejo's face and feel the micróbios festering inside him, and hear in the halls, children running by like fleeting sprites, like Mercedes, until someone tapped his shoulder and drew his attention away, or some pretty naked girl, with the most concerned expression, passed a rose under his nostrils, as if to bring him back.

Sometimes he came home in this state of mind, and then he would become anxious trying to avoid Alejo who, in those days after leaving the hospital, wanted to win back his friendship. As soon as Hector came home he went to bed. One time there was a knock at his door.

"Who is it?"

"Yo," Alejo said. "It's me."

"Okay, okay, what do you want?"

"I came to bring you something." Alejo pushed open the door and turned on the light. Holding a box, he looked at Hector most strangely, puzzled. "Is something wrong with you? You never go to sleep this early."

"Nothing."

"Well, I've brought you something." And he put the box on the bed. Inside were a pair of white sneakers, just like his.

"These are for you."

"Why?"

"Because you're my son."

"Okay, okay. Thanks, Pop."

Then Alejo tried to give him a kiss, but Hector turned away.

After Alejo left, Hector stayed up thinking about him and the sneakers and about looking like him. Hector couldn't sleep.

The rich kids' fathers were doctors and lawyers and book publishers. When they asked about Alejo's occupation, Hector always told them "chef," as Horacio always told people. But he was only a cook, and he smelled of meat. Hector got sneakers, but his friends were given stereos and sent away to resortlike colleges and to Europe. Hector went to Coney Island. So when Alejo asked, "Why don't you look at me? I try to give you things," Hector answered him roughly and demanded more. When he finally graduated from high school, which he had hated, he demanded a cash present, one hundred dollars, which Alejo managed to give him. Then Hector blew it on a girl in a bar. And even that wasn't enough. Nothing could equal the big parties, trips, and cash of his West End and Riverside friends.

Hector came to a point when he paid no attention to Alejo.

"Would you take a walk with me today?"

"No Pop, I'm busy."

And yet Alejo continued to try. Each time he went out, he returned with something for Hector. A pair of socks, identical to his own; a T-shirt, a sports shirt, or pants identical to his own.

"Come on, Pop," Hector always said. "I'm my own man."

But he wasn't. He wanted to get out of his skin and go somewhere. He was tired of the neighborhood: the hoods, the racists, the snotty college kids, the dope fiends, the booze, the drugs. He was tired of getting drunk with his neighborhood pals, tired of being high, tired of being like a Cuban Quasimodo. He wanted to go somewhere, but where?

One day in the late spring he started to think about Aunt Buita in Miami. She still sent him presents every Christmas and wrote the same letters each year: "I miss you very much and dream of the days when you will come to see me." So Hector badgered Alejo until he called Buita to arrange a visit that summer.

The very day Hector left for Miami, he said two words to Alejo, and passed much of his time pacing his bedroom, impatient to go. He looked in the mirror; he was the hip blimp wearing a gray flannel jacket and black turtleneck. "Don't you think you'll be hot in Miami?" asked Alejo.

"No." That was one of the two words.

And he had loaded himself down with a guitar and with a stack of records, rock 'n' roll—"heepie music," as Buita would call it.

"Don't you think you're taking too much?" Alejo asked him.

"So?" And that was the second word.

There were kids playing ball in the street and some neighbors waiting with Alejo on the stoop when the car came around. Alejo was wearing black pants, a belt that had been stretched very far, so that its holes were like oriental eyes, a T-shirt, and comfortable sneakers that gave him spring when he rushed to the car to get an embrace and kiss from Hector. He rapped at the window. Hector moved inside and waved him away. There were so many people around.

"Come on, I'm your papa," said Alejo, with his head so far inside the car that his slightly bristled cheek was right in front of Hector. "Come on, I'm your papa," he said again. But Hector ignored him, and Alejo went back to the stoop, waving like a mad man as the car finally drove away.

3

Alberto Piñon, Buita's bandleader-contractor husband, had aged grace-fully. His white hair was parted down the middle, and he had a suave moustache and clear blue eyes that were still the eyes of a young child. He was a calm man who attended to his responsibilities in an orderly fashion. He carried around a thermos of Cuban coffee and rum. He owned two Cadillacs and had taken Buita on a cross-country journey to Disneyland—not once, but twice! He owned a large house with central air conditioning, three remote-control color TV sets, a swim-ming pool, and a white baby grand piano on which, in his spare time, he composed simple melodies in the mode of the Cuban songwriter Ernesto Lecuona. He had thousands of dollars in the bank and had built houses everywhere in the Miami area. Looking over swampland, he would put his hand on Hector's shoulder and say things like, "One day I'm going to build a huge development for Cubans here."

He took Hector for long drives into the country, down to Key West or up north to the Hialeah brothels where he visited his "regular little girl, sweet as a spring peach." He didn't smell of meat. He was clean. He took showers, dried himself frantically, and then covered himself with clouds of talcum powder. He owned a huge gold watch with all kinds of dials. He had perfect white teeth. He was a member of the American Legion, and belonged to a weekly canasta club. In his garage he had pictures of himself seated at a table with Caesar Romero and Errol Flynn. He seemed to have gotten around. In stores he never looked at the price of anything, and not giving a damn about God, he ate meat on Fridays and did as he pleased when it came to church. He liked playing patrón. One night he took Hector to see a stripper in a nightclub. She was a tanned beauty with a perfect athletic body. "Lolita, the Cuban Goddess" stripped down to a mesh nylon body stocking and then tore it off and flung it out into the audience. She had gold-dyed pubic hair. Flowers covered her nipples, and glitters made two circles on her thighs. She danced for a time and then took a pack of cigarettes and shoved it up her vagina. Then she danced and wriggled and pulled the cigarettes out one by one, giving them to the men in the audience. For a finale, she placed a long candle up her vagina with the wick end lit and sticking out. As she lay down, men in the audience came forward and lit their cigarettes. Then music, curtain, and she was gone.

"You like it here, huh, boy?" Alberto asked him.

But Hector's time with Alberto was not always fun. To acquaint Hector with his business, Alberto took him out to a construction site and put Hector to work with a pick and shovel, digging ditches for thick, corrugated foundation cables. Hector did not mind. He enjoyed the dirty stories the men told during lunch time and liked the idea of working with Cubans who did not fall down. And he was flabbergasted one evening when, after work, Alberto took him to a secret meeting of Cubans who wanted to overthrow Castro. The men drank and reminisced about the old days, hissed like snakes with the pain of nostalgia, pointed at maps of Cuba. There was a discussion about landing spots for invasion along the southern coast of Cuba, a discussion of weapons. Then a tray of sandwiches and coffee was brought out, and dues were collected. Some of the Cubans considered the secret group to be like a social club; others were dead serious. Many of them, including Buita's "son," Ki-ki Delgado, were survivors of the Bay of Pigs invasion. They talked about killing "the son-of-a-bitch-over-there" and about the crucial mistakes that had been made because of Kennedy and Fulbright. Although Hector said not a word in the discussions, he felt himself part of an inner circle, around strong Cuban men.

Hector liked being away from New York City, in a clean place. Downtown Miami was slick, neon everywhere. He went to a movie house near Calle Ocho and saw a film about vampires. Hector liked the Cuban sandwiches, the air conditioning, the modern buses. There were no street gangs, derelicts, or junkies. No broken glass. He liked being near Cubans who did not stagger down halls; he felt protected. Strolling along the white sidewalks, under coconut and orange trees, he daydreamed about living this good life. Aunt Margarita, Ki-ki's mother, said that Alberto and Buita would buy Hector a car and send him to a nice school if he ever decided to stay with them in Miami;

he would be able to go swimming every day and go to the movies at night, and he could find himself a nice, wholesome girlfriend to marry and have many children. Here, in Miami, he stood at the edge of the water, thinking that Cuba was only 140 miles away.

As part of her scheme to keep Hector in Miami, Buita often recounted to him the crimes of his mother and the Santinio family's trials with her, while at the same time she bought him everything he wanted, promised him the world. Hector felt as if his eyes had been gouged out by her, as if his brain had collapsed. She was getting to him. He was believing her. "At night," she told him, "I have dreams about your poor father. Oh how he calls to me in his dreams, crying, suffering so...and you know why."

Then the old story again: "Ah, your mother...when she married him, and it turned out that he wasn't rich, she told everyone that she would make him suffer. He had his chance to come with me and Alberto but she wanted him to stay in that city with the lowlifes! With her kind! Not the fine Cubans you find here. Here he could have made something of himself, but now all he is is a cook. I thank God my father isn't alive to see that. Do you know how much time I spend wondering how your Papa can take it, being nothing and working with nothing and having nothing in the world...and in the richest country...and all because of that woman?

"I know he drinks. He drinks because he knows he has nothing and will go nowhere. He could have been many things, but now he's a cook, and he takes a drink. Not because the work is demeaning but because he comes home and she's waiting to take the money he earns from his pockets and because she ridicules him. Of course he takes a drink, who in Cuba would have ever thought these things would happen to him?

"When we came to New York, of course we tried to bring him into the finest Cuban circles in the city. We would take him to the grand ballrooms, where the cream of Cuban society gathered. The few times we took your mother, she made a scene. Of course your father was going to dance with someone else, how else could he have fun? Or come to know the important people? We didn't want to spoil his chances so we left your mother at home, but when we came back she always accused him of desertion, the poor man, just when he was trying to improve himself."

At this point in the story, Buita would pull Hector close and hug him, giving him many kisses. Then she would start weeping.

"And when you were born I was worried for you, because I knew all about the crazy things your mother had done to your poor brother, things too horrible to tell you—but she poisoned him once, and I saved him, you know, took him to the hospital and saved him. And do you know what, child? That woman never thanked me, even though someone's death is the worst thing in the world. And when you were born, I told Alberto, 'Oh no, she's going to do the same things over again.' I warned your father and told him 'Watch that woman, she's up to no good.' And I ask you, child, what happened? *You almost died!* Her thoughts were so scrambled that she couldn't even take care of you well enough to keep you in good health. You should have seen us crying here, the day your father called to tell us what had happened because of her negligence. No intelligent woman lets someone stay ill for so long and does nothing about it. It was her fault, no matter what she says to you, dear, it was her. She only thinks about herself, which is why you got so ill and almost died.

"We were ready to go to your funeral, but thank God you're here. We used to call up your mother but she never said a word to you about these calls, did she? Do you remember? Remember how your aunt sent you all those presents? And why? Because we love you so much and with a love like a mother's love, not like your mother, who used to take a look at you and feel disgust for you and contempt for your father..."

Buita was tricking Hector, trying to feed his antagonisms toward the old life. But she needed to do more to win him. She set up a lure: a blond Cuban girl named Cindy, who suddenly began to visit in the afternoons.

Cindy was a beautiful girl. She always sunbathed in the back yard, showing off her body in a tight black one-piece bathing suit. On hot days when the cracks of the sidewalk sent up whisps of steam, her skin would soon be covered with beads of sweat as she lay in the sun. Then she would come into the air-conditioned house, eat a snack, and inquire about the soap operas that Buita had been faithfully following all her days in America. Then, to torment Hector, she would put on some Beatle records and shimmy on top of a piano bench, the bathing suit pulling tightly on her buttocks. As he watched Cindy twisting her body all around, Hector wanted to sink his teeth into her flesh. Each day she seemed yummier and yummier. But even though she wore the tightest bathing suit that showed off her "wares," she was a virgin, so pure and Cuban, like the golden honey she swirled around in her mouth after lunch.

She was part of a dream. Always so cheerful and sure of herself, she shimmied through her days, while Hector remained quiet, shy, and gloomy. In his fantasies Hector became more like Cindy, part of the "good life" that Buita was offering him. Cindy dancing, Cindy in the cool air conditioning, memories of Alejo's melancholia on days when Hector ran from him, death and screaming, and heart attacks...the thought of returning to New York made him ready to explode. He wanted to tear off Cindy's bathing suit, go to a nice wholesome Dade County Community College. He kept thinking of Cindy's mouth and nice clean sidewalks and the clusters of trees around the park and Cindy's luscious hips and good productive Cubans everywhere and Cindy's tongue, soft and moist, gleaming in her mouth when she talked; the opportunity of joining Alberto's business and Cindy's cleavage and dear Aunt Buita and good Aunt Margarita and Cindy's plump thigh...

Above all, to Hector, Cindy was a nice, clean, Cuban girl with a modest, gold crucifix around her neck. He had believed in God once and was ready to go that route again, if necessary, to finding purification. He wanted to be cured of his sense of illnesses: inadequacy, stupidity, obesity, ignorance. He wanted to go to bed and wake up a Cuban in the Havana of 1922, run into Alejo as a boy. But he would settle for Miami. He would believe in God and all the things good people believe in. He would court Cindy, float in the clouds, get married, daydream watching the ocean, run off to a little Cuban-

American hideaway, fuck her on top of a piano bench and on a big silken bed with heart-shaped pillows, have children, and shimmy to the Beatles and boogaloo to soul and surf music.

The truth was, Buita was a close friend of Cindy's mother and had presented her with the appealing scenario of a future wedding and a good start in life. So Cindy's mother sent her over to Buita's house. Cindy, who liked the swimming pool and the air conditioning, did not really like Hector. When he tried to impress her by pulling a book from the shelf and pretending to read, Cindy would smile. But her smile didn't mean friendship. She had already gone through her "reading thing," as she called it, before high school. And when Hector suggested, "Why don't you come over when Buita's not around?" her nervous laughter didn't mean she wanted to. Not at all.

4

On the evening of the moon landing, Cindy and her mother came to Buita's house to watch the event on their huge twenty-five inch color TV. And that night Alejo called Miami from a new telephone he had had installed in the bedroom. He decided to call after Mercedes had told him about a bad dream in which Buita came at her with a knife. Waking in a nervous state, Mercedes began to worry about Hector. "Don't be worried," he told her. "Hector is fine." Alejo leaned against the wall, watched Neil Armstrong on the television, listened to the clicking of the long distance lines.

Buita picked up. "Buita! How is everything, sister?"

Buita and Alejo spoke for about ten minutes, Buita enumerating Hector's activities and hinting at a romance between Hector and Cindy.

"How good," Alejo said. "Let me talk to the boy."

When Buita called Hector to the phone, he was annoyed. Each time Cindy moved in her chair, the hem of her skirt lifted higher and higher, and Hector could not take his eyes off her.

"Your papa wants to speak to you."

Hector cringed, and his pale face turned red. He shook his head as if to wave Alejo's call away, but finally he went to the phone.

"Yeah?"

Alejo leaned against the wall. He was smiling. He was wearing checkered pants and sneakers just like the ones he had given to Hector. His elbow rested on the armadio. He was happy to speak with Hector. "How are you? Did you see the moon? That's something, isn't it? So how are you? Are you happy to hear from your papa? You know I miss you, boy." He kept speaking, but Hector was not really listening. He was paying attention to the television noises and thinking about Cindy. "You know I miss you boy...ai chico, are you there?"

"Yeah, Pop." But Hector did not say another word.

"Okay, good-bye, son," Alejo said finally and then Mercedes, with her screechy, high-pitched voice, got on the phone. She asked him to think of her often and told him to take care of himself. She said, "Your papa misses you," so often that he got tired of hearing it, and then he gave Buita the phone.

Hector did not think about Alejo as the days passed. If he wasn't following Cindy around, he would often take walks into the fields where the sunflowers grew tall, in the steam of the Miami afternoons. A few times he caught a bus downtown and went to the old-Havana style cafeterias. There he sipped sweet juices and smiled at the pretty gypsy-looking waitress who seemed tired of life, while the Cubans around him, old-timers, carried on their conversations. Sometimes they looked at him as if he were a tourist, definitely out of place, even though he tapped his feet to the jukebox and even though he nodded when they looked over. They resumed their talk again as if he were not there. Then he began to think about what he would need in this world to court the waitress, for example, and to make her smile the *Cubanita* way, as if she had just spent an exhausting night with him. What could Hector do to be more like the suave, lanky, young Cubans, smooth and untroubled, purposeful in their ways, gliding down the sidewalks? Everywhere he went in downtown Miami he saw them, men in bright-colored guayaberas and women in sleeveless dresses. Their Spanish flowed into his ears: "Hey Ramon, how did that chick turn out for you?" "She was hot, I jammed her and she screamed and her pussy just kept getting hotter and hotter!" "This is my daughter, Innocencia. She just completed her first communion. Innocencia, this is my old friend Maria. I knew her back when in Cuba." "Come to the house and we'll have a little party." "Rudolfo is looking for a job, he just got in from Spain. He used to be a mechanic in Havana, but they put him in the army. He's got a wife and two kids and doesn't care what you can pay him. He needs the work." "And you should see, for the marvel of your life, Disneyland. I'm telling you Consuelo, the marvels of American science are there! This country has more good than any other in the world!" "...and every time I fucked her, she wanted the old stick again."

But as he sat there in the cafeteria or in any other shop, the owners always asked "What would you like?" in English, or if they could not speak English, there was always a Cuban around to ask the same question in English for them. And Hector would play the American-American. When he did ask for something in Spanish, the response was always, "You speak good Spanish, for an American."

"My parents were from Oriente."

Looking him over, not believing a word of it, they would reply, "Oh yes?" But they didn't return to make more conversation, as he wanted; they just slapped down the bill.

Walking along Calle Ocho, he would think about what he should have said to prove his authenticity: "Look, my mother believes in the spirits and the Devil and Jesus Christ. I know about Santa Barbara! And the Virgin of Cobre! I know about the white cassava and yucca and arroz con pollo y lechón asado... Machado and Maximo Gomez... and my father came from San Pedro, Oriente province, home province of Fidel Castro, Batista, and Desi Arnaz. My father's a worker and Santiago is fifty miles south of Holguín. I know about the shadows and magic, how you court nice girls and get married, and drink only with the men, and the women are your slaves, and you look to the future and never fear death. You have the Day of the Three Kings instead of Christmas as the time for giving presents. You drink rum and don't take LSD, you walk straight and do not fall down. You don't cry and are very strong, and one gaze from your eyes makes women faint. Your sexes are enormous, the women are your slaves..." and on and on, until he felt himself fading away.

Soon he was thinking how good dear Aunt Buita was to him. She was offering him a life: college, a car, friends. If he stayed, he wouldn't have to go home and look at Alejo and Mercedes. He could forget everything—the medicines, the arguments, having no money. He wouldn't have to get drunk with his old buddies. But he wanted more. To crawl out of his skin, get a tan, get healthy, be Cuban, forget the shit—marry Cindy.

Hector started going places with Cindy at night. Buita paid for these excursions. One night they went to the Zebra Disco. The hall was decorated to look like an enormous Tarzan-style hut with strobe lights and stuffed zebras and zebra skins everywhere. There was a thick haze of purple smoke in the air, a refreshment counter where pizza, hamburgers, and Cuban sandwiches (pork, swiss cheese, turkey, ham on hero bread) were sold. The music was by the Supremes, Beatles, Four Tops, Rolling Stones. Cindy was wearing a pair of tight white slacks, and a striped halter top. She was dancing in absentia. She was standing in front of Hector but did not seem to be there. She was watching colors on a screen on the opposite wall change forms. She was chewing gum. Hector felt out of place, and in his dreams he was taking Cindy out on the beach and, under the moonlight, fucking her in the sand the way Horacio used to fuck girls under the boardwalk at Far Rockaway Beach and Coney Island. He daydreamed about finding starfish in the cleft of her bosom and about floating-in-water-love with her—kisses, gropes, all lust—but even while he dreamed this she was digging someone else: a sharp-looking Cuban a few feet away who was watching her and smiling. One second she was dancing with Hector and the next she was shaking her winsome hips for the other guy. She was giving off wisps of orchid scents and showing off her big white teeth and speaking to the other guy in Spanish.

"Who you with?"

"It doesn't matter."

"All right! Vaya!"

Hector was trying to be cool as Cindy and her new partner started to dance. Hector moved closer to watch them, but they moved away. This went on for two or three songs, and then Cindy and the Cuban went off to get a hamburger. Hector waited about a half hour and then went to the refreshment counter. There was a bamboo fence covered with fake orchids and ferns and a few rubber palms around the counter. She was sitting with the Cuban behind one of the trees, making out. Alejo would have been able to sweep her off her feet, Hector knew. At least Alejo should have taught him something about women. He thought of the way all the women gave Alejo the onceover whenever he walked into a room, how they all turned to look at him. He put Alejo out of his mind, walked back out onto the dance floor, and started to dance. He did a few turns like a spinning mannequin and then felt a fist slamming into his chest. Someone hit him, but no one was there. He danced again and, boom! there was the same punch. His arm had a spasm, and then the spasm went away. He sat down, off to the side, drank a Coca-Cola. He felt like a "lame," as the neighborhood kids used to call him when Mercedes would not let him out of the house. He waited on the bench for a half hour and then stood up against the wall. He watched the dancers, Cindy among them, as they swung around. Everybody was dancing but him. Some of Cindy's friends came over and pulled him onto the dance floor, saying, "Don't you know how to have a good time?"

So he started to dance again. Then he thought he heard his name being called out through the loudspeaker. "Hector Santinio. Hector Santinio come to the office." He went to the office. There was a phone call for him. "Margarita's coming to get you," Buita told him. But why? She told him nothing more. For a half hour he waited in front of the Zebra on a striped bench, and then Margarita came and they drove home. She was chainsmoking and looked very tired, as tired as she had looked in the days of her dead husband's illness.

"Where are we going, Tia?" Hector asked.

Margarita did not answer. At the house he packed. In the kitchen he ate a quick sandwich, bacon and lettuce and tomato on toasted rye bread. He kissed Buita good-bye. They drove to the airport. Margarita and Hector flew to New York. They did not say very much. In New York everything was quiet in the apartment. Paula and another neighbor were in the living room. A big fan was blowing the window drapery. Horacio was in the kitchen. It was very early in the morning. "Come on, let's go," Horacio said to Hector. His car was parked outside. They drove downtown to a square building and walked through a hall of tables. The hall was as large as an airport hangar. Their footsteps made echoes. They waited in a small room, facing a window booth with curtains. When a light came on they pressed a button, the window curtains parted. A table lifted into view. On it rested Alejo Santinio in a black shroud, eyes shut, arms at his side, dead.

Final Evening, 1969

1

The night before he died, Alejo Santinio could not sleep well. He kept waking up, gasping for air. There were no breezes in the room. It was a hot night and he kept getting up for a glass of water. At five o'clock in the morning, time for him to get ready to go to work at the hotel, he dressed before the mirror, brushed his thick curly hair, went to work, returned at three in the afternoon, tried to nap for a few hours, could not breathe, thought of Hector, was hungry, thought of Mercedes and Horacio, and of Cuba, and his job, and money and perhaps opening a store one day after all, and of the USA, ate steak with onions and thin French fries for dinner, read the newspaper and then, at 5:30 P.M., wearing his checkered pants went to his second job. For the last few years he had been working a dinner shift as a cook at the University Faculty Club restaurant, which was located on the roof of a tall neighborhood building.

According to one of the restaurant workers, he was "in a good mood." He was attending to a large pot of vegetable soup, stirring it with an immense ladle, when he turned to this man and said, "It's hot in here, isn't it?" And so the man opened the window. But Alejo was still too hot. Heat came from the ovens and from the steaming pots. "Why don't you get some fresh air?" suggested one of the waitresses. Alejo put down his ladle and went out onto the roof. He could see all the neighborhood, Harlem to the east and the river to the west. But Cuba was very far away. He could not see it, leaning at the railing and looking far away... The waitress, who had watched him from a roof doorway, later said that Alejo looked at the clear sky and took a few deep breaths. He was perspiring. When he noticed her, he smiled and nodded in his friendly way and then leaned against the railing again and took a few more breaths and then sighed as the artery inside his head abruptly burst and flooded his brain and sent a shock through his body making his right arm shake. He felt the spasm in his arm, looked around with a confused expression, and then fell down. It took five kitchen workers to carry him inside, where he was laid on the tile floor, black and white, just like his shoes. The waitress called Mercedes, who at the moment of his death was peeking out the window.

It was six o'clock. Horacio was pulling out of a McDonald's parking lot in Brooklyn when his arm started to shake. This shaking made him nervous enough to call Mercedes an hour later. By then one of the neighbors was in the apartment, trying to comfort her. She was not speaking. Her eyes were glazed. She would turn her head toward no one, whisper as if someone were there. Paula had heard her scream when the waitress told her the news. How do you tell someone that? When Mercedes heard the news she said, "What, no me digas eso? What did you say?" And the waitress repeated, "Your husband is dead," and Mercedes said, "What?" and sat down and then screamed *Dios mío* like a siren, and that left her without a voice. Then she became unable to hear or understand anyone. She lay down on the bed and curled up in fetal position and began to cry, the sadness and terror pouring out of her. Neighbors attended to details—calling Buita in Miami and Luisa in New Jersey, making coffee and cooking food, trying to calm Mercedes down when she started to shake, trying to make her respond to questions when she could not speak.

When Horacio arrived, he had no patience for Mercedes and left her in the care of the neighbors. He had to go to the faculty club restaurant. He got there and saw the large army blanket spread out in the middle of the kitchen floor. Under the blanket was Alejo. Around him workers were still cooking and rushing around and doing their best to get along, because the manager did not want to close the restaurant down. Horacio froze. He felt like a helpless fool standing over Alejo's body and moving out of the way as waitresses went by with platters of hamburgers and french fries and onion rings, salad, and Coke. He stood there looking down, then jingled change in his pocket and looked out the windows, asking, "When is he coming?"—meaning the medical examiner. Then he knelt down, pulled off the blanket, and looked at his father's face.

Horacio ran his fingers through Alejo's hair, touched his ears, his unmoving face. He tried to lift up Alejo's head, it was so heavy, and then he said, "A cook..." He started to think about Alejo's original ambitions or the way things worked out for him without the little store in the country or a color TV set or a pot to piss in, lying there, his head flooded with blood, when just a short time before he was strong enough to shake walls, punch and slap, to frighten the hell out of his children, strong enough to leave a little hick town in eastern Cuba and take an adventurous woman with him. But for what? To work all his life and then be laid down on a dirty kitchen floor? He didn't like to think about it because then he'd say fuck this fuckin' world, so when he looked down at Alejo's face he thought instead, "At least now he's peaceful." But everyone says that, even when they feel they're looking at a piece of stone, something for the worms, a stuffed man in a museum.

Horacio remained with Alejo for three hours, and then the medical examiner came, a tired Jewish man who carried a black leather bag. To declare Alejo dead he listened to the chest with his stethoscope for a moment and then opened the right eyelid with his thumb; the eye was like a cracked piece of glass.

The evening of Alejo's death, Luisa and her son-in-law Pedro drove in from New Jersey. Luisa tried to soothe Mercedes by rocking her in her arms, but Mercedes kept saying, "Now I'm going to join him," and then she would faint in Luisa's arms, and her pulse would seem to have stopped. Quiet for a while, she would then start screaming. Sometimes her nose began to bleed, her arms trembled and flailed as she insisted over and over again, "I didn't make him that way! God, why did you send me this man?" She wo ld shake and spit and cross herself so much that finally Luisa took her to the hospital, where the doctors shot her full of tranquilizers and kept her in a room for the night. When she returned the next afternoon, her skin was so pale and the look in her eyes, like those of a lizard, was so stony and glazed that Hector could not recognize her.

Suddenly Mercedes was the greatest invalid of all time, oblivious to everything around her. Horacio was suddenly in the position of patriarch, and he had to be strong. When Mercedes would not eat or lift a finger, he would take hold of her and shake her arms.

"You're not going to ignore this situation. You have to be here." And then in an unpleasant slip, he said, "After all, you did that to him, you killed him."

And that started her on a long string of denials. Now it took Mary, Luisa, and Paula to calm her down. As they clustered around Mercedes in the living room, Horacio and Hector went down to the funeral parlor to make the arrangements. Cousin Pedro made phone calls to inform people that Alejo was dead.

By the afternoon there was a constant flow of visitors through the apartment. The first to come were Alejo's drinking buddies from up and down the street, drunk but not too drunk, so much in sorrow that no amount of alcohol could undo the forlornness. These men wept irrepressibly, but without embarrassment. They made solemn promises to Mercedes: "Look, he'll come back." The same promise Luisa had made to Mercedes: "He'll come back the way Papa did. Don't you remember those ghosts in Cuba when we were children?"

His old drinking buddies drank some more and went outside, stood in front of the building, and told everyone Alejo was dead. One by one, neighbors came downstairs to offer their help. The worst shaken was Mr. Kent, who had ridden to work that very morning with Alejo. He began to drink, unusual for him because he reserved alcohol for the holidays. On Christmas and Thanksgiving, Mr. Kent would come downstairs and Alejo would get Mr. Kent, who was of New England Puritan stock, completely soaked in whiskey. Mr. Kent would sit in the kitchen, happily rapping his fingers on the table, as if hearing a song. He came downstairs now bawling and shaking his head. And he got so drunk that he could not leave his bed for the next two days.

When it was time to get ready for the wake, Hector complained that he had no black shoes. Aunt Luisa came up with an old pair of Alejo's.

"Dios mío," she declared, "I haven't seen these things since Cuba."

After some urging, Hector tried them on. The shoes were much too large, but they started to close in around his feet, and as the day went on they gripped him tighter and tighter.

Horacio dressed up in a black suit and put on the ring that he had removed from Alejo's hand. Then he kept pacing back and forth down the hall to the bathroom, copiously urinating even though he had hardly anything to drink. Smoking cigarette after cigarette, he kept having the impulse to wash his hands. He spent the morning looking everywhere for ways to make use of himself, as befitting the new head of a household.

And Mercedes? Helped by Luisa to dress, she stood before the bedroom mirror, staring at herself. Carefully she placed a medallion bearing the image of the Virgin of Cobre, a recent gift from Alejo, around her neck. Luisa was brushing Mercedes's hair and pulling lint from her dress. As she looked at herself, Mercedes kept wondering, "Who is that woman in the mirror looking so grieved?" over and over again, until it was time for the wake and she was led away.

2

The problem was that his body, stretched out in the coffin, was so imposing. Immense to begin with, in that coffin Alejo looked the size of two normal men. He was laid out in the blue suit he had purchased for Horacio's wedding. He was wearing a white shirt, a new tie, no socks, no shoes—his feet were hidden from view. His mouth was stuffed with cotton and his cheeks thudded with the touch of the hand. His eyelids were closed tightly and felt like leather. There was a lotion on his face that gave it a healthy glow. He might have just come from a walk in the park or from watching an exciting cowboy movie on the television. His hair was wavy and nicely curled, thick and full, like a young man's hair. His hands were folded one on the other. He did not look drunk.

Inside the coffin there were no birds or radios or televisions. There were no parks or shady trees or tables covered with foods that are bad for the heart, no whiskey or rum. There were no sea creatures or gently crawling caterpillars or lilac lotion bottles on a shelf. There was no Cuba, no San Pedro, no musicians strolling on Sunday afternoons, no New York, no beautiful women, no Coney Island, no sunsets, no stars. There was no morning, no night, no chilliness, no heat. There were no sweets inside the coffin, no music. And they were not in the coffin. Horacio and Hector were standing on either side. Calmer now, Horacio kept sighing and repeating, "It's hard to believe he's dead. At least it took a lot to kill him."

But Hector wasn't ready for this, and he did not really believe it. The room smelled of eucalyptus, flowers, and candles. The walls, the wood of the coffin, were cold to him. Alejo was not in this world, but he wasn't dead. Hector kept thinking, "I should have kissed him one last time." He remembered how Alejo had leaned into the car when he left for Florida, and how he had denied his father a kiss. Now that Alejo was dead, he became worried that Alejo's ghost would come after him.

Hundreds of people came to the wake. People kept coming up to Horacio and Hector, saying, "From now on, when I see you on the street, I am going to think of your papa." Everyone came by: neighborhood kids, priests, people from far away, Eliseo Hernandez, and other Cubans from all over the city. They came to take a look at him and left shaking their heads. For three days processions moved back and forth between the funeral home and the apartment, and there was always someone to say, "After so many years in this country, he didn't even own a car." People came forward, patted their backs, offered sympathy, departed never to be seen again. Diego, Alejo's co-worker, showed up dead drunk and stood for an hour whispering into the coffin. The union reps showed up. Then the family doctor. Women getting old but still curvaceous, who had probably been Alejo's girls at one time, came in, wept into their frilly handkerchiefs, and went out again.

195

In a chair, Luisa held Mercedes tightly. "Don't worry," she kept saying, "he had the sacrament." Meaning the priest had said words over his dead body. The female cousins and women from the neighborhood sat with Mercedes and tried to calm her down whenever she had a vision.

"He's moving! He's moving! My God!" And then she would almost faint.

For three days, they stood near the body. Alejo kept changing. He was good and kindly, and then the image changed so that he was pounding the walls. He seemed at peace. He seemed to weep. For Horacio, the worst had passed. He saw a tired man finally at rest. But Hector saw a frightened man who wanted one last embrace but died with his arm shaking. That was the detail that stood out in his mind.

"Are you going to kiss him when all this is over?"

"I don't know," Hector answered Horacio.

"You will, if you loved him."

At night sleep was not easy. Mercedes walked through the apartment, saying his name, as if his ghost would soon come. There was drinking in the kitchen, continuous phone calls, Hector had nightmares. Horacio kept trying to shout Mercedes back into the real world. Aunt Margarita could not sleep at all. Exhausted, she would sit with Hector in his room.

"When this is done with, child," she said in a low voice, "Buita will let you stay with her, and then you'll be happy. It you want to go. No one is forcing, you understand. But it would make her so happy, and you would be away from your mother... Oh your mother's good, but Buita would treat you so well."

But Hector had decided to stay. As crazy as she could be, Mercedes was still his mother. "Tell Buita I will come and see her again one day."

Margarita touched his face. She looked just like Alejo. She exhaled smoke from her cigarette, kissed his forehead, and then left the room. Even though she was not there, Hector could not sleep: an afterimage of her face, so sad, like Alejo's, lingered in the room.

The three days came and went, one no different from the other.

Sometimes, at the funeral home, the body in the coffin moved; that was all. People touched him. In the apartment there were all the old smells, of the meat and his cigarettes, persisting in the air. His shoes and clothes were laid out by Mercedes. Pictures of him were out. The contents of his drawers were dumped out: union cards, Havana cigars, old letters from Buita and Margarita, an old passport dated June 10, 1943, a folded-up chef's hat that smelled like his kitchen, a ring, boxes of Chiclets, a penny collection, some Trojan prophylactics, a few old pictures of Cuba, a lock of hair. "Yeah, these things were Pop all right," said Horacio peacefully.

On the morning they were going to close the coffin, Horacio said, "At least he won't be suffering anymore. You won't see him yelling or crying anymore. No more work for him. Now he's resting."

Nodding, Hector was thinking about bones, worms, dirty soil, and being in the coffin beside Alejo.

"You won't see him drinking rum anymore. You won't see him falling down the way he used to."

The degree of sadness in that room was unbearable, but one by one the family came forward to say a last prayer over him. There were the cousins and Aunt Luisa and then Margarita Delgado, who said to Mercedes as she left the room, "Let's forget the past." But Mercedes did not answer her. Then Horacio and Hector brought Mercedes forward to the coffin and held her as she looked down into the coffin. She began to whisper. They watched her kneel and touch Alejo's face and lips with her fingers, saying in the last moment, "I was good to you," and then withdrawing into her silence. Luisa led her away.

Then Horacio touched Alejo's hands and his face, as tough as leather, and then the hair, lively as the hair of a younger man. He leaned down, listened to his chest, and then kissed Alejo's closed eyelids and then his lips, which were cherry red. Standing with his hand spread over his face, Horacio began to cry and, shaking, remained beside the coffin some time before he stepped aside.

"Now it's your turn," he said to Hector.

But Hector couldn't kiss Alejo or begin to cry. Instead he touched Alejo's folded hands and his face. He stood there, anxious to go. And

197

then Horacio started to cry again, and Hector, thinking of good days, tried to cry but could not. Finally the priest arrived with some men who would carry the coffin to the hearse.

On the way to the church and during the funeral service, in which the host was lifted toward heaven to promote the soul's safe journey, Hector tried again to think of things that would make him cry: Alejo on the floor, Alejo yelling at Mercedes, "You are killing me. You are killing me." But nothing was there. "Pop, you did this to me," he kept thinking. He remembered resting beside Alejo when he was sick as a child, when he thought he would die. He was comfortable beside Alejo, touching Alejo's big belly and chest and feeling the hair and inhaling the mixed scents of meat, lilac lotion, and talcum. What had happened to those days of peace? The next moment he had opened his eyes and seen drunk men falling and Mercedes alone in the bed, suffering, and men with twisted smiles coming close and touching his hair and saying, "You're his boy? You're so Americano. Speak to me in Spanish." Alejo slumping in his chair at the table would reply, "Yeah, he's my boy. He and I are the same," repeating that with blood in his nostrils and saliva at the corner of his lips, bloated from eating and drinking so much. "Yeah, he's my boy," he would say, so drunk and close-eyed that the room must have been spinning and all faces glowing red and strange, repeating incessantly, "That one . . . I am the man, and he's the boy." *Try to cry? I'm trying, but it's no use, Pop, you made me this way.* Alejo would put his thick hands on the boy's face, pull him closer into the meat and booze smells, take the boy's hand and place it over his heart. Alejo would hold him so tightly that the boy could not pull away. The boy would close his eyes because he did not want to look, but there was Alejo's voice, low and calm, saying, "Look at me. Look at me." Or sometimes he would struggle down the hallway to the bathroom where he would lean one hand on the wall and piss in the toilet, then crash open the door to Hector's room and ask, "Do you love me, boy? That's what I have to know. Do you love me?" These memories went through Hector's head while the Latin rang out in the church, while Horacio and the others were crying. Hector was trying to cry, too, but he could not. He had dropped into a hole as deep as the earth. Inside the hole was the image of his father, Alejo Santinio, a man who always had to beg his son for kisses.

At the cemetery they lowered Alejo's coffin into a grave near a fence overflowing with blossoms. Mercedes dropped a bouquet of flowers into the hole and began to whisper, saying that she forgave him if he forgave her. Hector watched her with contempt, and the others bowed their heads and prayed. Horacio wept again, and one by one, the mourners passed and dropped flowers into the grave. Everyone cried except Hector. He had weeds in his mouth and in his heart. No tears. He was frightened and stood by the grave, not saying a word.

Ghosts, 1969–1975

1

The white blossoms that left Mercedes's hand and fell into the open grave might have drifted endlessly downward—into the clouds and sky of Cuba, long ago, falling down, carried in a breeze that swayed the treetops and scattered them on the road in Holguín. Mercedes was a little girl again, with a red ribbon in her hair, sitting in the garden of her family's grand house in Cuba. She was waiting for her papa, Teodoro Sorrea, to walk by, waiting for him to lift her into the air and give her many little kisses. When the blossoms from the sky fell on the road, she went out and gathered them up. She put one in her hair and then went looking for her father. She found him in the house, in the kitchen, reading the newspaper amid the blue smoke of his cigar and smells of food cooking in pots on the small white stove. The maid, Divina, with her lion's mane, was preparing the evening's meal.

"Look, Papa. Look what I found," she said. Teodoro took the blossoms. They were white roses. He held them up to the afternoon light that streamed through the window.

"Son bonitas," he said.

"They fell down from the sky."

"Ah, si?" Her father's brow furrowed, and then he turned toward the door as Doña Maria entered. She was wearing a plain, black-dotted dress. Her hair was in a bun, and she was holding a sewing basket.

"Ai, but you dream too much," her father said.

"She sleeps too much and the dreams stay inside her during the day," Doña Maria added with a sigh. "Now come along and put the flowers aside and help your mother."

Doña Maria and Mercedes went into the living room. On the long table there was a great pile of white cloth. Seamstresses were measuring pieces and cutting them out. Doña Maria sat down beside one of the seamstresses and gave Mercedes instructions. "Pay attention, dear, this dress is for your first communion." But Mercedes was distracted, and at the first opportunity, when she heard a noise in the hallway—a skittering mouse—she ran out. Rina and Luisa, in pretty white dresses, were in the yard playing with dolls. Mercedes joined them. She played with a Queen Isabella doll, pretending she herself was a Spanish queen. The yard with its high flowers and hanging lianas and orchid vines was the castle; the sun moving through the tree branches was the passing guard. They were moving the dolls under the leaves of the flowers, moving them in procession through a make-believe hall of mirrors when a few raindrops fell off the fronds of a spider palm and a wind smelling of rain swept through the yard. Being of more practical natures, Luisa and Rina went inside, but Mercedes stayed. As the rain came pouring down, Teodoro Sorrea stood at the window, fiercely motioning for her to come inside. When she finally obeyed he went after her with his belt.

"Why did you stay outside," he wanted to know.

"Because Queen Isabella loves the rain!"

He beat her anyway and left her crying in her room, alone.

That night she remembered the damp garden's smells and how wonderful the rain had felt on her skin. She fell asleep envying the flowers of the yard and their pleasant life in the sun and rain. She made a wish: "I wish I were a flower. Then I would have no worries."

That night, as she rested in bed, she felt herself becoming lighter. When she tried to scratch her nose she couldn't believe how wonderful her own skin smelled. "Something's going on!" she thought. Feeling around the bed, she found that in place of her legs there were long purple stems with wide petals. Trying to roll over, she found that she weighed practically nothing. She felt her head and found that it was made of flower skin and shaped like a bell. Orchid seeds were her eyes.

In the early morning her mother, Doña Maria, came looking for her. It was time for breakfast on the patio.

"Mercedes? Mercedes?" she called, looking around. She did not find Mercedes, only a large orchid in the middle of the bed, which she lifted up and put in a glass of water. She placed the flower near the window.

In the sunlight Mercedes became happy. She had no worries except that her mother and father would miss her. By the afternoon they were looking everywhere for her. Several times Teodoro came into her bedroom and looked in the closet and under the bed, checking over and over again. The last time he came in, he sat down on the bed and patted his sweating brow with a handkerchief. Seeing the worry and sadness in his expression, Mercedes could not hold back and called out to him, "Papa! Papa! It's me, Mercita, your little flower."

"Dios mío!" he cried out. But the serious frown left his face, and he called all the servants and Rina and Luisa into the room. "Do you see this? I've found my daughter!" Thinking of the consequences, his happiness suddenly left him. "This is fine now, but you have to be changed back..."

Then during the evening's meal he remarked, "Mercita, we'll have to make the best of this. Now that you're an orchid, I can take you everywhere with me."

So for years, gently wrapped in a handkerchief, Mercedes traveled around in his pocket. She went to the forests with him, to political meetings, on his journeys to Mexico and to the Dominican Republic. They went to church, to Santiago, and once even to Havana. When he stayed at home on Sunday afternoons, she stayed in the garden with her new companions, the roses and the chrysanthemums.

The years passed. Mercedes was an important flower in the weddings of her sisters, Rina and Luisa. And she had been one of the flowers clutched in her mother's arms when Doña Maria cried at Teodoro's funeral. When her father died, Mercedes wanted to be changed back, but her wish did not come true. She resigned herself gracefully. Since it was time for her to get back into the world, Mercedes began to frequent the park across the street from the Neptuna movie theater. She spent her mornings among the orange blossoms and was very content until she was captured by a peanut vendor, who tucked her into his hatband. When after a few days he noticed that he owned a flower that would never wither, he sold it to a friend, and the friend resold her, so that after a number of transactions she became part of the centerpiece of a government minister's dining table. Then one day when a servant opened a window wide, a wind whisked her up, carried her high over the treetops, and finally dropped her into the park.

By then Mercedes was of the age when she wanted a man. "The right man." How would she know him? By the way he held her and by the look in his eyes when he inhaled deeply of her. She waited in the park. Different men touched her. Most were handsome but too rough. One after the other, she saw these men come and go. Well-scrubbed, good-looking compañeros, but the one she fell for immediately was Alejo Santinio. Another wind had carried her out of the park and across the street, onto the pavement in front of the Neptuna movie theater ticket booth. Alejo was walking by. He bent over her, lifted her from the ground in just the right way, and she changed back into a woman in his arms.

Now that he, too, was dead, like her father, Mercedes wished the wind had carried her off that day, before Alejo had touched her with his hands.

2

With Horacio married and living in Astoria, Queens, Hector was left alone with Mercedes. He had graduated from high school, had a few part-time jobs, and had gotten into a community college, which he hated attending. But it was better than staying around the gloomy apartment, which Mercedes kept dark. When he was at home, she was either yelling and pacing in circles or going off into trances.

One evening Hector snapped his fingers before her eyes and she did not move. "Ma, Ma, please. Look who's here to see you."

Mercedes's friend Paula from next door stood in the living room, holding a pot of chicken cacciatore, aromatic with big pieces of green peppers and silvery onions. She came over every day with something for Mercedes to eat, but Mercedes never ate. Now Mercedes was sitting on the couch, oblivious.

"Ma, Ma," Hector kept repeating. "Paula is here."

Mercedes, all worn out, looked over at Paula, nodding slightly as she did with all visitors. Paula sat down beside Mercedes. "Hello, Mercita. Now be sensible, you have to eat or you'll get sick." She took hold of Mercedes's hands and looked into her eyes. "Don't worry I'm here with you, sweetie."

But Mercedes was wallowing in her own solitude.

Hector went into the kitchen, pulled out a few plates, forks, and knives, and set them on the table. Paula brought Mercedes in, pulling her along by the hand. Mercedes's hair was wild from turning in bed, and in the past three or four months her hands seemed to have aged. Thick veins showed in her fingers, and her hands were shaking as Alejo's had shaken when he fell down and died.

"Now eat, Mercita," said Paula cheerily. "I made this especially for you."

Mercedes took a few forkfuls but that was all.

"Ma," said Hector, "you have to eat." When she shrugged, he started shouting: "You have to fuckin' eat. Now fuckin' eat!"

"Sssssshhhh, child," Paula said. "She doesn't know where she is."

"She knows," Hector said. "Believe me she knows."

For months Mercedes had been driving him crazy. She liked the dark and often went into trances. She would watch the television without the sound, spend hours walking back and forth in the hallway, and spend the afternoon in bed staring at the ceiling. She didn't cook or clean, didn't eat, wept for nothing, and would wake up in the middle of the night from nightmares or because of ghosts. Sometimes she stood before the closet touching Alejo's clothes, which were still there—that annoyed and frightened Hector more than just about anything else, except for when Mercedes started to imitate Alejo's voice and held conversations with herself.

"Even so," said Paula, "you have to be good to her. She is your mother. Now *you* eat."

204

She filled Hector's plate, and while he ate dinner, she took Mercedes into the bedroom, brushed her hair, and then helped her to choose a dress to wear for the evening. "We can go upstairs and watch television in my brother's apartment," she said. "Or if you like we can go over to Broadway and see what's going on."

She was referring to the riots on the University's campus. For weeks reporters had roamed the neighborhood. There were pamphlets everywhere—against the Vietnam war, racism, capitalism, class exploitation. They were handed out by students who didn't really seem to give a damn about the people who lived right in their own neighborhood. Every night a high-pitched, mechanical-sounding voice from a loudspeaker somewhere down the street had come in through the window: lots of rhetoric, incitement to riot, revolutionary talk. Señor Lopez, the union organizer from upstairs, was in his glory. He too was out in the street, lecturing on the evils of capitalist exploitation. The tide of history was turning at last! Hector always nodded, listening intently, because Lopez was a good man and had been a friend to the family. At least Lopez was genuine. During the late 1950s he used to come home badly beaten up from organizing down on the docks. He was a Cuban Communist, not like Hector's relatives from Cuba. He was always preaching Marxism and thought the revolution was the greatest thing to ever happen to Cuba's poor people. Thinking about Lopez and his involvement with politics, Hector felt greater loathing for the college "revolutionaries" whose clapping and shouts could be heard coming from the campus.

"We could go there later," Paula told Mercedes. "Do you want to come along, Hector?"

"Nah." He didn't like walking around with his mother these days.

Paula picked a bright red dress from the closet for Mercedes to wear. "Try this on," she said. Listlessly, Mercedes put on the red dress. She stared in the mirror for a long time and then looked out the bedroom window. Her eyes got big and wide.

"Did you hear something in the courtyard?" she asked them.

"Only the cats, Ma."

Hector went into his room. There was a mirror in there, too. He didn't like to look into it. Staring disturbed him just as it disturbed

205

Mercedes. Sometimes he saw Alejo's eyes looking back at him, as if Alejo had sneaked into his body to play a game. Alejo was dead but not dead. He remembered how he had run his fingers over Alejo's closed eyes, pressing down and feeling them beneath the eyelids. They were hard and did not spring back like living eyes that are asleep.

"Hector," Paula said, hovering in the doorway. "We're going for a walk now." And then in a whisper, she added, "Don't be worried, child, she'll be fine. Give her a little time and she'll forget everything."

When they left, Hector took a drink. He kept bottles of whiskey under the bed. A swig, burning in the throat, and then relief. He had been drinking a lot. Everybody but everybody in the neighborhood bars bought him drinks; whenever he went to someone's apartment, he got stoned. That made him feel close to Alejo. It made him feel strong and large in every way.

Soon he went out into the street. He must have looked like he was still in mourning because passersby were always nice to him, even when he was stumbling drunk. Passing the wrought-iron fence at the corner, he thought, "That's where Alejo used to sit watching the people go by on the avenue." Passing the basement entrance, he thought, "That's where Alejo almost fell down that time."

He ran into Gonzales. Gonzales was drunk enough to be slurring his words. "My God, I thought you were your father. Do you know that? Oh man, that hurt me, when he died. He was good—you believe it, too. You only have one father."

"Yeah, yeah, I know that."

"You know what?" he said laughing. "I never told this to no one, but the same night he died, I saw him. He came down to the basement looking for me. Yo te juro. I swear on my mother's grave. He was wearing the same pants he died in. The checkered ones. And I've seen him twice since."

Hector felt contemptuous of Gonzales. He was wearing porter's clothes and a ratty hat, and he looked haggard, as if he hadn't slept.

"Everyone says they've seen him," Hector said.

"Don't believe them. They bullshitting you. But I was his friend, we were like brothers."

Meaning they used to fall off chairs together.

"Yeah, well look, I gotta go."

Hector walked off, but Gonzales ran after him, took him by the arm. Gonzales was an exhausted-looking man but tremendously strong. He gave a tug and stopped Hector.

"Look, it would mean something to me if you come and drink with me. I know it hurt you inside, but please come and drink with me."

"Maybe another time..."

"You come, okay?"

Hector was going to go down to the bar, but now he found himself walking behind Gonzales. There were many things he didn't like about Gonzales, but in some ways Gonzales reminded him of Alejo. They went down the rickety steps to the basement apartment where Gonzales and Alejo used to get drunk together. It was behind the boiler room and was very narrow. Gonzales had his own private little macho room off the kitchen, where his wife now sat reading the newspaper. On the wall were posters of big-titted women; on the ceiling a little fan whirling around. A small table, few chairs.

"I get you a drink," Gonzales said.

He got the drink and also threw a magazine in Hector's lap.

"You like the girls?"

Hector drank down his drink, flipped open the pages: all in color, women and men copulating and kissing each other in every imaginable way.

"Ha! Ha! That's nice, huh?" Gonzales slapped his knees and said, "You like pussy?"

"Yeah."

"That's good, that's good." And he slapped Hector's knee with his large bony hands. His eyes squinted in pleasure and he leaned back as if to remember. "Your papa used to come here all the time to have a little drink. Salud, to your papa!"

Every drink was a toast to Alejo, or their life together.

"Your father and me," Gonzales said, "we were almost the same. We were both workers and we could both read! To workers and working men everywhere." A toast. "Me and your papa, why, we had our fun. We played our lottery tickets, but best of all we had each other by the heart! And we could read, so never let anyone say that your father, or me, was illiterate . . . because we have no money. We just had bad luck!"

Gonzales's balance faltered for a moment and he almost fell off the chair. His voice was all gnarled up, spitting when he talked. Hector too was getting high and he was tempted to wrap his arms around Gonzales the way Alejo used to, but he couldn't imagine what could bring two men so close together, so brotherly, so affectionate in a manly way.

"Yessiree, we were like brothers!"

"But what made you that way?"

"What? I don't know." He rapped at his heart. "We knew each other's sufferings. Sufrimientos . . . that made us the best pals!"

"Yes? What kind of suffering?"

"I don't remember."

He was shifting back and forth in the chair. He laughed. "People look at me and say, 'There's Louie the drunk.' But, you know, your father always made me feel respected, no matter what I did or said to him—and sometimes I could be a shit. He always looked out for me. Always treated me with respect."

And then Gonzales started to cry. He was staring off into the corner just like Mercedes did, as if the welling of tears in the eyes was a camera being refocused, as if the resolution of vision would produce Alejo's ghost. He wept and repeated, "Pardon me, pardon me, I don't mean to be such a baby, but he was so good a friend for me."

And the more Gonzales cried, the more Alejo seemed to be there in the room. Hector couldn't see him, but perhaps he was waiting to step out from behind the door to tell his friend to stop crying. Why was Gonzales crying in the first place if he didn't expect Alejo to do this?

"Pardon me, I still cannot believe it." Gonzales got up to piss in the stinky, closet-size toilet, his urine making deep gurgling noises.

"Hey, Louie," said Hector, "I gotta go soon."

"Yeah, yeah. But have one more drink with me."

Hector looked through the magazine while Louie poured out more from the bottle. A guy with the biggest prick was fucking two women at the same time . . . juicy pictures. They reminded Hector that he had

had no girlfriend since Alejo died. And here was this lucky guy fucking around with two women at once.

"Salud," said Louie, raising his glass. "To your papa, who was a hell of a man!"

Then Hector got up to leave. On his way out he said hello to the señora again. He kept wondering: *Did Gonzales really see Alejo?*

Hector left the basement and went down to the bar to see if he could get laid. But there were few women around. Many of the old buildings had been torn down. The few available women were usually hooked up with cops. Then there were the university girls. Either they fucked only heavy-duty freaks or they were too good for everyone. In any case, he had to be drunk to rap, and girls didn't appreciate that. Sitting at the bar, he watched the ball game. The bartender always gave him a free drink, and even the racists who badmouthed everybody bought him drinks. Ever since Alejo died. Good people. People getting high because there was nothing else. Not much was happening. He played a game of pinball, got bored, left.

He went home to watch television from Alejo's old chair. The house was dark, so he turned on the lights. There were noises in the hall. He ignored them. On television: "Beverly Hillbillies," then "I Dream of Jeannie." Jeannie had a nice body: he wanted to fuck her. Thoughts of jerking off. Do Cubans do that? Can ghosts see that?

Around ten-thirty Mercedes came home. She and Paula had been over at the campus watching the riot police facing the students. Mercedes had sat on a bench watching without saying a word. Helmeted police with bullhorns kept telling everyone to go back; people jeered, trash was thrown. Paula, who wanted to get on television, had dragged Mercedes in front of a television news reporter. Mercedes stood behind her, as the reporter asked Paula his question, "Are the police too brutal in their handling of the situation?" Paula had answered, "The cops are wrong in hitting people with their clubs. But the students are wrong for looking down at the cops and calling them *pigs*, as if they were necessarily better." Afterward she and Mercedes bought ice cream cones, vanilla and pistachio, and then they came back home. When Mercedes came to the door, she spent a long time opening the tricky lock, went into the living room, turned off the lights. Went into the kitchen, turned off the light. Then she went into each of the rooms where Hector had turned on a light because he was afraid of the dark and she turned it off. As soon as he heard the clicking of the switches he was ready to start the same nightly fight.

"Turn those back on," he insisted. And she turned them back on. But then she turned them off again. He yelled. Back on, but then off.

"Why do you do that?" he asked her.

"Don't hit me," she said.

"Then don't turn off the lights."

He didn't want to tell her that he was afraid of the dark. He was afraid that Alejo would step out of the dark. He was conditioned by her to believe that forces lurked in the dark: spirits, micróbios. When it was dark he expected Alejo's dead hands to fall around his neck and to send surges of electricity through him. He was afraid to admit that Alejo was dead.

"Well, what do you think?" Mercedes said. "We're not rich!"

"Keep the lights on."

But when he fell asleep in the chair, she turned off all the lights around him. It was funny, in the dreams everything went abruptly dark. Something to do with illness and gardens, and an old woman patting his head, when all of a sudden . . . there was something in the room. He didn't want to open his eyes. What should he do? Run down the hallway, hoping that his father's ghost would not catch him? Should he hold the door against his father as he used to do, hoping that his father wouldn't crash through it? Or should he cry like Horacio and the others cried at the funeral? Or like Gonzales had cried?

He called out, "Ma! Ma!"

She was in her bedroom whispering, praying. When she said her prayers she made the Sign of the Cross and said her father and mother's names. Sometimes she would leave the bedroom and stand in the hallway trying to speak in the voices of her mother and father. One night she had imitated the voice of Eduardo Delgado with his terrible wheeze and coughing. On other nights she tried the voices of others she had once known and who were now dead.

"Ma! Ma!"

210

No answer. He got up and smoked a cigarette, went to his bed. A short time later he smelled Alejo: meat and lilac lotion, smells of the hotel kitchen. He imagined the front door suddenly burst open. He heard footsteps in the hall and then the scraping of a belt against the wall, like that of an enormous, exhausted man trying to drag himself along but not being able to keep his balance. He kept telling himself, "I'm going to have to do something about this," but he couldn't move.

Mercedes had gone to her bedroom window. She called out: "Alejo, Alejo!"

"Stupid ignorant Cuban," Hector thought, "don't you know that when a man dies he is put into the ground and goes nowhere? His body turns blue like rotting meat."

"Alejo, Alejo!" she called.

"Ma! What the fuck are you doing?"

More noises in the hall: More smells. But worst of all were the voices coming from her mouth. Her voice and Alejo's voice.

"You were bad to me!"

"I do as I please!"

"You hit me!"

"I am the man!"

"If you hate me, then leave!"

"I will leave!"

Hector couldn't take it anymore. He couldn't find peaceful sleep, and he had no where else to go. Trembling in bed, he wanted to crawl into one of the pictures Mercedes kept in the bureau, of the rain forest or of the house on Arachoa Street.

"I want a divorce!"

"You shut up!"

"Make me!"

"Go to hell!"

"This is hell!"

"Shut up, or I swear to God, I'll hit you!"

"Oh, big man!"

"Shut up."

"Do you think you're still in Cuba? Well, you were something there, but here you're only a cook . . ."

"Shut up!"

"And the way you're going—your face is changing so—you're going to die. And when you're..."

"Leave me alone!"

"...in the ground you're going to ask people to help you out, but you won't be able to move."

On and on, as Hector tried to sleep.

"Leave me alone, woman, I don't want trouble anymore."

"But you have it. You made it! I am going to rub your face in what you did to me."

Finally Hector decided to quiet Mercedes down but, as usual, when he reached the bedroom she was under the covers, staring up at the ceiling. The voices had stopped. She was finished playing her game. He was standing by the doorway, looking at her. His mother. His Cuban mother.

"She killed him," Hector had told Horacio.

"What?"

"She killed him."

"Who told you that?"

"Buita told me everything."

Horacio laughed. "You believe her? What did she tell you?"

"That Pop had his chances and she fucked it up for him. And when he failed in life he didn't want to live any more."

"You're dumber than you look if you believe her. She hates Ma. She crucified Ma in the old days. She always fucked Ma, and you believe her. That cold bitch."

"Yeah, well Pop's...dead."

"He was fucked up, too weak, and afraid of too many things."

"Well, it was because of Ma."

"You're fuckin' blind, deaf, and dumb! Ma's no saint, but neither was Pop! Or you for that matter. And Buita, she fucked Ma royally. Stop playing so dumb."

Hector watched Mercedes from the doorway, just dying to catch her speaking in Alejo's voice. But she remained in her bed, without moving, without speaking. He went back into the hallway. He was thinking about catching her and throwing her against the wall, making her stop. In the afternoons when he shouted at her, all the good neighbors came downstairs to tell him to treat her better. "She's your only mother," Doña Teresa from upstairs told him. "You have to love her. Your blood is her blood."

"You have to be good to her," said another neighbor. "It is your obligation. In Cuba we always looked after our mothers."

In his bedroom Alejo's presence seemed stronger, as if his ghost were standing a few feet away, hiding perhaps, inside the closet. Hector didn't want to touch the closet. He didn't really think Alejo was there, but then he imagined what Alejo would say: "Estoy aqui, porqué tu no crees en mi?"—"I am here, why don't you believe in me?"

Be rational, cool. Only stupid, superstitious Cubans see and hear the dead, fear the dead. But the smell of meat and the kitchen grew stronger. And while Hector was turned to the wall, he felt the mattress compress beside him.

"Pop? Pop?" Hector could not move. He had the ghost to scare him, the Cuban susceptibility to such things, but none of the Cuban strength, not even the skin of a Cuban... He tried to sleep but dared not turn. He was thinking about that Cuban susceptibility. It was like automatically sucking in anything put before you. The way Alejo allowed grief to enter him; the way Mercedes sucked all fear into herself. And Hector himself had taken in the micróbios from Cuba, was penetrated by them, in the same way that Alejo's spirit was going to penetrate him and take over, make him feel dead. Sometimes when Hector looked in the mirror, he had the sense that Alejo had stepped into him. Horacio said he had the same feeling, but he didn't let it bother him. He had a good feeling about Alejo, but not Hector.

"I feel bad for him," Hector had said to Horacio.

"Yeah, well you didn't even show it."

"What do you mean?"

"You didn't even cry for him."

"Well, I meant to."

"And it's funny, because you were tighter with him. He always looked out for you, ever since you were little."

"I was just too pissed off at Ma."

"Yeah, well she looked out for you even more than he did."

"Yeah?"

"You were her little prince. When you nearly died, she flipped. Went every week to the hospital."

"And Pop went, too."

"Brother, I told you. He never went. He was at home getting sloshed."

That made him cringe. He wanted to bury himself in the dark of the sheet underneath him. Alejo not caring for him. Alejo begging him for love. Alejo being such a pain in the ass. All this passing into him like micróbios.

Wasn't going to cry and let Alejo go inside of him.

Wasn't going to be afraid and let Alejo go inside of him.

But he was afraid, and was startled suddenly when Mercedes called out again, "Alejo! Alejo!"

Hector started to shake and grew red in the face, and he felt something entering, something stepping into him like a bather into the ocean. He got out of bed, paced the floor, punched the wall, shouted "Shut up, shut up!" and pushed the door open so forcefully that it crashed into the wall. He went down the hall knocking over things. When he got to her bedroom, Mercedes was standing by the window.

"Shut up! Shut up!" he told her.

"What did I do?"

"Stop calling him. Stop calling Alejo."

"Ai, leave me alone."

"No, you leave me alone! And shut up."

Then he took hold of her wrists and pulled her from the window and made her sit down on the bed. She held one wrist and began to cry.

"Shut up!" he told her.

But she kept on crying, so he started shaking her, and then he pushed her off the bed, and she fell. "Don't be such a saint. You killed him," he shouted. She began to breathe quickly and hyperventilate, like getting fucked, and she started screaming and carrying on, holding herself as if she had been slashed up with a knife. "You make me sick with your self-righteousness!"

She kept looking at her wrists, as though they were bleeding. She remembered how she had worried that Hector had almost died and how she had tried her best to raise him. But now he was going to explode and hit her. "Shut up! Stop crying!" he kept repeating. And seeing that it was making him miserable and maybe softer, she cried all the more and began saying in a whisper, "What luck I've had, what luck I've had..."

When Hector heard this, he felt bad and left her alone. Later, when he came back, she was still on the floor. He gave her his hand, but she wouldn't touch it. Instead, she told him, "You're crazy and bad to me. You're just like Buita and worse to me than your father ever was."

3

Another morning, any morning. Alejo's shoes sticking out from under the bed. The closet door open. Alejo's hat on the bureau. The bureau drawers pulled out. A pack of Alejo's cigarettes, a used coffee cup and saucer on the kitchen table. In the bathroom, wet towels slung over the racks, talcum powder on the floor.

"Ma, why do you try to make it look like Pop was here?"

"Not me, it *was* your papa!"

"Ma, that's impossible."

"No, no, no, no..."

Hector had to calm himself. He was afraid of hurting her.

"Look Ma, maybe you should go and visit Luisa for a few days."

"Why should I go? This is my home."

"But it would be good for you."

She went to the bureau and picked up a picture of Alejo and herself from the old Neptuna days.

"Good for me? No, this is where I live!"

"Well, at least you'll see Paula today, right?"

"I think so."

Mercedes was determined to continue mourning Alejo. After a year she should have begun to feel better. But she did not improve. When people came to visit, she sat around passively, expecting her friends to entertain her with news of the day and stories about how good she and Alejo had been to each other, how she had been a good devoted wife. At first there were visitors from the hotel, old family friends, friends of Alejo who came by to keep her company. She allowed these visits to become solemn occasions. When Alejo was around there had been laughter and endless talking and much food and drink. But now a visitor was lucky if Mercedes brought out a few cookies.

"It's not much, you see, but it's all I have since he died," she would say.

Then they would sit in the living room, not saying too much. Even the most cheerful souls left disheartened. Few people could stay very long. Friends and neighbors drifted in and out. Mercedes's outbursts of weeping and her excitability were exhausting. Luisa, in poor health those days, could not visit at all and her children were much too busy to come more than once a month. Other Cuban friends like Eliseo Hernandez, whom Alejo had helped, came over once, twice, but soon stopped showing up.

"You help them out, and they never return," Mercedes would say to herself. "They use you, you help them, and for what? So they can leave you alone."

But no one could blame people for staying away. Mercedes kept the house dark, behaved like a broken old woman.

Soon only Paula visited. Mary had moved away to Brooklyn, and Alejo's friends only nodded as they walked by the building and saw Mercedes's or Hector's face in the window. Horacio did not enjoy visiting and did not visit often. Everything embarrassed him: the furniture, the way the house looked, the food. He did not want his new wife, Marilyn, to know much about the family. Mercedes was in the habit of serving meals on plates she had forgotten to wash, of undercooking food...

So even though she was always fighting with Hector, Mercedes did not want him to leave, not even for part of an evening.

"Where are you going?"

"Out."

"Do you have to go out every night?"

"Yeah, I do."

One night he walked to the University, where there were still riots, and while he was standing around he met a girl. She was a pretty blonde whom he had seen around a few times before. He moved beside her and they started talking. "Would you like to go to the park?" he asked her. They went to the park, sat on a bench in a closure of trees facing the moonlit river, talked, started to make out, and then came back up looking for a place to go. Hector decided to bring her home. Mercedes was upstairs with Paula, watching color TV. Hector took the girl into his room. Hector took off the girl's blouse. They were lying on his chaotic bed; big full breasts in his hands, her whole body trembling, tight and honey-tasting; hair long and curling like the tresses of pre-Raphaelite virgins. She pulled down her pants and panties, he took off his pants, and she sat on him, much heat in her rump and a thick, hungry tongue and a mouth like some opened fruit, up and down she went on him, fucking him, inhaling, exhaling.

Upstairs before the glare of the color television, Mercedes felt an alarm going off inside her.

"Dios mío, Dios mío," she said to Paula. "I have to go now." Down the stairs she went.

Hector and the girl were making their way through a dense cloud of sensation when they heard Mercedes's keys jiggling in the door.

"Hurry and get dressed," Hector said.

Mercedes rushed down the hall and pushed open the door without even knocking. She saw the girl, gasped, turned away, and went into the hall. When Hector and the girl came out, Mercedes said, "How funny, you and a girl!" And she started laughing, a high, cackling laugh that Hector would never forget.

After that, Mercedes started spying on him: reading his letters, looking into his hiding places inside the closet and behind the desk. One day he came home and found her reading one of the letters Buita had sent him. The letters were all the same: "When are you going to come and see us? We can give you anything you want. When are you going to leave that woman?" He didn't answer the letters, but they kept coming. In the most recent ones Buita kept bringing up a casual promise Hector had made to Alberto when he was in Miami. He was supposed to find a certain drill for Alberto and send it to him. But since Alejo's death, Hector had been distracted. He had lost the ad, did not know where to buy the drill, did not care. Every letter mentioned the drill: "If you cared, you would remember your familial responsibilities." But in the end all the letters begged him to come live in Miami: "And you know that we will always love you."

Mercedes was reading this line over and over again to herself when Hector came into the room. The line was like the knife that Buita plunged into her heart in her nightmares.

"What the fuck are you doing?"

"Nothing."

"Give that to me!" and he pulled the letter away from her.

"Do you believe that? What she says? She doesn't love you. She doesn't love anyone."

"At least she didn't kill anyone!"

"I killed him? How could you say that?"

"It's the truth, you hurt him so much."

"Oh yes? And was it me who wouldn't even look at him. He cried because of that and because you told him to drop dead! He cried when you took his money, so you could go and see Aunt Buita. Don't make me laugh. Why don't you write her and tell her that?... Don't think I don't know. Buita took you and put lies in your head, and you believed it. Well, who took care of you? Who put clothes on your back and fed you? Buita? Don't make me laugh. You were nothing without us, so don't believe a word of what she says."

He wanted to hit her, but instead Hector took hold of her wrists and started squeezing them.

"And don't think that Alejo doesn't know what's going on. He sees how you abuse me."

"Ma, he's not here!"

"Oh yes, he's here. You just don't want to see him. You don't want to look at him because you are ashamed of the way you treated him. You don't want to see his misery! You hurt him! You looked down on him and he knew it. It hurt him in the heart! He loved you, and you thought he was nothing... Don't think he didn't know. He knows it now, and he won't forget."

Now she was speaking her Spanish one thousand words a minute.

"You think I don't know anything? That I dream all the time? I'm not like you. I treated my mother and father in a proper way. When my poor papa died I cried and cried for years, but you, you go out

218

and get drunk and you bring girls into the house and you abuse me! Instead of saying you love me, you get letters from this witch and you hide them from me. Your father knows these things. He comes to me and says, 'What's wrong with that boy?' It hurts him, he suffers because you had no respect for him in life and no respect for him in his death. No good Cuban son would do that, but you think only of yourself. You are so selfish you will make people suffer all your life...And Buita? She can go to hell! You want to go with her, after how she hurt me? You want her? Then go. Psssh, she's no saint and neither are you, so don't make me laugh."

Hector tried to be more helpful to Mercedes. They didn't have much money and were living on her widow's social security benefits, and on money she had saved over the years. Hector worked as a messenger for a weekly newspaper and used part of his earnings to buy better food. When Mercedes went shopping she returned with bags of the cheapest food possible: chicken necks and backs at twelve cents a pound, frozen, sinewy turkey wings and drumsticks that were impossible to chew at nineteen cents a pound, half-spoiled fruit and vegetables. Hector would come home with ice cream, pastries, meat loaf and ham sandwiches, and pizza. He cleaned the house a few times and took care of certain chores, but his energy soon dissipated from coping with Mercedes. He had tried to be a better son, but the same kind of arguments flared up over and over again. And at night, with the air swirling with Alejo's restless ghost, he could not sleep. Finally, Hector decided to move out. He had a friend with an apartment about ten blocks away. When he told Mercedes he was leaving, she begged him to stay.

"Please, I'm sorry. I'll do anything if you'll stay."

"No."

"Don't go, please, my boy, don't go. I'll be alone."

"You'll have Pop."

"Please, son..."

But he continued to pack up his junk. He was thinking about sex with that blond girl and about getting drunk without being harassed about it. He thought he would leave all the bad feelings behind, that he wouldn't think about Alejo anymore or hear Mercedes's voice at night or think about micróbios, or sense Alejo in the room, see Alejo weeping at the kitchen table, hear him falling, hear him crying. He thought these things would disappear like vapor when he left.

4

For a long time, things died inside the house, broke down as if because of her weeping. When the big television set died, it remained sitting there like a piece of furniture, never fixed, never replaced. On top of it she put a vase with some plastic flowers. She didn't want it to be hauled away even though it was dead. Perhaps she thought Alejo could still come at night and plop down on the sofa or into the easy chair and watch "Gunsmoke" on the ghost television. Certainly he often passed through the walls into the bedroom to see how she wept for him.

The purgatorial existence. Her suffering. He did make her crazy with worry and now she wept. Everyone knew he was going to die, and he died. One moment here, the next gone. And he was finally beginning to treat her better. "What a life. To think this would happen to me," she kept saying. In her dreams her fingers remembered the feel of his wavy hair, his chest hair, his broad shoulders, his back. She remembered his enormous strength, carrying her into that little room in Holguín, years before, his force, the warmth of his body.

Bones? No. Rot of body? Oh no! A shadow? Yes. A dappling of lights against the walls? Yes. Eaten by the worms? No. Covered by dirt and pebbles? No.

He would come to visit her around midnight. A regular suitor with gifts. He brought her flowers, a mirror, a camera. He would sit on the bed, touch her face and hair with his thick fingers.

"Don't worry, Mercita, you and I, we'll always be together."

Sometimes the dark hallway became the avenue by the park in Holguín, high royal palms, scent of orange, scent of tamarind. Everyone, dressed in his Sunday best, strolled in a parade on the street, amid coffee vendors, peanut men. Alejo and Mercedes walked along, laughing, whispering their love for one another. A pleasant breeze, kisses, mouths tasting of sweet juices, the sun up high, flowers in the path.

"You're the prettiest girl I know."

"You're crazy."

"No, I swear it's the truth."

"Well, you are the most handsome man."

"So that's why we make such a good couple."

The kitchen held the quiet afternoons in their house in San Pedro, where they played in bed. The smell of his hair, taste of his skin, his fingers over her body. She trembled, sighed as he spoke in his manly voice, possessing her, lifting her spirit, taking her into the most narrow of rooms, jammed with love and passion.

"Mercita, you're so beautiful . . . so beautiful."

The sound of the ocean up north. Spray of waves, touch of sand, so white and pure, carried in the wind. Crinkly seashells underfoot, scent of faraway places; mangoes and coconuts dropped down from the trees.

"Ai, I love the way you feel in my arms, Alejo."

The smell of fritters wafting out the window into the courtyard of Doña Isabel's house in San Pedro. Mercedes, pretty in a blue dress, so happy, until Buita steps out of the archway. Buita watching her, laughing at her, Buita with the knife.

"Alejo, Alejo!" the infernal call. Everything dark again, the hallway was dark. Leaning against the door, Mercedes held it shut to keep Buita out. Buita must be outside, waiting patiently for the door to open, and then she would plunge the knife into Mercedes's heart.

"Alejo, Alejo!"

She felt his warm hand on her trembling face. "Don't be afraid. I'm here," she heard him say.

And only then could she open the door in the hallway. Buita was not there. And if she had been? He would turn Buita away. "This is my wife, and you are not to hurt her," he would tell her. "I love her with all my heart and soul. She is my love forever. Now, you go away."

Bones? No. Rotting flesh? No. Mercedes knew exactly what would happen to Alejo now that he was dead. It was the same with her mother and father. People you love return.

In the cemetery in Long Island, among the greenery, the rows of stones, and the shading trees, it was five-thirty and time to go to work.

221

He opened his eyes. He wasn't in the apartment. Something is wrong, he told himself. He got up, stretched himself. It was very bright; the sun came up over the eastern hills, and the trees sounded with life. He found himself walking into the brilliant sunshine, the light passing through his hands. Everything was so clean. The flowers that were everywhere smelled so sweet. Not tired anymore. No more *trabajo*. No more bad heart. No more yelling. Now only the comforts of love.

He walked around silently, confused at first, but soon he took on the confidence of a saint. His face looked purified, like Jesus's, and he was calm as he went about making his appearances: to Horacio, to Louie, to all the people who loved him. And now he visited Mercedes. He was her lover boy, dead.

Voices from the Last World

1

HORACIO: Ma's always telling us about her dreams, but I had my own the other day. In my dream, I was standing over the coffin touching Pop's face when he opened his eyes and asked, "What's happened to me?" I told him. He sat up in the coffin and looked me over. He saw that I was wearing his wedding ring, the one that he bought the year he came to the States, in 1943 or 1944, and he said, "What are you doing with that, Horacito?" "You gave it to me, Pop, don't you remember? You said, 'If I die, it's yours.'" He thought about it for a moment and said, "Okay, you're right." He got out of the coffin and we walked out of the funeral parlor to the street, then down Broadway to Riverside Drive. That's when it started to be a nice dream. I felt the same way I did as a kid when he would take me out, both of us slicked up in suits and hats, riding the bus all the way downtown to visit his Cuban friends. That was before he started to take things out on me. It was a sunny day, not a cloud was in the sky. We were walking down 116th Street into the park when he asked me: "What are you doing these days?" So I told him about my job and my son, Stevie, and he asked me, "Where is he?" I said, "At home, Pop." And then I said, "You want to come to my house, Pop?" "Sure," he said, but we kept walking into the park.

There was no logic to this dream; instead of going to my house Pop wanted to sit in the grass and watch the boats passing on the river. On the way down the hill, I saw Mr. Hess, our old super, and waved hello to him. It wasn't until we reached the bottom of the hill that I realized Mr. Hess had been dead for a long time. We found a shady place to sit and watch the boats. It then occurred to me that this was a day I had forgotten for years. In 1952, when I was seven years old Pop took me to look at boats on the river. He was as happy as a lark about something and bought me two ten-cent Good Humor ice creams, one of them coconut, the other chocolate malted. Man, I was happy that day. Now, years later, in the dream he was doing the same. As we sat in the park a Good Humor truck came by. Pop got up and returned with ice cream for us both. When he went back for seconds, I stopped him and went instead. I told him: "Pop, from now on I'm going to take care of you."

We sat in the park for about a half hour and not once did I think of him as dead or as an apparition. He didn't say very much while we sat there. He was basking in the sunlight, with his face raised to the sky. Then he said, "I want to see my grandson." So we went back up the hill to where my car was parked. He had never owned a car and was very impressed by my white Coupe de Ville. We drove to Astoria with the windows rolled down. His eyes grew big looking at all the houses and the scenery. When we came to my home, it was as if little Stevie had been waiting for him. Stevie ran down the path with his arms outstretched, yelling, "Grandpa! Grandpa!" and that made Pop smile. His face even turned red, and he lifted Stevie up and kissed him and we went into the house where I showed him everything, from my color TV to the electric saws in my workshop. He was impressed by everything in the house. Then we sat out in the backyard. I watched him, and again he raised his face to the sky in order to enjoy the generous sunshine. Marilyn was in the kitchen cooking up an old-fashioned Italian dinner, and Stevie was playing by Pop's feet. Then I just had to tell him something, and I said, "Pop, remember how you cried for me the night before I went into the Air Force? That meant a lot to me." And he nodded and looked over at Stevie and smiled. "Hey Pop, why don't you take Stevie for a walk down the street?"

Pop took Stevie down a few blocks and bought him an ice cream cone, which dripped down his shirt. Pop was wiping away the stains with his handkerchief when Marilyn stuck her head out the window to announce that dinner was ready. We went inside and had a great meal. Afterward Pop said to me, "I have to go." He kissed everyone and I blinked my eyes and he was gone.

I woke Marilyn and told her about the dream and she said the dream was a sign that I was at peace with his soul. I could not sleep the rest of the night, thinking how lucky I was. I felt contented not just because I had material things that Pop never had, but because he seemed to know what I had done with my life. I did not turn out to be a bad man, and it was because Pop, deep down, really loved the family. If he had hated us I would have burned out. But we went beyond survival. He gave me something that was simple. I keep saying it, the ability to feel love. And having that makes it easy to give. The next day I told Stevie about how Pop was a chef in a fancy hotel and that he had come from Cuba and that Stevie was also half Cuban. I treated Stevie the way I had always wanted Pop to treat me. And I was thinking about how I had done in this life and about how, with luck, Stevie will end up with more than I.

2

HECTOR: Sometimes I go to a certain house. Dead kids are hiding in the hallways. They wander the halls and are afraid to join the world of adults...of the Cubans. When I see my mother in his house, she is forever laboring over the kitchen stove cooking chicken with the paper wrapping on and the innards intact and sour milk puddings. Or she is sweeping piles of dirt from one side of the linoleum floor to the other, then trying to mop out stains of thirty years. I feel like telling her, "Forget it," but she is a good woman. I am the one who believes the stains will never come out. "Ma, don't mop anymore," I could tell her a thousand times, but she would keep on going.

Pop is sitting at the kitchen table, slumped over, worried about something. He's in a T-shirt, with a can of beer and a Kent cigarette between his fingers burning down to the filter. I know he is going to call me over, so I leave the kitchen. But in that house, which is memory, I can't escape him. In the living room he is sitting in the easy chair and moving his lips while he reads the *Daily News*. In the bedroom he is fretting over bills that he has spread over the bedsheets, or he is asleep, drunk, naked on the bed. I see him with numbers slips, awaiting that one big *numerito* to come along and solve his problems. In the bathroom he is shitting with the door left open. In all cases my mother is not far behind, accusing him of one thing or the other. There is yelling.

But a few spots in this house are beautiful. For example, streams and streams of elegantly dressed Cubans who give me quarters and pat my head come in through the door. My Pop is sober when he greets them. They dance in the living room, the air is filled with wonderful perfumes and the aroma of food. Pop spreads his arms open for me. In my bedroom are my soldiers. I play with them under the light of the window. That light is something: In its caress I roll over on my side and enjoy its warmth. I feel myself transported by that light into another world before awareness of problems. I'm not in the apartment anymore, but in Cuba, in Aunt Luisa's house. The sunlight is no longer caressing me; Aunt Luisa is caressing me, massaging my side which has started to hurt. I'm naked and rolling around on a bed and looking up into her smiling face. Cuba radiates in through a window. Peeking out I follow the path of a long silvery hill with its trees and colorful houses. I take in the scent of the flowers and of the bakery making its soda crackers and loaves of high-rising puffy bread. Squirming in Luisa's arms, I am let go. She lets me run naked around in front of the house. I jump over the squirting break in the line of a garden hose that's lying on the sidewalk. My brother, Horacito, has just sprayed some white-suited señor on his bicycle with the hose and is getting a spanking from Uncle Manny. Aunt Luisa's voice, sweet as music, calls me inside.

I feel mesmerized by this notion of the past. I want it forever in my house, but it fades away.

I always come back to the present, and I write my thoughts down in a black-and-white composition notebook, the kind my mother writes poetry in. Looking at these notes I think that one day I would like to write a book, something that would so please my mother and my Pop, if he was still alive. He didn't read very much—only newspapers and magazines, never, never books. But I know that he would have been pleased with the idea and say, "At least you're not scrubbing floors."

In the morning I ride to work on the old IRT subway, probably the same one that my Pop rode years ago. Sometimes I think of his scarred, burned, cut hands holding on to the same poles, and I feel connected to him. But our lives are much different. I am almost twenty-five years old. At that age, I've been told, he was running some kind of mail route by burro in southeastern Cuba. Me? I work down on East Forty-seventh Street in a tall building with a sloping glass front. It's just three blocks north of the hotel where my father used to work. He used to burn up his hands and smell of meat, but I spend my days with a yellow notepad and IBM typewriter, writing promotional copy for a travel agency that sells vacationers dream packages to places like Hawaii and the Virgin Islands. It's an okay job, but not what I want to do for the rest of my days. Perhaps I will be lucky enough to do just what I want to do—write.

I did graduate from college. But it took me five and a half years because I kept dropping in and out to get my head together and travel around to see something of the country—the Grand Canyon, Disneyland, Niagara Falls—places my mother and father, for all their years in America, had never seen. (I think they went to Miami once, and New Jersey three or four times.) When I did well in school I felt that I was going against my family grain, which, to my mind, was to fail. Maybe that was Pop's influence, maybe my mother's. It kills me that they never had a chance to get what they wanted out of life; that my mother, for all her talents, never had the chance to realize herself; that my father, for all his simple desires, died on a rooftop. I guess real luck has to do with not being afraid of your own future. My Pop was like that when he first came here more than thirty years ago, but he was not like that when he died. He had changed.

Perhaps that's why I'm so happy to see my mother these days. I still live in the same noisy neighborhood. My girlfriend tells me I'm crazy for not living on the chic East Side. My brother says I've never really left home. But even though I live just a few blocks away in an apartment very much like my mother's, I've been living my own life, and I have my moments of detachment, of disbelief that I ever lived with her and Pop at all. She's the same, at times like a little girl, at other times like a grieving old woman. I like being near her. She always has the same stories to tell. Sometimes when I see her superstitious ways, her Old World ways, I remember my troubles with her, remember her fear, and I almost leave. But I never do. And when I write in my notebook I feel very close to her and to the memory of my father. I go back to that certain house, I go back to my beginning. I remember my mother and father—"Pop" always "Pop." At night, I still dream about feeling his warm, heavy hands touching my face.

3

MERCEDES: My poor mama, Maria, used to see a little mouse in the room, and she would say, "Mercita, look at that mouse running along most happily." I would go and look for the mouse, and he always came out from his hiding place to stare at me, with his crooked teeth showing from his mouth and his little smile. How hardworking he seemed to be, digging everywhere with his crinkled little hands. Sometimes he looked at me with his cute little face and moved his nose around and smiled, and I would say, "Oh see Mama, he really knows about this life." Then after we looked at each other for a while, I would go my way thinking about the mouse and how happy he seemed to be.

I suppose if I were a mouse, my mama would have said I moved most happily alone. That was her way of describing all the creatures— the pigs, the dogs, and the cat. One day Mama called me into the kitchen to show me the cat eating the mouse, most happily.

That was a lesson for me. As Mama put it: "See what happened to that little mouse? He was playing and then...psssh, now he's the cat's dinner." She walked away slowly and turned around a few times to see if I knew the meaning of the poor mouse's passing. I did. I went and got my sister Rina and we buried the mouse by the roots of a tree in our yard.

"But don't be too sad," my mother later told me. "Because that mouse will probably come back. Heaven knows where it'll turn up next."

"What do you mean, Mama?" I asked.

That was when she told me about reincarnation, when you die and come back as someone else. She told me, "In my past life, I was a brave soldier's wife. That was during the Moorish wars. When I died I was a ghost for a hundred years and then I came back into this life. You were someone, too. And you'll remember who, one day."

It must be true that people have other lives because we pass so easily from this world. As soon as I speak of this to a friend or visitor, he always has a past life to tell me about. I have friends who had other lives as princesses, or who were daughters or sons of the very wealthy, with big mansions and all the riches in the world. One of my friends claims that she was Cleopatra. That makes me laugh!

My other life was long ago, in the time of Queen Isabella and Christopher Columbus. I lived in a small house near the castle and worked there, cleaning the floors in order to bring home money to my mother. I had very little time for simple pleasures and I didn't have a husband—that made me sad. One day Queen Isabella saw me sitting on the steps of the castle, taking a rest, and she decided to cheer me up with a little present. Soon a servant came up to me with something I had seen in my dreams—a mirror. I spent the longest time looking at myself, trying to find out if I was pretty or ugly and if a man would ever want me. But I still felt very tired and that tiredness showing on my face made me feel very sad.

"Why are you so sad?" Queen Isabella asked me.

"Because I love the flowers so much and I have no time to be around them. I would plant a garden if I could and spend my time caring for the flowers there," was my answer.

So she made me an attendant and ordered me to her court where there were many flowers, and I spent many days sitting at her feet, sighing, because I wanted to be as pretty as she.

One day when I was in a happy mood, I began to sing. And the

queen liked it so much that she ordered me to sing before all the
wealthy and important people of the court. They applauded and threw
gold pieces, which I brought home to my mother. This happened
again and again. But we needed the money for food, so I was never
able to buy new dresses. I always wore tattered dresses, and the women
made fun of me.

"Why are you sad now?" the queen asked one day. I told her about
the cruel women's jokes, and she took me to an enormous closet filled
with row after row of velvet dresses. "You may choose one dress to
keep," Isabella said. She was such a good woman. She reminded me
of the Holy Mother. She had large blue eyes and long brown hair. She
wore a blue veil and was always smiling kindly and very patient as
she waited for me to choose a dress. I took one that was studded with
bells and bright stones. It made me so happy that for days I did nothing
but thank Isabella.

But, as my mother used to say, when people come out of their own
sadness they see the unhappiness of others. Another day when I was
scrubbing the floors but singing most happily, the queen said to me,
"I wish I could find happiness so easily." And when I asked her why
she was sad, she pointed down the long dark hall toward the chamber
of the king.

My mother used to say, "A person's position in life has little to do
with inner happiness." And it is true.

The king, Ferdinand the Catholic, was a bent-up, crooked man,
with a terrible illness that would make him cough all night. Sometimes his coughing was so terrible that no one in the castle could sleep.
That morning Isabella pulled me aside and asked, "Esmeralda"—that
was my name at the time—"do you have a man?"

"Oh no," I told her.

"Well," she confided, "even though I am married to the king I don't
have a man either."

Then she broke down crying. She placed her head on my shoulder
and told me how she had been promised to Ferdinand as a little girl
and had never fallen in love with him. As she continued to weep, I
touched her hair and began to daydream. You know, I could see things
in those days, just like I used to in this life in Cuba. In the daydream

I saw a handsome red-haired man with broad shoulders kissing her in the olive grove, and I knew that she would soon have a man to love her. I told her to have faith because her suffering would soon end.

One afternoon as she held court, Christopher Columbus knelt before her. Beside him was another man, thin and tall with big ears, holding a bundle of maps and charts. That was Alejo. In those days he was called Capricorn.

Everyone in the court laughed as Columbus presented his case. He claimed that the world was as round as a ball. In that time everyone believed that God had washed the world clean of sinners during the great flood and that all the drowned animals and men were swept off the edge to the land of the dead, where their bones were to that day. Ferdinand thought that Columbus was crazy, but Isabella listened to his every word as if he spoke the Bible truth.

To plead his case for ships to sail the world, Columbus came to the castle three or four times a week. Isabella took an interest in him and soon began to meet him secretly in the evenings. She and Columbus would sneak down a twisting stone hallway and lock themselves inside a narrow room, so deep inside the castle that they could not hear the king's terrible cough.

I used to stand watch by the door, and that is how I came to know Capricorn. In both lives my Alejo was so handsome and very romantic. One evening while we waited outside the room, listening to the queen and the mariner sigh and kiss, he took my hand and said, "Señorita Esmeralda, I think you're very beautiful." And that was the beginning of our mutual love.

As for Columbus, Ferdinand's jealousy helped him on his way. The king knew the castle gossip and would storm around calling Columbus a "seducer." He would have killed Columbus if Queen Isabella did not calm him by taking him into her bed. The poor king had a twisted spine and was so pathetic that this always put him into a good mood. On one of those evenings, soothed by the queen's kisses, he decided to get rid of Columbus by giving him the money. It would make Isabella happy, and he believed Columbus might sail off the earth's edge.

By then Capricorn and I were quite a pair. We would go to dances and ride through town together on horseback. He would come to my house and sing to me. We walked down to the harbor to look at the stars. I think he was going to ask me to marry him, but then one day he came to my house and told me he was going to sail to China with Columbus.

I remember the crowds by the harbor as the ship left the port. I made some extra money that day by selling flowers and fruit from a cart. Men would pass by and ask me for prices as they touched the fruit, but my thoughts were on the departing ships. Capricorn was on the *Santa Maria*, the little one, hardly fifteen feet long. He watched me from the deck as the three ships pulled away toward the horizon.

People say we must suffer in this life, and that is true. Isabella and I passed our days watching the sea from the tower. We feared that a storm had drowned them, because there was no news for months. Crooked Ferdinand was of no help. He would limp into the throne room and happily announce that a storm had been sighted over the Atlantic, or that the bleached bones of fifty men had been found in the belly of a whale. He made us so sad. There was always a story about dragons that flew low over the water, or winged women who carried sailors away to cook meals of terrible food for them, or about the Devil himself whom some thought was Neptune.

But one night as I dreamed I saw my Capricorn. He was sitting on a barrel in a dim room on the rocking ship, writing a letter to me. Then suddenly I saw him walking in a plaza in Cuba in the 1930s with a bouquet of flowers... But that's how dreams are, one second here, the next second there—it makes me laugh. From the dream I knew they had not fallen off the edge of the world, and the next morning I went to tell Isabella. That made her happy. But time passed and we heard no more news. A year went by. Then a messenger rushed into the castle with news that one of the ships had been sighted two days' distance away. Ferdinand did not take the news well, but Isabella and I danced. We were at the tower window the day Columbus arrived. We went down to the street and saw the procession from the ship. We saw Indians in feathers and all manners of trees from the New World. There was talk everywhere of gold cities and people who lived in the treetops. Columbus came to the court, and when I had my chance I asked him about Capricorn. He looked at me sadly and said in a low voice, "He went down with the *Santa Maria* in a storm off the coast of Cubanacan four months ago."

I felt the worst pain in my life then. I have only felt a pain like that once in this life. Capricorn was my first love, and even though we were not married, I took to wearing black. All my friends told me that I should forget him, but all I could do was think about him. Then I began to have certain dreams. My Capricorn was walking in a garden of prickly trees in a place that I had never seen. Then I knew that he had been saved. Maybe he had lived in a whale's belly or had been taken to shore by a mermaid. Or he had been saved by the Virgin Mother like those fishermen at Cobre. Sometimes at night I would hear his voice calling to me, "Esmeralda, Esmeralda. I am waiting for you in the distance where no one else can go."

I did not look for another man. I was always crying and did not eat. That was why Isabella took pity on me and asked Columbus to take me with him to the New World.

That voyage is hard to remember. Overhead there were endless constellations in which the sailors tried to see the faces of their loved ones; there were banks of clouds, bottom-heavy as a drenched awning, receding forever into the distance. And below there was the sea, rippling like the tongue of a lizard, as uneven as a cobblestone road after a bad storm. There was lightning, and comets dropped out of the sky. I saw these streaks of light as the souls of the dead, as angels, even though the others were frightened. I became so ill from the movement of the sea that I took to standing at the railing of that tiny boat. Sometimes when I looked down I saw golden fish and women like mermaids receding into the water. I saw the columns of public buildings like those in Santiago, and sometimes, looking back from a depth far below and waving his hands for me to continue on, my Capricorn.

We had been at sea for a few months when the lookout alerted everyone by shouting, "Over there, I see Cubanacan. I see Cuba!" And I looked myself and realized that it was the most beautiful place on earth. But where was my Capricorn? When we landed, I went to Santiago, to all the houses and churches, asking for him. I went down all the alleys, calling out his name, but I never did see him. Everywhere I looked there were Indians dragging stones for building, but no

Capricorn. Everywhere there were men on scaffolds constructing walls for new houses, but no Capricorn. I decided to stay and got a job measuring out flour and grains for a merchant. I sold fruit, too, but nothing else because there was little to eat. The Spanish soldiers would not touch the Indian food because they thought they might be poisoned. And the Indians feared the Spanish soldiers as gods.

As for myself, I had decided to remain alone. Every man in that city knew me, but I wouldn't let anyone touch me. After two years of the most terrible solitude, in the market I heard a voice very much like my Capricorn's. Then the voice came closer. I closed my eyes and felt a strong hand grasping my chin. When I opened my eyes, Capricorn was standing before me.

He looked older and worn out, and one of his legs was missing. He stood on a peg and moved with the help of a crutch. I did not care. We found a priest to marry us and that very night we went back to my house as man and wife. Of that life I remember little. At first we just stayed at home, kissing and hugging as young couples do. We spoke much of the future. Capricorn had a four-stringed *guitara* that he sometimes played in the saloon. But otherwise he did nothing to earn money. He said he could not find regular work because of his one leg. One day when I complained that he did nothing around the house he took me by the arm and said, "From now on, you'll have to work for me." And that was how my time was spent, working by day in the market, cleaning the house and cooking at night, and then, at a much later hour, entertaining the men in the saloon with some of the songs I had performed in the court of Isabella.

It was a life of few satisfactions, but through it all I never stopped loving my Capricorn. Inside him, I knew another love existed: the one whose soul I came to know in my present life. The good Alejo. In his other life he died in a delirium, filled with a fear of the dead. He clutched my hands, asking my forgiveness as he succumbed to a fever. That was God's answer to him for having mistreated me so; and God made up the balance in this life. As I had worked for him in that life, he worked for me in this life, worked so hard, the poor man.

I remember watching the Angel of Shadows entering that room where Capricorn rested long ago and how she passed her hand over his face and removed his fear. Then it was my turn to die. Years had passed. It was raining outside, I remember, and I had no one to watch over me. I was afraid of being alone in the last moments, so afraid in the dark of my fever, without anyone to hold my hand. But the Angel of Shadows came to me and showed me a clear path to the garden where my Alejo waited, a path of light and flowers.

Just before he died, I told my Alejo, "If you suffered in this life, it is because you were bad to me in another life." And that was the only reason for Alejo's sadness. "When this life passes, you will awaken to the brightest day," I told him. But he just looked at me with doubt. "Don't be afraid," I said. "You and I will die but death will not separate us."

And then there was the day of proof. He had been buried for three days, and I was afraid to close my eyes for fear of seeing skeletons. I was turning in bed when I heard his voice. "Mercita...Mercita! It's me. Do not be afraid."

He was standing at the doorway and he smiled. "Mercita, I am happy to see you again."

And then he told me about his ordeal. I do not remember everything he said, only that he had closed his eyes and then had felt himself passing through a fire, *quemándose, quemándose— burning, burning*, and that he had been confused and had been walking on a long road, like a blinded man, until someone passed a hand over his face. Then he could open his eyes and see.

"Do not be afraid," he kept telling me. "Do not be afraid."

FOR THE BEST IN PAPERBACKS, LOOK FOR THE 🐧

In every corner of the world, on every subject under the sun, Penguin represents quality and variety – the very best in publishing today.

For complete information about books available from Penguin – including Puffins, Penguin Classics and Arkana – and how to order them, write to us at the appropriate address below. Please note that for copyright reasons the selection of books varies from country to country.

In the United Kingdom: Please write to *Dept JC, Penguin Books Ltd, FREEPOST, West Drayton, Middlesex, UB7 0BR.*

If you have any difficulty in obtaining a title, please send your order with the correct money, plus ten per cent for postage and packaging, to *PO Box No 11, West Drayton, Middlesex*

In the United States: Please write to *Dept BA, Penguin, 299 Murray Hill Parkway, East Rutherford, New Jersey 07073*

In Canada: Please write to *Penguin Books Canada Ltd, 2801 John Street, Markham, Ontario L3R 1B4*

In Australia: Please write to the *Marketing Department, Penguin Books Australia Ltd, P.O. Box 257, Ringwood, Victoria 3134*

In New Zealand: Please write to the *Marketing Department, Penguin Books (NZ) Ltd, Private Bag, Takapuna, Auckland 9*

In India: Please write to *Penguin Overseas Ltd, 706 Eros Apartments, 56 Nehru Place, New Delhi, 110019*

In the Netherlands: Please write to *Penguin Books Netherlands B.V., Postbus 3507, NL–1001 AH, Amsterdam*

In West Germany: Please write to *Penguin Books Ltd, Friedrichstrasse 10–12, D–6000 Frankfurt/Main 1*

In Spain: Please write to *Alhambra Longman S.A., Fernandez de la Hoz 9, E–28010 Madrid*

In Italy: Please write to *Penguin Italia s.r.l., Via Como 4, I-20096 Pioltello (Milano)*

In France: Please write to *Penguin France S.A., 17 rue Lejeune, F-31000 Toulouse*

In Japan: Please write to *Longman Penguin Japan Co Ltd, Yamaguchi Building, 2–12–9 Kanda Jimbocho, Chiyoda-Ku, Tokyo 101*

A CHOICE OF PENGUIN FICTION

The Swimming Pool Library   Alan Hollinghurst

'Shimmers somewhere between pastoral romance and sulphurous confession ... surely the best book about gay life yet written by an English author' – Edmund White. 'In more senses than one a historic novel and a historic début' – *Guardian*

On the Golden Porch and Other Stories   Tatyana Tolstaya

'There are thirteen stories in this collection and every one's an absolute gem of emotion ... It's not hard to see why quite so much fuss is being made over Tatyana Tolstaya' – *Time Out*

Mother London   Michael Moorcock

'A masterpiece ... it is London as we know it, confused, vast, convoluted, absurd' – *Independent*. 'A vast, uncorseted, sentimental, comic, elegiac salmagundi of a novel ... His is the grand messy flux itself, in all its heroic vulgarity, its unquenchable optimism' – Angela Carter

Eva Luna   Isabel Allende

'Isabel Allende [is] a latter-day Scheherazade, a true descendant of the skalds, a Teller of Tales' – *Guardian*. 'Fact, fiction and glorious exaggeration merge easily against a brilliant setting: legend becomes real, while superstition blends with political reality into the forging of characters larger than life' – *Options*

Libra   Don DeLillo

David Bell's rise as New York's youngest TV executive had been meteoric. Drawn by the power of his 16mm film camera, the citizens of a small Kansas town become willing actors in the bizarre movie that he begins making in his motel room... '[A] swift, ironic and witty cross-country nightmare' – *Rolling Stone*

FOR THE BEST IN PAPERBACKS, LOOK FOR THE

A CHOICE OF PENGUIN FICTION

A Far Cry From Kensington Muriel Spark

'Pure delight' – Claire Tomalin in the *Independent*. 'A 1950s Kensington of shabby-genteel bedsitters, espresso bars and A-line dresses … irradiated with sudden glows of lyricism she can so beautifully effect' – Peter Kemp in the *Sunday Times*

Love in the Time of Cholera Gabriel García Márquez

The Number One international bestseller. 'Admirers of *One Hundred Years of Solitude* may find it hard to believe that García Márquez can have written an even better novel. But that's what he's done' – *Newsweek*

Enchantment Monica Dickens

The need to escape, play games, fantasize, is universal. But for some people it is everything. To this compassionate story of real lives Monica Dickens brings her unparalleled warmth, insight and perception. 'One of the tenderest souls in English fiction' – *Sunday Times*

My Secret History Paul Theroux

'André Parent saunters into the book, aged fifteen … a creature of naked and unquenchable ego, greedy for sex, money, experience, *another life* … read it warily; read it twice, and more; it is darker and deeper than it looks' – *Observer*. 'On his best form since *The Mosquito Coast*' – *Time Out*

Decline and Fall Evelyn Waugh

A comic yet curiously touching account of an innocent plunged into the sham, brittle world of high society. Evelyn Waugh's first novel brought him immediate public acclaim and remains a classic of its kind.

A CHOICE OF PENGUIN FICTION

Moon Tiger Penelope Lively

Penelope Lively's Booker Prize-winning novel is her 'most ambitious book to date' – *The Times*. 'A complex tapestry of great subtlety ... Penelope Lively writes so well, savouring the words as she goes' – *Daily Telegraph*

Jigsaw Sybille Bedford

'This is a wonderfully absorbing book. The events described are so astonishing that it would perhaps be asking too much that they be merely imagined; Sybille Bedford's childhood is beyond fictive invention ... considerably moving ... it seems inevitable and absolutely real' – *Sunday Times*

Fludd Hilary Mantel

'Fludd is a curate sent to assist Angwin – or is he? Loving beauty and language, sowing scandal and unrest in Fetherhoughton, might he not be the devil?' – *New Statesman and Society*. 'I loved this book. I loved its humanity, its humour, and its elusiveness. I have read it twice, and I would read it again' – *Literary Review*

A Gentle Occupation Dirk Bogarde

1945. The war in South-East Asia is ended. But on one island in the Java Sea, 400 miles south of Singapore, the fragile truce is plunged into the chaos of violence. As an empire crumbles, those who remain to keep the peace must fight the hardest to survive... 'A triumph' – *Daily Telegraph*

A Lesser Dependency Peter Benson

'On a night in September 1971, Maude, Leonard, Odette, Georges and all remaining Ilois left Diego Garcia for ever...' 'Peter Benson, through the experiences of this one family, shows how heaven turned to hell ... this account of a shocking, shaming business smoulders with quiet anger' – *Time Out*

BY THE SAME AUTHOR

The Mambo Kings Play Songs of Love

'The book is a hymn to music, to heterosexual love . . . There is hedonism and pain, ecstasy and despair, devotion and lechery . . . A fantastic novel' – *Evening Standard*

'A world as exotic and enchanting as that of García Márquez . . . You won't find a wrong note from beginning to end' – *Blitz*

'Dripping with nostalgia and longing . . . it makes you want to get up and dance' – *Sunday Times*

'Sad, passionate and compelling . . . it leaves its readers feeling that they have not just read another book, but that they have lived other lives' – *Independent*